THE RUSSIA

A *Ben Sign* Crime-Espionage Story

By
Matthew Dunn
FORMER *MI6 SPY* AND *BEST-SELLING* AUTHOR

ALSO BY MATTHEW DUNN

SPYCATCHER SERIES
Spycatcher
Sentinel
Slingshot
Dark Spies
The Spy House
Act Of Betrayal
A Soldier's Revenge
Spy Trade
Counterspy

BEN SIGN SERIES
The Spy Whisperer
The Fifth Man
The Kill House
The Spy Thief

PRAISE FOR MATTHEW DUNN

"Terse conversations infused with subtle power plays, brutal encounters among allies with competing agendas, and forays into hostile territory orchestrated for clockwork efficiency...." ---- *Washington Post*

"Great talent, great imagination, and real been-there-done-that authenticity.... Highly recommended." ----Lee Child, author of the *Jack Reacher* series

"Dunn's exuberant, bullet-drenched prose, with its descriptions of intelligence tradecraft and modern anti-terrorism campaigns, bristles with authenticity.... Save for the works of Alan Furst, good thrillers have been thin on the ground of late. Mr. Dunn has redressed this balance with an altogether gripping book." ----*The Economist*

"[Dunn] makes a strong argument that it takes a real spy to write a truly authentic espionage novel.... [The story] practically bursts at the seams with boots-on-the-ground insight and realism. But there's another key ingredient that likely will make the ruthless yet noble protagonist, Will Cochrane, a popular series character for many years to come. Dunn is a gifted storyteller." ----*Fort Worth Star-Telegram*

"Matthew Dunn is [a] very talented new author. I know of no other spy thriller that so successfully blends the fascinating nuances of the business of espionage and intelligence work with full-throttle suspense storytelling. ----Jeffery Deaver, author of *The Bone Collector*

"Just when you think you've got this maze of double-dealing figured out – surprise, it isn't what you think. All the elements of a classic espionage story are here. The novel moves with relentless momentum, scattering bodies in its wake." ----*Kirkus Reviews*

"[Dunn has] a superlative talent for three-dimensional characterisation, gripping dialogue, and plots that featured gasp-inducing twists and betrayals." ----*The Examiner*

"A real spy proves he is a real writer. This is a stunning debut." ----Ted Bell, author of *Patriot*

"Not since Fleming charged Bond with the safety of the world has the international secret agent mystique been so anchored with an insider's reality." ----Noah Boyd, author of *The Bricklayer*

"Once in a while an espionage novelist comes along who has the smack of utter authenticity. Few are as daring as Matthew Dunn, fewer still as up to date…. Is there anyone writing today who knows more about the day-to-day operations of intelligence agencies in the field than Matthew Dunn?" ----John Lawton, author of *Then We Take Berlin*

"The two most important days in your life are the day you are born and the day you find out why." – Mark Twain

PROLOGUE

Moscow. Fifty years ago

In exactly twelve minutes and thirty three seconds time, female twins would be born. They'd never see each other again. One of them would be named Jayne; the other Susan. Jayne would return to England with her English parents. Susan would vanish.

Backtrack fourteen minutes. The pregnant mother was gripping her husband's hand in a grimy Russian medical centre. The pregnant woman was Elizabeth Archer. She was a professor of Russian Studies & Culture at Oxford University. Her husband, Michael, was also a professor at the same university. They were gifted and contrarian types who'd travelled to Russia despite Elizabeth's advanced stage of pregnancy. Before planning the trip, she'd had her last scan at St. Thomas's Hospital in London. The hospital had advised her not to travel. Elizabeth and Michael never did what anyone in authority told them to do. They ignored the advice, didn't tell the airline booking agent that Elizabeth was heavily pregnant, and boarded a nine AM Aeroflot flight to Moscow. They wanted the offspring to enter the world in unusual circumstances. They thought it would be cool if the delivery took place in Russia.

That decision was a dubious one. Elizabeth had gone into labour three weeks ahead of schedule. And she'd done so while undergoing a routine health check in the medical centre. There was no time to get her to hospital. The delivery had to take place in the underequipped and staffed centre. The Soviet Union medical centre was underfunded and overstretched. Paint was peeling off dank walls. The place was crowded with patients who were elderly, or young, malnourished, drunk, injured, or suffering internal symptoms they couldn't explain to the staff but were nevertheless agonizing. The noise in the small complex was deafening. Patients were shouting; trollies with metal containers were rushed back and forward, a loudspeaker system blurted out instructions every few seconds, doctors were barking orders at stressed nurses, fights periodically broke out, a receptionist was screaming at a man in crutches to wait his turn in the queue, and all the time tinny music was played at full volume from the centre's speakers in each corner of every room. The music was designed to calm the occupants of the building. It had the opposite effect.

It was a miracle that Elizabeth was given a private room to give birth. As well as her husband, a midwife, two other nurses, and a doctor were in the room. She was very lucky to get this amount of attention. Still, the whole situation was horrific. Elizabeth was in agony while lying on a bed that smelled of urine. One nurse dabbed a cold flannel against Elizabeth's brow. It didn't help. The midwife stood at the business end of the birth, callipers in her hand in case her baby twisted in the womb and needed to be wrenched out. The callipers looked like a medieval torture instrument. The doctor was leaning against the wall, a clipboard in his hand. For the most part he looked bored and exhausted, though now and again he'd mutter an instruction to the nurses, who in turn would look at him over their shoulders and exclaim obscenities at the useless man.

Michael was sweating nearly as much as Elizabeth. His hand felt like it had been squeezed of all blood, due to the strength of his wife's grip. Now, more than ever, he wondered whether the trip to Russia had been a good idea. But, it was too late for regrets. He stayed by his wife, telling her that everything would be alright, when in truth it seemed like the opposite was the case; saying anything that came into his head and, like all fathers in this situation, fundamentally failing to say anything meaningful. There's nothing meaningful to say to a woman who feels like her body is being torn apart.

Elizabeth – normally an elegantly dressed woman, with platinum blonde hair, high cheek bones, blue eyes, and a curvaceous yet trim figure, now looked a mess. Her hair was matted, some of it clinging to the soiled sheets underneath her. The radiant shine she'd obtained towards the latter stages of pregnancy was now replaced with an oily paste of moisture that made her skin look like the seal fat lather applied by long distance cold sea swimmers to their bodies. Her eyes were red. And her lips were bloody from her teeth clenching in to them.

She didn't care what she looked like. Nor did she care that her legs had been forced into the most un-ladylike position. She just wanted this to be over. Fast. What she did care about was the room. It stank. Not from her, but from previous patients. She had no medical training, but it didn't take a genius to work out that the room was totally unhygienic. The nurses weren't wearing gloves; bloody swabs were tossed into a metal bowl that already contained other crimson swabs that were not from her; the room smelled of cheese, decay, iron, body odour, shit, and piss. This wasn't a place to bring a child into the world. Still, she wasn't going anywhere now until the job was done.

She stared at the midwife. The woman placed her hands between Elizabeth's legs and helped her guide the baby out. The baby's umbilical cord was cut; the baby was washed, wrapped in sheets, and placed into a cot.

After that, everything changed.

Crimea. Four years ago.

Petrov Asina was a twenty seven year old Russian man who'd joined the army age eighteen to escape the humdrum of his impoverished upbringing and resultant boredom of having to survive every day in an apartment in the outskirts of St. Petersburg. The flat was in a tower block that was thirty stories high. There were twelve other apartment blocks nearby, each looking, he often reasoned, like an old person's decaying tooth. The buildings were grey, except when the rain came – then the exteriors turned black. He grew up in a one bedroom home that housed his parents, Petrov, and his sister Natalia. His parents were smart but poor. Father was a teacher; mother a poet who wrote all day but barely made more than a few roubles for her work. They were tired and had long ago run out of puff. There was no chance they'd get a second wind to carve a new life. But, they adored their children and wanted them to have a better life. The problem was they were conflicted. Petrov and Natalia excelled at school. However, their parents only had enough money to pay for one of them to go to university. And even that was a stretch. His father had to take a night job as a security guard, getting only a few hours' sleep here and there to accommodate his day job as a teacher. His mother gave up poetry and got a job as a shipping clerk. Still, they had to choose which child they would financially support and which child they would condemn to a life comparable to theirs. Petrov had lost track of the number of times he'd heard his parents arguing about this subject in the kitchen while he and his sister tried to sleep on their blow-up air beds on the floor. The siblings knew their parents were significantly stressed. And they knew how much they loved their children. They should never have been placed in this situation.

Petrov had the academic rigour to go to university. So did Natalia. Sometimes in life choices have to be made by others, because those mostly affected by the choices presented to them simply cannot decide on the right course of action.

Petrov did what he thought was the honourable thing to do. He took the choice away from his parents. On his eighteenth birthday he entered an army recruitment office in St. Petersburg. He had no idea about the army; had never expressed an interest in any matters pertaining to the military. But he had a clear vision. In the army he'd get fed, clothed, and would be able to sleep for free in barracks. He'd be paid but wouldn't need much of his monthly salary. The cash could help pay for a cottage, on the coast, a few miles west of the city. His parents and sister could live there. This was their only way out of the hellish existence they'd endured for so long. The army recruitment sergeant eyed him with a look of disdain. He told Petrov that his hair was too long and that his physique was scrawny. Petrov had replied that hair could be cut and muscles could be expanded. He looked at posters on the wall – sailors smiling on the decks on battle cruisers; marines storming beaches; pilots disembarking from fighter planes, weirdly, a big breasted blonde on his arm as they walked across the runway. It was all bullshit. But, one poster caught his eye. It looked more serious; more real. It was a photo of a man jumping out of a plane, high above the ground, his arms and legs outstretched, equipment and guns strapped to his back, no parachute deployed. The man looked like a diving bird of prey. More importantly, he looked free. Petrov pointed at the poster and said he wanted to be that man. The sergeant laughed, saying that to be that man Petrov would have to serve in one of the parachute regiments before surviving selection into Spetsnaz, Russia's Special Forces unit. Petrov was undeterred. He liked the idea of freefalling through air, no matter what it took to get that qualification. And when the sergeant told him that elite forces get a higher pay than regular units, he was rifle-shot focused on joining the paras. The sergeant wasn't convinced that Petrov would make it past day one of training. But, he had a job to do and that included meeting quotas of military applicants, regardless as to whether they were suitable for the job in hand. He signed Petrov up for a pre-selection assessment with the 106th Guards Airborne Division, headquartered south of Moscow.

A week later, Petrov attended the assessment course and passed. Two weeks later he began his training in earnest. It was brutal, exhausting, and lasted six months. He earned his parachute wings and was top of his intake. He was officially a paratrooper. And by now he was physically bigger and the fittest he'd ever been. He was a man. Life in the Airborne Division was relentless – constant training exercises, deployments to various parts of Russia, sniper schools, HALO and HAHO qualifications, unarmed combat drills, and excruciating physical training that involved running, mountain climbs, swimming in freezing waters, gym PT, and twenty mile marches with one hundred pounds on his back. He couldn't say it was boring. But – elite or not – back then, Russian military units never saw combat. And though Petrov wasn't a bloodthirsty type, he'd increasingly wanted to test his skills in war. It made no sense to do all this training and not put it to good use. Also, he was changing. Maybe it was because his testosterone levels had increased; possibly it was because he'd been carved into a warrior who had no fight to fight. For three years, that was okay. He carried on doing what he was doing and each month saved up his money for the coastal cottage he wanted to buy his parents. But, boredom is a killer, even if it's crammed with twenty hour days of non-stop activity. Petrov wanted more.

He was twenty two when he applied to Spetsnaz. In Russia, for the most part the concept of Special Forces is very different compared to SF in, for example, the UK and US. In fact, Spetsnaz doesn't translate to the western term *Special Forces*. More accurately it translates to *special soldier*. And there are tens of thousands of Spetsnaz soldiers spread across Russia. Most of them are embedded in regular units. They are not Special Forces. Instead they are soldiers who are tasked with doing things that the rest of their unit haven't been trained to do – parachute insertions at night, reconnaissance, intelligence gathering, and other things. They are highly trained but Petrov was aware that they were not as good as the elite British Royal Marine Commandos or Parachute Regiment soldiers. They were certainly nowhere near as good as SAS, SBS, SEALs, and Delta. Petrov wanted to better himself, rather than move into a unit that thought it was special but wouldn't survive contact with a superior Western unit. He did his research and discovered there were three Spetsnaz units that were completely autonomous from the regular military units. Instead, they worked for the SVR, GRU, and FSB, the foreign and domestic intelligence agencies. These units were small, spent years honing their skills, and only allowed the very best operators to apply to be in their ranks. The units were Directorate "A" (Spetsgruppa Alpha), Directorate "V" (Spetsgruppa Vympel), and Directorate "S" (Spetsgruppa Smerch). Alpha was a counterterrorism and assassination unit. Vympel was a counterterrorism and counter-sabotage unit. Unlike Alpha, it primarily operated on Russian soil. Smerch was a capture or kill unit that operated primarily in the North Caucasus, tracking down bandits, though they also operated elsewhere in Russia. Alpha, he'd heard, was the unit most comparable to Western SF, given it could work anywhere in the world.

He approached his commanding officer in the Airborne Division. While stood to attention in his CO's office, he said, "Sir, I wish to apply to Directorate Alpha."

From behind his desk, the CO looked at him with a cold stare. "That doesn't surprise me. You're one of my best men. Why wouldn't you wish to climb several rungs up the ladder? But, look at it from my perspective. If you succeed in Alpha selection, and that's a big *if*, I'd be losing a highly effective paratrooper from my regiment."

"Are you blocking my request to undergo Alpha selection, sir?"

The colonel drummed his fingers on his desk and looked away, deep in thought. "No." He looked back at Petrov. "I have a son your age. He's not in the military. That doesn't matter. What does matter is how I would respond to him if he approached me and told me that in his heart he wanted to take a huge risk in order to pursue his dreams. What would I say? Would I say he didn't have my permission? He'd hate me for life, and would ignore my stance." He clasped his hands. "Sometimes in life we parents must bite the bullet and let our children fly to their zenith or nadir. You have my permission, corporal. I will arrange matters. That will be all. Dismissed."

Two months later Petrov turned up at Alpha's training establishment. Out of an intake of forty applicants, only three passed the six month selection process; a process that would make other combat units in the Russian military drop their jaws. It wasn't like anything that Petrov had experience before. Airborne Division selection and training was a walk in the park compared to Alpha training. He was one of three people who passed. He felt proud. But then he had to receive continuation training by serving Alpha troops. They gave him no quarter. To them, he was a newbie who hadn't proven himself. In their minds it was simple – when they went into combat they had to have the right man by their side. Petrov had done Alpha selection; but now he was back to square one – he had to show his colleagues that he was up to the task. He was. He served with distinction for three years.

It all changed in 2014.

Russia's neighbour Ukraine was tearing itself apart. The new Ukrainian president was seen as a Western lackey; half the country liked the shift in politics, the other half yearned for a return to communism; war broke out in the eastern peninsula, particularly the Crimea; Russia couldn't tolerate the collapse of the Ukraine into Western democracy; more importantly, it needed to secure the Crimea to ensure that Russia had a land channel to its fleet in the Black Sea. Russia decided to take action. It had the support of the Ukrainian rebels, but they were for the most part amateurs. Russia needed to send specialist troops in to the Crimea.

It did so. They were nicknamed 'Green Men' due to the fact they wore green army uniforms with no insignia. There were rumours in the Ukraine and the West that they were elite Russian troops; but Vladimir Putin, the president of Russia, didn't admit that until months later. Some of the green men were airborne guards, tasked to protect airports and other installations, others were Spetsnaz tasked with arming and supporting rebels. Alpha was sent in with a very different remit. The political landscape of the Ukraine was on a knife edge. Russia needed popular opinion to side with the pro-Russia rebels. And the best way to do that was to make the Ukrainian government and its forces look like a travesty.

Petrov didn't know why he and eight other green men were monitoring a village on the Crimean border with Russia. He assumed it was because there was some kind of strategic value to the zone. He was prone on the ground, on a hilltop, watching villagers in the valley below go about their daily business. His rifle was pointing at them, even though he could perceive no threat. The villagers didn't know the green men were only a quarter of a mile away. The green men were camouflaged, hiding amid bushes and trees.

Petrov wasn't in charge of the eight-man unit. He was a sergeant and was outranked by the captain leading the platoon. So, he had to follow orders, even though he didn't know what those orders were. He waited for several hours, maintaining his surveillance of the village.

The captain gave his first and last order. "We move in to the village now and kill any human we see – men, women, kids, old, young, it doesn't matter. Kill them, and then we extract over the border. This is for Mother Russia, and this is for our ally the Ukraine. When we get back to base I'll tell you why this needed to be done. Meanwhile, don't blink. Do your job."

He led his men down the escarpment above the village. The green men were armed with assault rifles, grenades, and pistols.

Petrov knew this was all wrong. But, it's very hard to disobey orders when you've spent years getting in to the unit you've dreamed to be a part of. Alpha was his family. All that sweat and toil to get into the unit couldn't be wasted. Even though his stomach was in knots, he continued walking, telling himself that he was kidding himself if he thought organisations like Alpha never did black ops. The captain was right, he reasoned. There had to be a purpose behind this. It was part of the bigger picture. He could either follow what he'd been taught in training, or he could follow his conscience. He chose to grip his rifle and stand shoulder-to-shoulder with his comrades.

When they reached the village, the captain was the first to unleash hell. He tossed a grenade at a group of women who were clustered together around a well and were beating dust out of their homes' rugs. The grenade exploded. So did the women.

All of the Alpha men opened fire, except Pavlov.

Men, women, and children were running haphazardly while screaming. Some of them fell to the ground, injured or dead. Others sought cover in their houses or behind walls. Where they hid didn't matter to Alpha. They torched buildings, burning occupants alive, shot people in the head, despatched wounded villagers who were lying on the ground, killed their goats and sheep, and grabbed an elderly man who they assumed was the village elder and hanged him with a length of climbing rope.

It was a massacre. What Petrov was seeing was a set of images that would were being branded onto his brain and would stay with him for the rest of his life. He wanted no part of this slaughter. And he wanted it to stop. He ran to a house that hadn't been torched. Other Alpha men were oblivious to him. They were smiling, just focused on their quarry, shooting and killing like madmen. Petrov went to the top floor of the house. He was alone in there. He guessed the people who lived here were already dead on the street below. He raised his rifle and aimed it at his captain.

The captain was moving further down the central path in the village. Petrov was in no doubt that he was either a madman, a psychopath, a sociopath, or any other label one could apply to a sick fuck. The captain hurled another grenade, this time at a bunch of kids. Petrov counted. One, two, three, four. The grenade would go off in two more seconds. All of Alpha's grenades had been primed for a six second detonation. There was nothing Petrov could do to save the kids. But, he could try to make this end. He counted two more seconds, the grenade went off, obliterating the children, Petrov pulled his trigger, the captain's head was turned into mush.

Petrov ran out of the house, screaming, "Sniper! Sniper!"

The Alpha men stopped in their tracks then darted for cover.

Petrov grabbed the dead captain under his shoulders and dragged him back toward the escarpment. The other Alpha men scanned windows and other places with their rifles as Petrov stayed out in the open and continued hauling the captain's limp body. The Alpha team thought it was the bravest thing they'd ever seen.

One of them shouted, "Let's get out of here!"

The Special Forces men retreated, their job done. Most of the village was ablaze. At least forty people were dead.

They reached Petrov and the captain four hundred yards up the escarpment. The captain was on Petrov's shoulder. Petrov was breathing fast, struggling up the hill towards the Russian border.

One of the men put his hand on Petrov's arm. The man was a highly experienced operative. "We'll carry him from here. What you did was incredible. You should be dead. I'm going to recommend you for the Gold Star Medal." It was the highest award that could be bestowed upon a Russian, and was also known as *Hero of the Russian Federation.* "I can't guarantee you'll get it. We were never here. The captain's body will be disposed of by us. So, if it's impossible for you to get a medal, know that Alpha can picture that medal on your chest."

They took the body off Petrov's shoulder and hauled him up the hill. Petrov spent a moment catching his breath, bent over, his hands on his knees. He looked back at the village. It was a sight no man should have seen. He turned and followed his colleagues towards the border.

Before they got there the captain's body was burned until it was a crispy and molten carcass. It was then tossed into a pond, weighed down by rocks. It was the kind of burial they all expected. They left him there and escaped to Russia.

Three months' later Natalia Asina was in the kitchen as she watched her older brother take a walk along a remote footpath alongside the clifftop close to the cottage he'd bought for his parents. The cottage was ten miles west of St. Petersburg – far away from the hurly burly of city life; close enough to long distance city rail and airplane hubs. Natalia was twenty three, a brunette, fluent in English and French, had no boyfriend or any meaningful friends for that matter, was career-driven, had recently graduated from St. Petersburg State University with a degree in politics, and had passed the gruelling selection process to join the SVR, the successor to the KGB. In one week, she'd be moving to Moscow to start her training.

Her parents had paid for her education.

Petrov had paid for the cottage.

The timing of both events had been awful. Her parents had used up every last penny to give their daughter a better life. Petrov had hoped to give his parents a retirement home. But, their father keeled over a year ago with a heart attack. He was dead before he hit the ground. Their mother had contracted pneumonia. If she'd had any money left she could have paid for hospital care and drugs. She was broke, mentally and physically. She died on her bed, Petrov and Natalia by her side.

Natalia had made a pledge to herself that she would repay the debt to her family. Petrov was all she had now. He couldn't last forever in the army. She'd look after him when she could. And if he had any future money problems, she'd help him out.

Something was wrong with Petrov since he'd been granted a four week holiday before he was required to return to Moscow. He seemed distant, forced himself to smile but in doing so had a grin that looked like a cracked porcelain vase, would never talk about his work, and he drank vodka day and night. When he was sleeping in the two bedroom house, Natalia could hear him from her room. He'd shout out noises that had no meaning, with one exception: several times every night he'd yell, "This is wrong! Stop it! Stop!"

Natalia watched him from the kitchen window. After walking over a slight rise in the footpath, he disappeared from view. She was cooking beef stroganoff for dinner, with plenty of potatoes on the side. She hoped the carbohydrates would soak up the alcohol in Petrov's system. He'd never been a big drinker before. And since he'd joined the army he'd been a fitness fanatic. Now, there was something wrong with his state of mind. But, she had to tread gently with him. Petrov was her intellectual equal, they'd been extremely close as children, never judged each other, and always helped each other and their parents. Maybe that was because the family had grown up in poverty. Or maybe it was simply because they loved each other unconditionally. The last thing Natalia wanted was to cause an argument with her brother.

The only reason she knew he worked in Spetsnaz was because it was mentioned to her by her vetting officer, as part of her recruitment into the SVR. She never told Petrov that she knew which unit he worked in. It didn't seem relevant. He'd tell her himself, if he wanted to, she'd reasoned. She was proud of him before he joined the army; proud of him when he joined the army so she could go to university; proud of him now. But she was worried. Something was troubling him.

She went upstairs to use the bathroom. She was not the prying type, though that would have to change when she became a spy. Petrov's bedroom door was ajar. She didn't want to go in there, but something was telling her that she should. She entered. His bedroom was a mess – bed sheets and blanket twisted into a shape that resembled a coiled python; sweat stains on the bottom sheet; soiled clothes strewn on the floor; empty vodka bottles on a bedside cabinet; the rest of his clean clothes unpacked, within his open suitcase. This was so unlike him. He was always previously meticulous, even before he joined the army. Growing up with parents in a one bedroom flat typically induced almost OCD-like behaviour. It had to be that way – every inch of space had to be accounted for and kept functional and clean.

She closed the door, used the bathroom, and returned downstairs. He needed her, she decided. But how could she help him if she didn't know what was wrong? She knew that Spetsnaz Alpha was an extremely tough gig. They were the most elite special forces that Russia had to offer; always first in and last out. It didn't take a rocket scientist to work out that Petrov had been to the Crimea. But the Russian government was still denying any involvement in the Ukraine crisis. She wouldn't know what happened in the Crimean Peninsula until she joined the SVR. Even then, it might take months, even years, before she was granted clearance to know the truth.

The stroganoff was slowly simmering. The potatoes were boiling. There was nothing more she could do until she served dinner in thirty minutes. She decided to venture out and meet her brother. She put on her walking boots and a coat and leisurely followed the coastal footpath. Though it was cold, the air was still and the sky was clear. She glanced back at the cottage. Petrov had chosen well when he purchased the property. It would have been idyllic for their parents. Mum and dad loved the sound of sea, the smell of heathland, solitude, peace. It broke her heart that her parents didn't live long enough to enjoy their new home. She carried on walking, going over the rise where she'd last seen Petrov, and following the route down on the other side. That's when she stopped. Petrov was sitting on the edge of a cliff. The drop beyond was eighty yards. Ragged rocks were on the beach below.

She forced a smile and walked to him. "Brother, dear. Dinner's nearly ready."

He looked at her. His expression was odd. It seemed to Natalia that he didn't recognise her. He had crimson bags under his bloodshot eyes, his face was pasty, his hands were white as they gripped tufts of grass where he was sitting. His legs were dangling over the edge of the cliff.

"Why don't you come back to the house? It's getting cold out here and the sun will be going down soon." Natalia tried to sound jovial and matter-of-fact, though internally she was scared. "Come on Petrov. I know you're a tough guy, and all that, but even you can get ill if you're not on the move."

Petrov opened his mouth. No words came out.

Natalia frowned. "What is it? Are you drunk?"

Petrov shook his head. He spoke. "No amount of drink can make me drunk."

She crouched beside him and placed her hand on his hand. "I've heard that the downtime is always the worst for soldiers like you. Maybe you shouldn't have come here. It might have been better if you'd stayed in Moscow and gone out for a few beers with your army friends."

Petrov shook his head. "They're not my friends."

In a gentle voice, Natalia replied, "Oh come on. You love their company. You once told me that no one understands a soldier as well as another soldier."

He bowed his head. "I was wrong." He looked at the sea and inhaled deeply. "I wish you well in your new career. But know this: one day you'll realise you're working for a bunch of barbarians. They think they're clever. They're not. They're inhibited by a necessary bloodlust that's determined by a need to exert power on others, both domestically and overseas. That's Russia's Achilles heel. Elections are rigged. We don't care. All we want is the tough man in power. He gives us what we want, even if there's a trail of blood behind him."

"Petrov. You're not making sense. Maybe it's the vodka talking."

Petrov sniggered. "Vodka. It's my medicine. But it doesn't work. Nothing works. Not fucking walks up here, not the quiet, not noise, not company, not books, not TV, not bullshit newspapers, not food, not fucking life itself!"

Natalia's smile vanished. All attempts at trying to convey a calm persona evaporated. She took his arm and tried to pull him to his feet. "Back to the house; food; I don't mind if you drink; sleep; tomorrow's another day."

Petrov pushed her away, with sufficient force to cause her to fall onto her back a few yards away from him. He shouted, "Three months ago my unit was sent into the Crimea. It was a top secret mission. The Russian president was the brains behind our task. But, I didn't know what the task was, until it was too late. The Alpha men with me slaughtered a village. I wouldn't help them. So I killed my captain and pretended it was done by someone else. A fucking village of innocent people! The idea was to make it look like the Ukrainian forces had done the job. That way there's more support for the rebels. And Russia gets what it wants." His voice became quieter. "I watched kids... you know, kids, turned into a million pieces; old people trying to hobble to their homes, but getting sprayed with automatic gunfire in the back; men acting as human shields to protect their families, but all of them getting wasted; people burning to death. The fucking fire. Smell of burning flesh. Screaming. Gunfire all the time. Bangs. And all because of a fucking chess move by the Russian government." Anger was in his voice as he added, "Go and work for the Russians. Do their bidding. But know this: you'll be working for a bunch of psychopaths who don't care about you or anyone else. They sent me to slaughter people. Why? Why would they do that?"

He turned to face the sea.

Natalia screamed.

Petrov launched himself off the cliff.

His body smacked the rocks below.

He was broken and dead.

CHAPTER 1

Modern day.

It was late summer and early evening in London. Tourists remained in the capital, either staying overnight in hotels or intending to catch the last train out of the metropolis and head home or to cheaper accommodation. Their presence doubled the population of London to sixteen million. After a day of sightseeing, they were now seeking relaxation – going to west end theatres, dining in Soho or elsewhere, strolling along the River Thames embankment, riding the London Eye so they could see the city from on high as the sun went down, having a few pints of beer or glasses of wine in alfresco bars or pubs, sitting on pleasure cruisers, or taking their kids to Leicester Square so they could enjoy illuminated fun fare rides. Londoners eschewed most of these activities in favour of heading to various parts of the city so they could be at home, though some of them had a couple of post-work drinks with their colleagues before jumping on a tube. All Londoners know that the city is actually a multitude of villages, glued together at the hip while retaining their autonomy. A north Londoner rarely knows much about south London, and vice versa. Ditto east versus west versus the centre. And even within those zones, the diversity is incredible – different cultures, classes, property prices, shops, restaurants, history, dialect, crime-levels, types of crime, and jobs. London is not a *melting pot*, as it's often described. It's a series of different identities that are held together by a spider web of interconnecting transportation links. And it's also one of the loneliest places in the world. Tourists come and go and mean nothing to Londoners beyond the fact that visitors clog up streets and encourage tacky street vendors to set up their stalls. Residents might occasionally socialise together, but for the most part they scurry to their bolt holes at the first opportunity when they've completed their day job, like rats darting in every direction after they've fed on a tasty carcass. A person could live in a part of London all his or her life and not know anything about a residential street that was only four roads away. Everyone under the age of forty should live in London at least once; everyone over the age of forty should move out.

Not everyone complied with that mantra.

Ben Sign was forty nine years old and lived on the top floor flat of a converted Edwardian terraced house in south London's West Square, in Southwark. He was a former senior MI6 officer, tipped to be the next chief until he resigned because he refused to buy-in to the backstabbing power-hungry nature of those who wished to get to the top in Whitehall. A year ago, he'd set up a private detective consultancy. His business partner was Tom Knutsen, fourteen years his junior, a former Metropolitan Police undercover operative. There were two bedrooms in the West Square flat. Sign slept in one of them; Knutsen the other. Sign was a widower. Knutsen was to be married, but his fiancée was murdered. They knew all about loss and grief. West Square was their base of operations. It was also the location where the two men, with wholly different in backgrounds and outlooks, could keep each other company, eat good food, put the world to rights while sipping a post-dinner Calvados, walk the streets of London, and challenge each other's way of thinking. They were two lonely men who'd been given a second chance at finding true friendship. And that's what they were: colleagues and friends. Nothing more; nothing less.

Sign was tall, slender, had clipped brown and grey hair that was singed at the ends by a barber in St. James's in order to produce a perfect cut, spoke with an aristocratic accent, and bought his suits and casual attire in Saville Row. And yet, he was from humble origins. His father was once a merchant navy officer, always travelling, before becoming an academic. His mother raised him with very little money. His brilliant mind was his way out of his modest but loving upbringing. He got sponsored to go to Oxford University, gained a double first class degree in politics, philosophy, and economics, and was tapped on the shoulder to join MI6. He was regarded as the most successful spy of his generation. Now, out of MI6, he still had a hotline to the prime minister, foreign secretary, defence secretary, home secretary, Met police chief, and heads of MI6 and MI5. They weren't going to ignore his talent. If they had a problem they and their officers couldn't solve, they'd call Sign.

For the most part, Knutsen was different, though, like Sign, he had a good intellect and had gained a first at Exeter University before joining the police. While he didn't possess Sign's brilliance, he complimented the former spy master very well. And that was why Sign had chosen him to be his business partner, over and above a number of other candidates from the intelligence agencies, police, and special forces. Knutsen had energy, could mingle with folks from all walks of life, had the advantage of not being as posh as Sign, could run a hundred metres in ten seconds flat, and was still young enough to not overthink the consequences of putting a bullet in a man's skull. He was an expert marksman and a dab hand at unarmed combat. So was Sign. But Sign had inflicted and seen too much death and destruction in his career. These days he preferred to think; not maim or kill.

Knutsen was nearly as tall as Sign. He had short blonde hair, an athletic physique, spoke with a working class London accent even though he grew up in the West Country, and owned one suit that he'd bought at a discount price in Marks & Spencer in Oxford Street. He knew London like the back of his hand – years of infiltrating ruthless gangs will grant a cop that knowledge – but didn't have Sign's grasp of the world, nor his ability to deduce the solution to seemingly intractable problems from the comfort of his chair. Sign was his mentor, there was no doubt. Knutsen didn't feel awkward about that. He was bright enough to realise that there was so much he could learn from the former spook. He also realised that a lifetime spent with Sign would barely scratch the surface of Sign's brain. That didn't matter. Knutsen was here for not only companionship; he was also here for the ride. It is rare for a man to be in the presence of brilliance. That said, Sign could be a cantankerous so and so at times. At home, Sign had his strengths. He was a superb cook, meticulous with his ablutions and keeping the flat clean and tidy, for the most part polite, and could regale Knutsen with mind-blowing tales about his past exploits. It was never boring living with Sign. But, Sign also had a propensity to irritability when their only cases were mundane – investigating potential infidelity, financial fraud, the vetting of potential employees, and the like. Sign hated work that didn't flex his intellect. He grew morose and snappy when he didn't have a job that made his head hurt.

Below them there were three other flats in the building. Sometimes they were temporarily occupied by students and city workers. Right now they were being refurbished by the landlord and were empty. Sign and Knutsen were glad of that. They liked being left alone. And their apartment was a treasure trove. The bedrooms, bathroom, and kitchen were modest in size, though Sign had transformed the kitchen into a chef's paradise. There were meat hooks attached to the ceiling, holding pans, ladles, clusters of garlic, vines of tomatoes, and, on occasion and when the season dictated, pheasants and other game - bought in nearby Borough Market - that needed hanging for up to a month before cooking. On the kitchen windowsill were pots of growing chillies, basil, tangerines, and lemons. A magnetic strip was attached to the wall and held knives that were old yet razor sharp, one of them having been used as a murder weapon in Jaipur in nineteen fifty six, another that had been used by an unfortunate adventurer to cut open a dead bear in Canada so that the man could sleep inside the animal rather than freeze to death, and the rest a collection of blades that had been used by a Chinese knife thrower within a circus in Hong Kong. Upon moving in to the flat, Sign had ripped out the useless electric cooker that the landlord had installed. He'd ordered a top-notch gas cooker. A reformed strangler who called himself Hip Hop had helped him fit the new cooker and dispose of the old one. Hip Hop owed Sign a few favours. It was the least he could do. But, it was the much larger lounge that was the centrepiece of the property. It was stunning; least ways for two bachelors. Women would probably say it needed a female touch. Sign and Knutsen didn't care. They currently had no women in their lives. They were blokes and they could live how they damn well liked. The room had antiquities sourced from Burma, Mongolia, France, Patagonia, and Japan. Three armchairs were in the centre of the room – two facing each other next to a fireplace; the third on the other side of the room. On the walls were paintings, framed military maps of various parts of the world, bookshelves containing academic journals, leather-bound out-of-print works of fiction, poetry, non-fiction, and a diary written by a British naval officer during his voyage to America in 1812. Persian rugs were on the floor. The curtains adjacent to the double window were heavy and crimson. The mantelpiece above the fireplace had candles, oil lamps, a revolver that had belonged to a Boer soldier, and an Arabian dagger that had its tip embedded in the mantelpiece's wood and was vertical. There was a tiny dining table, about the size of an average table in a Michelin Star restaurant, that was in one corner of the room.

It was six forty five PM. Sign and Knutsen were in suits, shirts, ties, their shoes polished. They were expecting a female guest for dinner and had to look the part. Sign was roasting and steaming shark, boiling potatoes and vegetables, and making a gravy consisting of sweated onions, fresh herbs, red wine, a homemade vegetable stock reduction, and a stick of aniseed. Satisfied that the meal was underway, he turned his attention to the dining table. With precision, he laid out a starched white table cloth, used a hot iron to flatten it, added pristine silver cutlery and two sets of polished wine glasses per person, set mats, and placed a bottle of white wine and a bottle of still mineral water in the centre – both in ice buckets. He went to the drinks cabinet – a Victorian piece of furniture he'd purchased in Kenya – and withdrew a bottle of French Cognac. He poured some of it into two brandy glasses.

He said, "Mr. Knutsen. Our guest arrives in less than ten minutes. Before she arrives we shall have a sharpener while sitting in our armchairs."

Knutsen took his drink and sat in his chair, facing Sign. "Why the VIP treatment?" He pointed at the third armchair in the room. "Normally you sit clients on that, and then tell them to bugger off after they've told us their sob story."

Sign sipped his drink. "I don't recall ever telling a client to *bugger off* or variants of that vulgar phrase."

"What about that bloke who thought his wife was possessed by the devil?"

"Oh, yes. He was wasting our time. I admit to being a tad curt with him." Sign swirled his drink in his brandy glass. "Why the VIP treatment on this occasion? Our guest is Jayne Archer. She's fifty years old, British, and single, no children."

Knutsen smiled. "So, the fancy meal and dining table placements are because you might just have the hots for her?"

"Hardly. I want to show her respect. She's a very senior MI6 officer who's just been promoted to head up the service's Russia Department. It's a plum posting. She knows me, and I know her, but not that well. Our paths rarely crossed due to the different nature of our work in MI6. And just to clarify – I do not have the *hots* for her and nor does she have the hots for me. Romance is not an emotion that features in her prevue, nor mine for that matter. All that matters to Archer is her work. Be careful of her. She's sharp."

"As sharp as you?"

Sign waved his hand dismissively. "I'm just a buffoon who gave up the opportunity to have the best job in Britain in favour of working a poorly paid business in partnership with an out-of-work cop."

Knutsen laughed. "We all make mistakes. But, I came out alright from your faux pas. I got a place to stay and a bit of cash in my pocket."

Sign smiled. "You've never made mistakes in your life?"

"Not really."

"You executed your fiancée's murderer in cold blood, could have been imprisoned for life, but instead got sacked from the police."

"Oh yes, there is that." Knutsen stated, "Any minute now a government servant is going to knock on our door, hoping to engage us on a case. I imagine she's on a good salary, but how's she going to be able to afford to pay us? With our running costs and personal draw-downs from our company, we're operating at a twenty K per month overhead."

"She has family money. She can afford our fees."

The downstairs intercom buzzed.

Sign said, "Mr. Knutsen. Would you be so kind to let Miss Archer into our humble abode?"

One minute later Jayne Archer was in the lounge. She was medium height, slightly plump, had blonde hair that was cut into a functional bob, was wearing the smart brown skirt and matching jacket that she'd worn to work in the day, and wore black shoes that had a centimetre high heel. From distance she looked plain. But up close there was no mistaking there was something special about the woman. Her eyes glistened and flickered as they took in everything around her. She radiated a weird aura – it felt like a kinetic energy. Her expression looked benign; but if one examined her with greater perception it was one of a person who knew she could outwit everything around her. Knutsen thought she reminded him of a crocodile, waiting partially submerged in water, its fake grin visible to prey, immobile, letting the quarry come to the reptile, and then striking with deadly speed. Sign was right. Be careful.

Sign sauntered up to her, his arms outstretched. "Hello gorgeous. I hope you like our digs. It's an oasis of calm amid a sea of madness." He embraced her and kissed her on both cheeks. "Will you have wine or something stronger? Dinner will be about ten minutes."

In a well-spoken voice she replied, "I'll have a whiskey with a dash of water."

"Quite right."

She looked at Knutsen. "Who is this handsome man?"

Sign placed his hand on Knutsen's shoulder. "Tom Knutsen; my business partner; former cop; undercover mostly; preferred conforming to criminal gang culture rather than the gang culture of the Met; left the police after a rather unfortunate lapse of judgement; joined the business a year ago; single; messed up in the head; loyal to me, and only me; university educated but can play the part of a bruiser; very useful with a gun; kills people for me." He looked at Knutsen. "Have I missed anything?"

With sarcasm, Knutsen replied, "Cheers. You've summed up my life in a nutshell."

"Excellent, dear chap. I'll let you two get acquainted while I serve up dinner. I do hope, Miss Archer, that you're not averse to fish. You haven't gone all mid-life crisis vegan or some such nonsense?"

"Fish is fine", she replied.

When Sign was in the kitchen, she sat opposite Knutsen, her drink in her hand. "I heard that you and Ben broke two very big cases within the last year."

Knutsen nodded. "I just did the donkey work. It was Ben who solved the problems."

"Does that rile you?"

"Nope. I know my strengths and weaknesses."

"Why did you join the police?"

"Would you like me to reel off a bunch of clichés? Stuff like, I wanted to protect and serve; get an adrenalin buzz; see parts of London that most people don't know; risk my life for others; that kind of shit. Truth is I wanted a job. And I wasn't dumb. When I joined there weren't many graduates entering the police. They thought I was a wonder-boy, even before I started my training. I thought it was a load of bullshit. But, I needed the cash."

Archer's eyes were locked on Knutsen. "And yet you eschewed more cash by gaining fast track promotion in favour of staying a lowly undercover cop. That says something about you."

Knutsen shrugged. "Undercover work gets extra pay and is all expenses paid. I don't need much beyond a room, bed, and a bit of grub in my belly. I had no need to become a superintendent or chief constable. Like Ben, I've never been power-hungry. We're not like you. "

"I don't seek power. I seek answers. You, however, seek solitude. You are like a monk. But one day you'll pine for more." She looked over her shoulder and called out, "Ben – would you like some assistance?"

Sign entered the room, two plates of food in his hands, the third nestled in the crook of his arm. "Nonsense! Since when do guests help their hosts?" He placed the plates on the dining table. "Dinner is served. I will pour the wine. It's a lovely 2016 Canapi Pinot Grigio. I selected it from my vintners in High Holborn. If one examines one's palate when sipping the wine one can detect tropical fruits and citrus. It is the perfect accompaniment to a solitary shark which has lost his way off the Dorset coast and yearns for warmer climes. Please be seated. We must have rules – no business talk while we eat. We can discuss why the three of us are in the same room when we have our post-dinner coffee and brandy."

After tasting the first mouthful of food, Jayne said, "This is delicious, Ben. You were always a good chef. Do you remember when you cooked us camel in a sand pit in the Yemeni desert? You, me and twenty eight other recruits. We were so naive back then. Well, all of us except you. I remember you unearthing the camel after it had been slow cooking for three days in charcoal. Goodness knows how you sourced the camel. I guess it was road kill. You carved it and served the meat alongside rosemary potatoes, juniper sorrel, chick peas infused with star anise, and dreadful wine you'd stolen from the nearby police station. You'd built a bonfire out of the trunks of sun-baked trees. And before we ate you sang us an old Yemeni song about a pauper's feast. You were always designed to be unusual."

Knutsen asked, "You both trained together?"

Sign tucked in to his food. "For six months, when we joined MI6. Then poof! We were sent our separate ways, like dandelions blown into a wind of multiple directions and agendas. We were carried across all parts of the world. Most of us never saw each other again."

Archer looked at Knutsen. "We were all superb. But Ben was different. He was top of our class. He saw the world and its possibilities in a light that even other brilliant MI6 officers couldn't fathom. Still, you had your flaws, didn't you Ben?"

Sign smiled as he ate. "The head of the training program felt he was an expert in all matters espionage. I told him that I'd pay for him to have a two week holiday in Hawaii if he could stop me sleeping with his wife. If he lost, he had to do me the honour of making me the top student of his batch. He accepted the bet. He said I didn't know where he and his wife lived. His wife had been faithful to him for nineteen years. He thought he was on to a winner. That was until he found me in his house, asleep alongside his wife on their double bed. Of course, I never touched his wife. But, I did sleep with her. He lost the bet." Sign sipped his wine and giggled. "Poor old William. I don't think he recovered from that. Part of me wishes I'd had the opportunity to apologise; part of me thinks he was a fool to take on the wager. Still, I regret that he passed away last year."

Archer addressed Knutsen. "In MI6 we are encouraged to take on the impossible and make it our mistress." She looked at Sign. "How have you been since you left the service?"

Sign munched on his potatoes. "It depends on what day of the week you wish to analyse me. Over the last year I've been broke, solvent, sad, lonely, happy, brimming with energy, slothful, intellectually stimulated, bored, charming, irascible, and happy. How have I been? I've lost a few strands of hair since I left the service. Apparently, in men, it's either due to too much testosterone or too little. My barber estimates I've lost two percent of my hair, compared to a year ago. I know for a fact I've lost nine thousand and eighty three hairs – not enough for anyone to notice. The average head has at least one hundred thousand hairs, more if you're blonde or a red head." He looked at Knutsen. "How have I been since I left the esteemed MI6?"

Knutsen looked at Archer. "I didn't know him when he was in your organisation. All I can say is that ninety percent of what Ben says is utter bollocks; ten percent is so precise it hits you like a sidewinder missile."

Jayne smiled. "The ninety percent is the chaff to deflect attention away from the ten percent." She looked at Sign. "Isn't that correct, Ben?"

Sign tucked into his shark. "I am like anyone else. I lie up until the moment I tell the truth. How have you been Jayne?" Sign didn't look at her.

Archer smiled. "You always were the brightest boy. I've been better, but I don't want your pity."

"You won't get any from us." Sign poured more wine for Archer and Knutsen. "We're candles, Jayne. We burn with ferocity, we shed wax, we extinguish. Are you extinguishing?"

I'm…" For the first time Archer looked unsettled. "I don't know." She composed herself, her poker face back on. She said to Knutsen, "Anything I say to Ben must be treated in the strictest confidence. Your police security clearance isn't high enough to be privy to matters pertaining to British Intelligence. Still, if Ben trusts you then I have no problem talking in front of you, providing you stick to the rules."

Knutsen shrugged. "When I had to pretend to be someone else while I spent quality time with a bunch of psychos who would have cut my head off if they found out who I really was, I got used to keeping my mouth shut. Security clearance or not, I wonder if you've spent chunks of your life living in fear."

"I have." Archer carried on eating. "As you both are aware, I've recently been promoted to head up the service's Russia Department. Even though I was born in Russia and speak the language fluently, I'd never served in the department before. I suspect the service wanted an outsider to run the show. MI6 has a long track record of being contrarian."

"Congratulations on the appointment." Sign slashed his knife into the shark's flesh. "Any fellas in your life?"

Archer laughed. "I have plenty of *fellas* in my life – male colleagues, my hairdresser, doctor, the chap who serves me wine at my local brasserie, my bodyguards when I'm overseas, and others. But, I certainly don't have a lover. What about you, Ben?"

Sign carried on eating. It seemed to Knutsen that he was deliberately being cavalier. "Two women dead. Two chaps left standing. Mr. Knutsen and I are not yet in the mood to start courting pretty ladies. That may or may not change." He finished his food and placed his cutlery on his plate. "So here we all are – loveless entities." He smiled. "I bought the camel off of a Bedouin. It was riddled with disease and parasites, and was dying. I purchased the unfortunate creature with a carton of cigarettes. Did you notice that I didn't eat the animal? I hoped I'd poison the rest of the recruits. I reasoned some of them would die; others would be hospitalised for a sufficient duration to render them unable to continue their training. I had everything to gain, because I'd be the last man standing."

Archer looked at Knutsen. "He may be lying; or he may be telling the truth. You and I will never know."

Knutsen nodded. "I'm getting used to it." He stood. "I'll clear the plates and put the coffee on."

"Excellent idea," exclaimed Sign. "Let's retire to our sumptuous armchairs. I have a smashing Lemorton 1972 Calvados. It won't conflict with the coffee. The calvados will be our *Le Trou Normand* – our means to obtain a hole in our stomachs after a hefty meal, though traditionally Le Trou Normand refers to a spirit that is served in France midway through a meal, not at the end. But we shall defy convention."

Two minutes later they were in their armchairs, coffee and calvados on small tables adjacent to each chair.

Sign said, "And now to business. You have a problem, Miss Archer – one that your peers, subordinates, and superiors cannot solve,"

Archer sipped her calvados. "I have two problems; both of them delicate."

Sign rubbed his hands. "Excellent. Juicy intrigue or salacious indiscretions. Or both."

"Ben – stop being flippant." Archer winked at Knutsen before looking back at Sign. "We can all playact and be chameleons. You don't need to put on a performance for me. I will see through it."

Sign nodded. "It's the layers beneath that you'll struggle to discover." He closed his eyes, clasped his hands, and leaned back in his chair. "Proceed."

Archer addressed Knutsen. "MI6 is a cell-like structure. Think of it as a honeycomb. I do things that my boss isn't cleared to know about. He does things I'm not cleared to know about. In headquarters there are people in the room next to me who have no idea about my work, and I've no idea about their work. There are different departments. None of us knows what another department does. Most importantly, none of us know about each other's foreign agents. It has to be that way. Secrecy is paramount. So, what I'm about to tell you is information that is only privy to a small number of security-cleared individuals. If you break my trust, Tom, I'll crucify you."

"Get on with it, Jayne. We have no time for melodramatics!" Sign remained deep in thought, with his eyes closed.

Archer kept her eyes on Knutsen. "I'm about to break the law by telling you something. If MI6 found out why I was here, they'd put me in prison and throw away the key. Breaching Section 1 of the Official Secrets Act is no trivial matter. It's one step away from treason."

Sign was getting impatient. "And yet here you are and here we are. And if we all have to spend quality time together in clink, you can look forward to the possibility of me telling you one day how I really sourced the camel. I'll give you a teaser – it involved me donning a chequered silk dish-dash and riding the beast across fifty miles of desert. It was very *Lawrence of Arabia*."

Archer sipped her coffee. "I run a female Russian agent. She's SVR, posted to Russia's London station. She's only twenty five years old."

"Her access?" Sign's tone was curt.

"She knows the names of every Russian spy in Britain."

"Her motivation to spy for you?"

"She hates Russia. Or more precisely, she hates the Russian regime." Archer placed her cup back onto its saucer. "Her brother was in Special Forces. He was deployed to the Crimea. He witnessed his colleagues commit a state-sanctioned massacre. He killed his captain, though his colleagues never found out it was him who pulled the trigger. He was riddled with guilt, took to drink, and committed suicide. My agent saw him take his life."

"And at that moment, his guilt transferred itself into her. She spies for you because it is her only was of slowly but surely bleeding the guilt out of her system." Sign opened his eyes. "But, something's gone wrong."

Archer nodded. "Without doubt, she is the best agent the Russia Department has. Only I am allowed to see her. She's single-handedly giving us the ammunition to dismantle not just the Russian spy network in Britain, but also its presence in France, Germany, and elsewhere in Europe. Plus, she has knowledge of Russia's footprint in the States. Some of this information is in her head. Other names she has to steal from files and by the use of interpersonal guile. It's a fraught task. She's walking a high wire tightrope. We all know what would happen to her if she got caught."

"Yes, we do. Why has she stopped spying for you?" Sign was looking straight at Archer.

"I didn't say she had."

"I'm accelerating proceedings. If she'd gone missing and you simply wanted us to find her you wouldn't have given us the information you've just supplied. Instead, you'd have spun a cock and bull story about why she's of value to you and why you need her back. No. You want us to get into her head. She's stopped spying for you and you want to know why."

"Correct." Archer was cautious. "I don't know if I'm doing the right thing, being here."

Sign huffed. "What's her name?"

Archer said nothing.

"What's her name?!"

Archer looked at Knutsen, then Sign. "Okay. So this is the bit where I break the law. Her name is Natalia Asina."

Sign took a swig of his calvados. "Given her age, she's of a low rank in the SVR. But, given her access to the names of Russian spies, she has a highly confidential, but desk-bound job. She's not yet been unleashed to be a front-line operative. She's an analyst. Correction – she's a human resources specialist. She has to monitor Russian spies in Europe and elsewhere. Her remit is welfare. If a Russian spy needs help, she directs support to that spy."

"Yes. But, not all spies. She's only cleared to know the identities of low to medium ranking agents in Britain. She has to manufacture access to the names of the top Russian spies in the West."

"Of course. But, at great risk to her wellbeing, until recently she was able to do that and pass that information to you. Now, she's got stage fright. You want us to work out why."

Archer looked cold as she replied, "The *why* is pertinent but not paramount. I just want her to continue to do her job."

"The *why* is most certainly pertinent if we are to tear apart her brain and ascertain the reason why she's no longer cooperating." Sign dipped his finger in his drink and placed it in his mouth. "How many MI6 officers are privy to the identity of Natalia?"

"Alongside me, the chief and four other high ranking officers."

"What are their views on this matter?"

"The chief is putting enormous pressure on me to get Natalia back on track. The others have offered to meet her. But, I've declined that offer. She'd clam up further. Probably she'd flee to Russia. She only trusts me."

"That must change." Sign said, "Tell me about her personal life and character."

It was clear that Archer didn't like being interrogated in this way. "She's single, though she had a boyfriend at university. She split up with him when she got the job offer with the SVR. Her parents are dead; she's pretty; no financial problems, though she's on a meagre salary; fluent English; intelligent; perceptive; lives in a one bedroom flat in Battersea; no pets; likes to go to nightclubs on a Friday night, but only to dance; drinks alcohol but not to excess; doesn't smoke; has never taken drugs; listens to music."

"What music?" asked Knutsen.

"Indie music. My Bloody Valentine, The Orb, Primal Scream, The God Machine. And other stuff that I'd never heard of until I met her."

Knutsen looked at Sign. "I like her."

Sign shook his head, a look of disdain on his face. He asked Archer, "What are her Achilles heels?"

"Hatred of Russia and vulnerability. Both can produce in her emotions and skewed decision-making. A woman bearing anger and fear can feel very frightened. She's terrified of herself and of others."

"As a result, we have the measure of her." Sign slowly exhaled. "Miss Asina is lost in the world. The only mentor she has is a manipulative MI6 officer. She's being raped by the system, on a daily basis. But, that's not why she's stopped spying for Miss Archer. No. There's another reason. We must determine the cause of her volte face."

Archer nodded. "I want a second opinion. Will you meet her? I would set up the meeting and say you are both serving MI6 officers."

"As you wish."

Archer's poker face was gone. "Ben – I'm asking you to do this because I respect your judgement. If anyone can get through to her, it's you."

"My dear, of course. Now, you have a second reason for being here."

Archer nodded. "I was born in Moscow in extremely insalubrious circumstances. At least, that's what my parents told me. My parents were professors at Oxford University. They specialised in Russian politics, language, and culture. After I was born, my parents returned with me to England. They raised me well, educating me, inspiring me, and teaching me many matters Russian. It's why I'm fluent in the language – both spoken and written. They taught me. They encouraged me to work in government, in some capacity. In particular they wanted me to one day get a job where I could combat the excesses of Russian regimes."

"Russian or Soviet Union?"

"In my parents' minds they were one and the same. By the time I was at university, they told me that it was my decision, and my decision alone, as to what career I chose."

"But, the ground work had been done." Sign placed his fingertips together. "They'd brainwashed you into hating Russia. No doubt they paid for your university education. And they'd been fabulous parents throughout your life. You felt you'd let them down if you didn't pursue a job in a government department."

"Yes."

"But, there would have been a trigger point for their hatred of Russia. And it would have been something that was personal to them."

Archer both loved and hated the fact that Sign was always so damn accurate. "My father died six years ago, of natural causes. My mother is in a care home in London. Her brain is completely lucid, but she suffers from a multitude of physical ailments that render her unable to look after herself. I visit her regularly, work allowing. The last time I saw her was a week ago. I'm hoping that she will soon be able to move into my house. But her medical tests need to be complete before she can be discharged; plus, I need to convert the interior of my house to accommodate her disabilities – a stair lift, walk-in bath, handrails throughout the property, panic alarms, et cetera. The reason I mention my last visit to see her is because that was when she told me something that shocked me. Before I tell you what it is, I must reiterate the my mother's brain is as sharp as it always was and her memory is rifle shot precise. She doesn't have dementia or false memories."

Knutsen asked, "What did she tell you?"

Archer breathed in deeply. "She told me that I wasn't the only one to come out of her womb. I have a twin sister. Her name's Susan. I came out first. My birth was straightforward. Susan's birth was complicated. My mother and I were sent to hospital. Susan was kept in the medical centre where we were born, allegedly to be monitored by doctors and nurses. Something happened. My mother and father never saw Susan again. She was snatched by the Soviet authorities. My parents and I were forced to get on a plane out of Moscow. They had no choice. Soldiers made them leave. Ever since, my parents had no idea if Susan was alive or dead."

"Which is why your parents hated Russia and why they indoctrinated you to think the same way." Knutsen asked, "Before a week ago did you have any inkling, any suspicion, that you had a sister?"

"None whatsoever. I was in shock when my mother told me. I'm still in shock."

Knutsen leaned forward. "Why didn't your parents tell you about Susan before?"

Archer raised her hands. "What good would it have done? Telling me that I have a twin who may be alive or dead in Russia is hardly information that a good parent would wish to impart to their daughter."

"So, why tell you now?"

It was Sign who answered. "Because Jayne's mother knows that her daughter has just been promoted to head up MI6's Russia Department. Jayne is an adult who's now in a position to potentially find Susan. Her mother felt the time was right to burden her daughter with her secret."

"Yes, that's right." Archer smoothed her hands over her skirt. There was no need to do so. Her skirt was immaculate. "My mother is security cleared by the service. I was allowed to tell her about my postings within MI6." She lowered her head. "I wondered if you could help me find out what happened to Susan. I realise that I'm presenting you with two wholly different cases – Natalia and Susan. What are your fees?"

"The cases may have some crossover."

Archer frowned.

Sign said, "If it's a government or corporation, we charge a fixed rate: half up front, half upon successful completion of the job. If it's a private client, we charge variable rates, depending on the circumstances of the client. What steps have you taken to find Susan?"

Archer looked frustrated. "I've tasked my analysts to do traces on the name Susan Archer, and to see if we have any details of the birth of British twins in Moscow in the month I was born. They've had zero results. I've spoken to the man who was third in command of our Moscow station at the time. He's retired and is in his eighties. He doesn't know anything about the incident. The second in command and the head of station died a few years ago. I've also spoken to two KGB defectors who were based in Moscow when Susan went missing. They couldn't help. I believe they don't know anything."

"Have you asked Interpol or the Metropolitan Police to submit a formal request for assistance to the Russian state police?"

"Yes. Russian police were helpful. They said that details of births in the Soviet era were notoriously inaccurate. Many were not even recorded. They couldn't find any records of Susan's birth."

"Could your mother be lying to you?"

Archer sighed. "I knew you'd ask me that. No, she's not lying. She has no reason to lie. She was crying when she told me about Susan. They were genuine tears. She was shaking. Her face was flushed. Plus, my mother has never been good at lying."

"She's kept this secret from you for fifty years. She clearly has some ability in deception."

Archer looked angry. "She withheld a secret that was deeply personal to her. That's very different from lying."

Sign smiled. "I agree." He crossed his legs, glanced at Knutsen, and looked back at Archer. "Our terms for both cases will be as follows. You'll pay us nothing up front. But you will pay us all expenses incurred during the investigation. And if, as we dearly hope, one or both cases are successfully resolved, you can then pay our company a success fee of your choosing, depending on what you can afford."

Archer was silent for a few seconds. "That's… that's very kind. I realise it's not your normal terms and conditions. Are you doing this because I'm an MI6 officer – helping a fellow pilgrim and all that?"

"No. I'm proposing this arrangement because I don't want us all to end up in a god-awful British prison. If we take a chunk of money from you upfront, and it's discovered why we received that money, we don't have a leg to stand on in the eyes of the law. Discretely pay us after the event, not before." Sign stood and walked to the mantelpiece. Next to the embedded knife was a small wooden chest encrusted with platinum patterns of cacti, won by him in a game of Texas hold 'em poker in a Moroccan souk. He opened the box. Inside were seven mobile phones. He withdrew one of them, and its charger lead, and handed it to Archer. "This is your hotline to us. It's deniable. There's only one number stored in the phone. That number reaches one of my phones, also deniable. Never use your name when calling. Never text or email."

"I know how to conduct tradecraft!"

"Yes, but you've never broken British law!" Sign towered over her. "Follow my instructions to the letter, pay any expenses we require, set up the meeting with Natalia, do so in a way that doesn't scare her off, and," he checked his watch, "get an early night tonight."

Archer tried to hide her anger. "As you wish. Good day to you gentlemen." She shook hands with Knutsen and Sign and left.

Sign slumped into his armchair and sipped his calvados. "What do you think?"

"I think you were very hard on her."

Sign shrugged. "People like Archer must not be given a millimetre of due deference. To do otherwise would mean they'd snatch a mile of our souls. She'd have the upper hand. We'd be slaves. I couldn't allow that to happen, and she knew that before she set foot in this room. She doesn't know me that well but she knows *of* me. She knew she'd be intellectually outgunned."

"God, you can be an arrogant bastard."

"Not arrogant. Arrogance is a propensity to look down on the weak and not help them. I don't look down on anyone; and I help people. And when I help them I do need them to surrender to their rescuer. When a person is drowning in a lake, and a lifeguard comes to that person's rescue, it is no one's interest for the drowning person to panic and try to fight off the chap who's trying to haul the person to shore. When a client engages us, they must submit to our ways of doing things."

"You mean you mentally break them?"

"I put them in their place. Then I start work. And at the end of a successful investigation, no one is more delighted than me when I see a client has a beaming smile on his or her face."

Knutsen asked, "How will Archer set up our meeting with Natalia? She's already told us that Natalia's skittish and will most likely do a runner if anyone else in MI6 tries to meet her."

"Jayne Archer is like me. She nudges the world into a direction of her choosing. That said, getting Natalia to meet us will not be easy. I suspect she won't say anything to Natalia. She'll bounce us into the meeting. Almost certainly the encounter will take place in a hotel room."

"God, you bloody spooks!" Knutsen laughed. "Mate — that was a nice dinner tonight. I'd score you at least five out of ten."

"Five?!" Sign had a twinkle in his eye. "The meal was perfect."

"I'd have preferred gravy rather than that sauce thing you made."

"Gravy with fish?! You heathen."

Knutsen asked, "Why is Natalia so important to Archer? I get the sister thing; but Natalia? That's just business."

Sign undid his tie. "Being an MI6 officer is a peculiar job. We know our agents better than we know our colleagues. Agents trust us with their lives. We communicate with them in English or their language, hold their hands, hug them when they're crying and scared, talk to them about their families, talk to them about anything that matters to them in their private lives, offer them hope, assistance, tell them they should only trust their handler, buy them nice dinners, cheer them up with a drink or two, talk about the latest Strictly Come Dancing results or any other mundane nonsense that comes into our heads, take them shopping, pheasant shooting, fly fishing, buy them perfume, or any other activity that flicks their switch, and all the time we do that because we want them to betray their countries and risk their lives. It's a contract between handler and agent. We look after them and make them feel special; they spy. The agent signs up to the contract, as does the MI6 handler. And the agent knows that the charming and considerate handler is sending them to their death. But, at the same time it's a marriage of sorts. Platonic love is a constant. Both handler and agent share one overwhelming fear: failure. Together, they try to make the relationship work." He arched his back. "Natalia is special to Jayne. She gives Jayne what she needs – information. But the marriage is on the rocks. Jayne doesn't like that. She's come to us because she thinks of us as mediators. Jayne's pride is at stake. She doesn't want the marriage to fail."

"Because it would damage her career?"

"No. Because she doesn't want Natalia to be sad."

Knutsen stood. "I need to get out of my suit. Once I'm in jeans and T-shirt, are you up for a couple of pints at our local boozer, and a game of darts?"

"One hundred percent, sir. But, I must warn you that I've been practising darts at the pub, without you knowing."

Knutsen laughed. "You really do talk bollocks."

CHAPTER 2

The next morning, Archer entered the care home that housed and treated her mother. It was located in Godalming, a forty five minute train journey south of Waterloo station. The place was on a hill, close to the prestigious Charterhouse School, and was once a sixteen bedroom private house, with six acres of beautiful grounds, that – during its two hundred and twenty three year existence – had been lived in by a high court judge, film star, opera singer, general who'd seen active service in World War Two's Operation Market Garden, American evangelist who'd turned the place into a venue for his religious cult, and a Turkish billionaire. The property had gone into receivership after it was discovered that the billionaire was avoiding UK tax and was making most of his money by illegally buying and selling blood diamonds, ivory, and vulnerable black girls and young women from Africa for use in European brothels. After five years in prison, the billionaire was thrown out of Britain. That's when the care home took possession of the property. The new owners, husband and wife, were Quakers, doctors, conscientious objectors who'd served in numerous battles in the Vietnam War as combat medical soldiers, subsequently worked for NGOs in Central and South America, set up their own malaria treatment hospice in Papua New Guinea, and could afford to buy the property after the wife's father, an investment bankers whose principles she loathed, had bequeathed his daughter five million dollars in his will. After he died, the husband and wife agreed that the money earnt via greed needed to be fed back into society. They bought the three million pound property on Charterhouse Road, spent a substantial sum on getting it converted, employed highly trained staff, and opened for business as a care home. It was their retirement of sorts. The husband and wife were now in their eighties. They were no longer up to the task of 24/7 looking after others – younger people did that for them – but every day they'd visit the fifteen occupants of the facility to check they were okay, were being cared for, and to see if they had any special needs. The home was one of the most expensive in southern England, but it had to be that way. The location was beautiful, the grounds were stunning, and the staff were highly paid because the Quakers only wanted the best for their residents. Their staff included two groundsmen who'd previously worked at Kew Gardens, a chef who'd trained in a Michelin Star restaurant, two on-call doctors who could have taken other highly lucrative jobs in the UK or overseas, nurses who were on twice the pay they'd have received if they'd stayed in the NHS, two Polish cleaners who were given free accommodation in a lovely cottage on the grounds, free food, and a healthy salary, and two mechanics who ensured that all medical machinery in the home were operating correctly. Thirty percent of all profits from the business were donated to the NHS, ten percent to the local church and state schools, and the rest was used to run the impeccable facility.

Some of the patients were here long-term; others were brief visitors who stayed until they were able to be safely cared for by their family. Jayne's mother was somewhere in between both camps. She wanted her mum to live with her in her house in south west London, but she also needed her to be fit. Jayne couldn't keep a constant eye on her; she was summoned overseas at short notice; and she wasn't medically trained.

Jayne approached the reception desk. She smiled. "Hello Ricky. They've got you working front of house today."

Ricky shrugged. "Gives me a chance to put my feet up. I've clocked seventy hours doing nursing duties this week." He held up his phone. "Since I've been here from six this morning, I've managed to get to level seventeen on Call of Duty. How are you Miss Archer?"

"I'm just checking in." She patted the carrier bag she was holding. "I've brought mum some Belgium chocolates and an academic thesis on how massive landmass, frightening winters, a depressed population that is spread out, alcohol and other substances, and an overwhelming sense within the population that life isn't worth living, will inevitably produce a collective sense of being inhuman. It doesn't refer specifically to Russia. It doesn't need to."

Ricky munched on an apple. "You sure know how to cheer your mum up." He nodded toward the corridor. "Usual place. She's had breakfast."

Jayne walked into the communal lounge. It was a very large and sumptuous yet eclectic room that had a mixture of old and modern fittings, with large bay windows overlooking the grounds' manicured lawn and array of bushes and trees that were trimmed into different shapes – Jayne always thought of the gardens as indicative of a set from Alice In Wonderland - , leather armchairs, oak side tables, gold rimmed paintings of city and county side scenes from 1920s England, widescreen wall-mounted television, Nintendo Wii which could be used by residents between the hours of ten to eleven AM so that patients could exercise their limbs by playing bowling, white-water rafting and other video games, a library containing books that ranged from the classics to popular modern-day fiction, a green-felt-clad table that was used for communal games of bridge and other card games, and The Heaven Telescope, as it was nicknamed by residents. The telescope was long, mounted on a tripod, was pointed out of a window at the sky, had once been owned by an eighteenth century astronomer who'd discovered previously unknown stars, and the more religious residents of the home liked to think it gave them a glimpse of the place they'd be going to when their presence on Earth was no longer needed.

Simon Doyle's face lit up when he saw Archer. He was the co-owner of the care home. Eighty three years old, holding a cane, the American was, as ever, immaculately dressed. Today he was wearing purple corduroy trousers, brogues, shirt and cravat, and a waistcoat with a time piece attached to a chain nestled in a breast pocket. "Jayne my dear. How's my sexy broad doing today?"

Archer laughed. "I keep telling you not to call me that. Your wife will be jealous. Anyway, you're too young to be referring to me as a *broad*. I think that term went out of fashion in America in the forties."

Doyle looked mischievous. "Some terms stand the test of time. I'm an old fashioned guy. Anyway, my wife's back in the kitchen, checking on the lunch menu with the chef. She doesn't know about our little affair."

Archer smiled wider and put on an American accent. "Do you think you've got enough left in your pants to keep up with this gal?"

Doyle shrugged. "We won't know until we find out." He hobbled over to her and put his arm on hers. He looked over his shoulder. "She's in her usual spot at this time of day – in one of the bay window sections, by the table, reading. Hey, we're serving tea and coffee in a few minutes. Do you fancy a hot one?"

"That would be lovely. How's she doing?"

"Pretty much the same as before. She gets tired after dinner, wakes early, can get in to a chair and bed but has to summon a lot of energy to get out, incontinence remains an issue but she and we are managing that, her blood pressure's a bit low, occasional dizzy spells persist, speech and cognitive faculties are good, muscle wastage is constant but slow, no signs of cancer or any other terminal disease, and she's in good spirits." He rubbed Archer's arm. "It's just old age." He patted his hip. "And I know all about that. This hip replacement of mine is a nuisance; it's on the side I always used to like to sleep on. I keep forgetting. Wake in the night feeling like I've been bitten by a rattlesnake down there. Mrs. Doyle never swears except when she's lying next to me in our bed and I wake her up at three in the morning because I'm yelping like a pig that's been shot in the arse." He looked at Elizabeth, who was on the far side of the room. Elizabeth was reading, oblivious to her daughter's presence and out of earshot of Doyle's conversation with her. "The only thing that's changed is she's getting dehydrated. We have to administer fluids via intravenous drips. She's on one now. At the moment it's not a twenty four hour thing. The doctors and nurses have judged that she needs a top up only twice a day. It's not your ma's fault – she drinks plenty. It's just the liver and kidneys aren't processing stuff as well as they should." He looked back at Archer. "We can't release her into your care just yet. But, I don't see why she has to be here for much longer. Once you've finished getting your house converted it will be fine, providing either you or a care worker can be with her when she's awake. Even when she's not awake, you'll need to think about night time routines. She'll want to pee fairly frequently. And other bodily functions."

"I know." She embraced Doyle and stood back. "How are you and your wife doing?"

Doyle laughed. "We're not spring chickens anymore. But we've got good people working this gig. All me and my gal do is potter – check on menus, chat to the residents, write quiz questions for Thursday night's residents competition, sit in front of our accountant and listen to him telling us how much this place costs to run, sign documents, have a nap in the afternoon, take a walk around the grounds before dinner, get one of the gardeners to drive us down to Waitrose once a week. Our days of heavy lifting are long gone. But, we like it here. Two crazy Yanks living the life in leafy Surrey. We only came here because my gal thinks she came from English stock. She isn't. I researched it. She's part Irish, French, Italian, Scandinavian, and Austrian. She knows that I know that. But, we don't talk about it. What's the point? Her heart's in England." He nodded at Elizabeth. "Go and sit with her. I'll make sure you get two cups of tea. Let's keep swapping notes. I'll let you know when your mother's ready to be released; you let me know when you're ready to have her." He was about to attend to his duties but hesitated. "Jayne. I know you've spoken about this before, but don't feel guilty about putting Elizabeth into a care home. You haven't got someone to help you out, you're busy, and your ma does need medical supervision. She likes it here. And she needs support. *Professional* medical support. Better this place than being in a hospital bed, trust me."

"I know. I just wish my damn job wasn't pulling me in all directions right now."

"Even if it wasn't we wouldn't recommend releasing her just yet from medical care. I'm not saying that because I want your money. We don't operate that way. If you didn't have the bucks to pay our fees we'd still keep het here for free if you wanted. Or we'd refer her to the NHS."

"Bless you Simon. The world's a better place with you and your wife in it." Archer walked to her mother. "Hello Mum. Mind if I join you?"

Elizabeth looked up. "Jayne, my dear. I wasn't expecting you for a couple of days. Is everything okay?"

Archer sat next to her mother. "I just thought I'd stop by for a cup of tea with you. Also I have news."

Elizabeth gripped her daughter's hand. "Susan?"

Archer chose her words carefully. "Finding out what happened to Susan will take time. But, I am on the case. I've engaged an expert to look into the matter. He's ex-MI6."

Elizabeth placed her book to one side. "Does he know Russia?"

"Yes. And he's the smartest person I know."

Two orderlies came to Elizabeth's chair. One of them removed her drip, while the other poured tea. When they left, Elizabeth sipped her tea. Her hand was shaking from nerve damage. "Being smart is one thing. But, does he have the capabilities required to find out what happened to Susan?"

Archer nodded. "He was on the fast track in MI6, tipped to be the next chief. He threw it all away to become a private consultant. He's significantly better than anyone if have at my disposal in my department. Plus, he has the advantage of being independent."

"He can break laws to get to the truth."

"Correct."

Elizabeth slowly placed her cup and saucer on the table, careful not to spill the drink. "Do you trust him?"

"He's very discreet."

"Do you like him?"

Archer pondered the question. "We joined the service at the same time and did our training together. After that, our paths rarely crossed. From what little I've seen of him, and what I've heard about him I'd say he's charming, ruthless, kind, rebellious, results-driven, hates boredom, feels dislocated from people, and carries sorrow in his heart. It's hard to answer your question. He's a chameleon who changes shades depending on the environment he finds himself in. I suspect it would take me a long time to find out who the real person is beneath his various disguises."

Elizabeth raised an eyebrow. "He's not the only one in your world who has multiple personalities."

"True."

"How will he go about establishing what happened to Susan?"

"He didn't tell me and I didn't ask him." Before her mother could interject, Archer held up her hand. "He'll have his methods and he'll want to keep them private, for two reasons: first, he won't want me interfering; second, if he does have to break rules, he'll want to do so without implicating me."

Elizabeth laughed, making no attempt to hide her sarcastic tone. "How very noble of him." Her expression changed. In a softer voice she said, "He does sound like the right person for the job. I shall think of him as a solitary falcon, watching everything from high altitude, and waiting to dive to Earth when he spots his quarry." She rubbed her arm and winced. "Be a darling and get me a new set of bones and muscles. All that prancing around like an idiot, with the other residents, in front of the Wii box while pretending to be skiing down a slope at Whistler, doesn't seem to be having the desired effect on my body. If anything, it just puts more aches and pains in my body."

Archer could feel herself getting emotional. She kept it in check, just. Elizabeth wouldn't have wanted to see her daughter cry. She had enough on her plate without having to comfort a distraught daughter. "Simon told me that you're making good progress. The only reason he'd like you to stay here for a bit longer is because the staff want to monitor your levels of hydration. But, if you still need the IV drips on a daily basis, that won't stop you from moving in to my home. I can administer the IV. The doctors and nurses will teach me, and teach me other things. They've very kindly said that I can do a week's medical course here before you're discharged."

Elizabeth smiled. "I do like it here. The staff and facilities are excellent. It's peaceful, but also stimulating." There were four other residents in the room. They were watching TV or chatting. They couldn't hear Elizabeth and Jayne. The rest of the patients were out in the grounds or receiving check-ups in the onsite medical centre. She pointed at each resident. "After Gordon graduated from Eton he was a batsman for the England cricket team, a fashion photographer in the sixties, a school caretaker, a failed polar explorer, and a ship's captain who used to smuggle marijuana from Morocco, Mexico, and Nigeria. Muriel helped design and build Apollo 11, the first craft to put men on the moon. Before then she was a folk singer, occasional prostitute, and a campaigner for black rights. She was a rebel with a Harvard-educated brain that excelled in rocket-science. Toby was unofficially the first man to swim the entire length of the River Thames. He did so after a drunken bet with his friends. He went to Cambridge University, and was kicked out for punching a don in the face because the academic had declared that sodomy had no place in a Christian society. He joined the French Foreign Legion and was court martialled and severely beaten after he skipped parade in the Legion's Djibouti base in favour of erecting a huge placard overlooking the military camp saying 'All Frenchmen Are Closet Homosexuals'. When he was released from military prison, he returned to Britain and ran a safe house for rent boys. He educated them and got them back on their feet. He was awarded an OBE for his sterling work. Yvonne owned two casinos in Bogota, moved to Ireland in the nineteen seventies, made bombs for the IRA, then became an special branch informant, moved to London, married a film director who cheated on her and died in mysterious circumstances, and hit the headlines when she walked down Oxford Street, topless, campaigning for the sale of untampered milk." She smiled. "Look at us now. We're old. All we have is the memory of the trails that we blazed in our past."

Archer looked at Gordon, Muriel, Toby, and Yvonne. "You might find it boring living with me."

Elizabeth shook her head. "Gordon's got cancer and wouldn't survive an operation. Muriel has dementia. Toby has Parkinson's Disease. Yvonne keeps trying to kill herself. People here come and go. Most of them go out in a box, so to speak. I will miss the people in this room. But, we're all resigned to the inevitable. Plus," she drummed her arthritic fingers over Archer's hand, "who'd want to miss out on spending time with Jayne Archer? One of the most brilliant students of her generation at Cambridge University, a knowledge of Russian history, language, and culture, that would make most academics extremely unsettled, a glittering career in government, travelling the world, informing and changing government and international organisations' policies, identifying that spy ring in Munich, so many other huge achievements, oh, and putting that KGB defector in the boot of your car and driving him across the border between Pakistan and Turkmenistan. You could have been killed then, and so many other times. But, you held your nerve." Elizabeth sighed. "I just want to have a hot bath without medical staff standing in the same room. I'll be happy and mentally stimulated in your home in Putney. I'm looking forward to driving my mobility scooter down the river promenade. When the sun's out, the Thames glistens like a huge excitable shoal of silver bass, chasing food just beneath the surface. And when it's dark, the river becomes moody yet alluring, it's black surface only visible from the Victorian lamps that straddle the Thames. I like to think the river is grumpy at night yet asleep. I adore that. It reminds me of your father when he was alive." She waved at one of the orderlies before looking back at Archer. "It's that time of day where I'm required to go for a stroll in the grounds. When will you come back?"

"Anytime you like. Same time tomorrow? I want to update you on progress with the new fittings in my house." She held up her carrier bag. "By the way – chocolates and a book. I'm not sure if sugar and a psychological analysis of the human condition is what the doctor ordered, but to hell with it." She placed the bag in front of Elizabeth.

Elizabeth smiled. "Same time tomorrow, but only if your work allows." Her smile vanished. "When I look at you I look at Jayne Archer, and I also look at Susan Archer. Every day, I've carried that burden for fifty years. I look at you, I look at her. It's been torture."

Archer kissed her mother on the cheek. "It's the bravest thing I've ever known."

That afternoon, Archer was back in London. For two hours she spent time in MI6's headquarters in Vauxhall Cross, checking in on her department, reading telegrams, and attending a meeting in a board room with other senior members of the service. After that, she left to attend an agent meeting in Mayfair.

She approached Duke's Hotel. The old building was tucked away in a short cul-de-sac within the heartland of one of London's wealthiest districts. It was hard to find unless one took a cab to the venue, was only a five minute walk from Buckingham Palace, was small yet luxurious, old, had a solitary and creaky lift, and a tiny bar that was world renowned for its martini cocktails. She took the elevator to the fifth floor. There was no one in the corridor. She walked past rooms until she got to where she wanted to be. She looked left and right. Satisfied she wasn't being watched, she knocked three times on the door, waited five seconds, and knocked twice.

Natalia Asina opened the door a few inches, though kept the chain lock in place.

Archer asked, "Would you like a coffee?"

The phrase was the pre-agreed code between Archer and Natalia that it was safe to meet. If Archer had asked, "Would you like to have a cocktail downstairs at six?" it would have meant that she suspected she was under surveillance. In that case, Natalia would have shut and locked the door, opened the room's sash window, walked twenty yards along the twelve inch wide exterior ledge, opened another window, and entered a room that was three rooms adjacent to hers. Then, she'd stay in the back up room that was paid for by Archer. Archer would meanwhile try to draw the surveillance team away from the hotel. And when the time was right, Natalia would leave the premises. But, it wasn't a failsafe routine. The drop from the ledge to the concrete ground was eighty yards; Natalia was scared of heights; and there was no guarantee that a surveillance team would leave the hotel when Archer aborted the meeting. Still, it was the only escape plan available to Natalia.

Natalia fully opened the door. Archer entered. Natalia closed the door and bolted the entrance.

The room was small, contained a double bed, chair and desk, wardrobe, chest of drawers, and a bathroom. Archer sat on the edge of the bed. Natalia sat in the chair.

Natalia puffed on a vaporiser electronic cigarette. Normally she smoked tobacco cigarettes, but smoking was not permitted in the hotel. "Why did you wish to see me?"

Archer thought that Natalia looked tired. Normally the pretty young Russian's face was taught and brimming with health. Now there were bags under her eyes, her face was pasty, and her posture was hunched, as if her body was fatigued and craved sleep. Archer replied, "I wanted to see that you're okay. Are you okay? You don't look like you're firing on all cylinders."

Natalia opened the tank of her vaporiser, squired in double menthol e-liquid, closed the tank, sucked on the device, and blew out a large plume of vapour. "The embassy's running on empty. There's so much damn work. Doesn't matter if you're SVR, GRU, or a mainstream diplomat. Lines between us are getting blurred."

She was referring to the Russian embassy in Kensington Palace Gardens, London, within which were twenty three undeclared SVR officers and GRU officers. GRU was the military wing of Russian Intelligence.

Archer nodded. "We're giving the Russians lots of headaches; the Russians are giving us lots of headaches. How will Brexit affect trade deals with Russia? Will the British ever be able to prove that the Novichok nerve agent poisonings in Salisbury were sanctioned by Vladimir Putin? What's our latest stance on Syria? What's Russia's next move in the Middle East? Are we going to maintain sanctions against Russia? Will billions in dirty Russian money laundered in our banks be unfrozen? The list goes on and on and on."

"It does." Natalia looked at the corner of the room. "Some of those issues are above my paygrade. But, I can tell you that our embassy's the busiest I've seen it since I moved here three years ago."

Archer felt like a mentor to Natalia. The Russian was young and relatively new to the secret world. By comparison, Archer had seen so much in her vocation. And if there was one thing she'd learned during her lifelong career as a spy it was never to be surprised by the surprising. In due course, Natalia would embrace that truism. But not yet. She was still learning. Archer asked, "Have you thought about what I said in our last meeting?"

Natalia was irritated. "I told you then and I'm telling you now – I can't do this anymore."

"But, you haven't told me why you won't work with me anymore."

Natalia threw up her arms in exasperation. "What is there to say apart from the obvious fact that if I'm caught, I'll be chopped up into little pieces, put in hundreds of parcels, and posted to all four corners of the world?!" She inhaled on her e-cigarette, in an effort to calm her emotions. "I've given you a lot so far."

"You have. You've given me the names of half of the undeclared Russian spies in the London embassy; ditto the embassies in Paris, Berlin, Vienna, Washington DC, and other places. There's still a lot more I need from you. I need to know the senior SVR and GRU intelligence officers in the embassies."

"I don't know their names! They use aliases. Most of them don't even tell low-ranking people like me that they work for the SVR or GRU. They pose as diplomats to you and me. They ring fence themselves because they're petrified that one of their own, in this case me, might talk to someone who'll cut their balls off."

"With a bit of effort and ingenuity, you could establish their true identities. Plus, it's imperative that we find out the identities of the sleeper cells in The Netherlands, New York, Manchester, Rennes, Madrid, and Zurich."

Natalia huffed. "The sleeper cells are ghosts."

"You're still responsible for every agent in each cell."

"Via cut outs, usually three or four people. I can't get direct access to the ghosts."

"Identify the last cut out in the chain who has that access. Give me that person's name. Then we can come up with a plan to take it to the final level and get each ghost's name."

Natalia bowed her head and rubbed her eyes. "I made a decision two weeks ago that I can't do this anymore. I'm tired, scared, trust no one except you, and don't want to fucking die."

Archer leaned forward and said in an earnest and calm tone, "You're not going to die."

"Really?! Can you promise me that?! Jesus!"

"Natalia. I know you're scared. And I know how that feels like. I was scared every second of every day when I served overseas. And for the most part," She waved her arm, "it wasn't in swanky places like this. I've served in warzones, famine-ridden countries, crumbling cities where secret police were hunting me while I hid in grimy apartments, deserts in Iraq where there were insurgents on my heels, and mountains in Afghanistan where my special forces protection detail got blown up by surface to surface missiles and were butchered by the Taliban. I know fear. Dukes Hotel in Mayfair is not a place to be scared."

Natalia shook her head. "Then you know nothing. My people can get to traitors wherever they are. You were lucky to escape the Taliban. There is no luck involved if Russia deploys an assassination unit. You and I would be dead before we knew what had killed us."

Archer breathed in deeply. She was getting nowhere and needed to change tack. "I hear what you say. You're exhausted. You need some time off. I'll give you that. But I also need you to do something for me in return."

Natalia was still but said nothing.

"I want you to take care of yourself. And I want you to allow me to see you tomorrow so that I can check on your wellbeing. It will be a different hotel." She wrote the hotel name on a piece of paper.

Natalia looked at the paper, withdrew a box of matches, and burnt the note.

"Is that okay?"

Natalia nodded.

"Good." Archer looked Natalia up and down. "What is your cover for being out of the embassy this afternoon?"

"I told my boss that I was researching an anti-surveillance route between Piccadilly Circus and Harrods. I said I may need to go shopping on foot between both locations, in order to define the reason for my route if a British surveillance team was watching me. It's the usual tradecraft – give the surveillance team some explanation as to why you're doing what you're doing."

"That's a perfectly plausible lie as to why you needed to walk the route. But, we have a problem. You have no shopping, two of your nails have cracked polish, your hair looks shit, you have no expensive sample perfume on your throat, and your face is desperately in need of a makeover. You need to return to the embassy with a huge smile on your face and the image of a woman who's shopped until she dropped."

"*Shopped until she dropped?*"

"Don't worry about it; it's just a phrase that refers to women who had a good time buying stuff."

Natalia looked at her phone's clock. "I only have four hours before my absence will be viewed as unusual."

"Then we must engage runners. I'd estimate you are a size six. Shoe size four. Is that correct?"

Natalia looked confused. "Yes on both counts."

Archer picked up the room's phone to the concierge. When he answered, she said to him, "I need you to do me an enormous favour. The guest in the room I'm calling from is a relative. We're in a bit of a pickle. She's just received a marriage proposal and has been invited out to dinner this evening to meet her fiancé's parents. She needs to look the part. We need a size six skirt and jacket from Harrods, Channel No. 4 perfume from Harvey Nichols, a hairdresser, manicurist, and beautician who can come right now to her hotel room, dresses and size four court shoes from Oxford Street, and do make sure that all clothes purchased are kept in the branded shopping bags. I will pay. This is an emergency. Do you have people up to the task?"

This was the most unusual request the concierge had ever heard during his twenty two years of service at the hotel. For a while, he was flustered. Then he said, "It is difficult, but I will see what I can do."

"Just get it done. I'll pay you extra if you achieve results. This is my daughter we're talking about. And she doesn't want to look like a bag of shit pulled up in the middle when she meets her prospective parents-in-laws." Archer slammed down the phone and smiled at Natalia. "So, now you can become a princess spy. I've just saved your ass and dignity."

Over the following three hours Natalia was pampered by the manicurist, hair dresser, and beautician. She was also fitted for the clothes purchased from Harrods. The garments needed tailoring in her room. Alongside Natalia and Archer, there were five people in her room. Archer sat on the bed, watching the workers buzz around Natalia like bees trying to make their queen the best she could be. At the end of the process, Natalia was transformed into a woman who resembled nothing short of elegant style and class. After the people left, Archer rang the concierge and gave him her credit card number. It wasn't in her name. It belonged to MI6.

Archer looked at the tasteful paper and twine shopping bags lined up in the room's corridor. "Go now. You paid for all of this out of your own cash. The receipts are in the bags. You can claim all money back from the Russian embassy. You'll get two thousand and sixty two pounds in compensation. That's what's come off my service's credit card; and that's what's going into your bank account when your accounts department pays up. Tomorrow your embassy closes at one PM. You'll meet me at three PM in the other hotel. There will be no need for all this rigmarole." She pointed at the bags. "Tomorrow it's your afternoon off. You can do what you like without being worried about explaining your absence from work."

The mobile phone that was Sign's lifeline to Archer rang at sixty forty five PM. Sign answered and listened to Archer.

She gave him details of the meeting with Natalia tomorrow. "Today I played a sleight of hand. Normally when we meet it's always one-to-one in hotel rooms. This afternoon I changed that. I told her that she hadn't covered her tracks correctly. That was true. She's naïve and has a lot to learn. But more important to me was that I wanted her to get used to the presence of others during our face to face meetings. It was a test. I got other people in the room. They were just hotel staff and beauticians. But it was a step in the right direction. Tomorrow we significantly up the ante." She told him what she had in mind.

"Good. We shall see you then." He ended the call and entered his flat's kitchen to make a cup of tea. Knutsen was out, collecting Indian takeaway for their supper. Sign was deep in thought as he stared at the kettle while it heated water.

Thirty minutes later, Knutsen arrived clutching a white carrier bag containing cartons of food. The aroma of Indian spices was unmistakable. Knutsen placed the bag on the kitchen counter and withdrew the cartons. "You told me to use my judgement and choose wisely. I've got us beef madras, tandoori chicken, Kerala prawn curry, lamb biriyani, turmeric potatoes, sag aloo, saffron basmati rice, chickpeas and lentils, mint sauce, and papadums. Oh, and I got four ice cold bottles of Henry Weston cider."

Sign looked at the mountain of food and smiled. "Are we expecting company this evening?"

"I was hungry. Help yourself to what you want." Knutsen grabbed a plate, heaped food on to it, opened one of the bottles, and carried his food and drink into the lounge.

Sign stared at the open cartons. "Which one is the joker in the pack?"

While sitting in his armchair and devouring his food, Knutsen called out, "Don't know what you're talking about, mate."

Sign wasn't buying that. "We do this once a month. Every time, and I mean *every* time, you smuggle in one dish, amid the others, that is so potent it is like eating molten lava. Last time we had curry, I lost the lottery and picked the joker. My body was perspiring more rapidly than it would have done if I'd been sitting fully clothed in a Swedish sauna."

"Just man-up and get on with it."

Sign served up a bit of everything. He reasoned that playing the numbers game would ensure he could push the lava to one side after a mouthful and at least have a near-full plate of less noxious food to fill his body. He grabbed a cider and sat opposite Knutsen. He sampled the meat and prawn curries. "Oh, you cad! There is no joker in the pack this time because you've tampered with them all."

Knutsen giggled. "Yep. I asked the restaurant to make sure they were hot enough to make putting your bollocks into a fire feel like a pleasurable experience." He couldn't stop laughing as he saw Sign breathing rapidly and sweating. "Work through the pain, mate. It gets easier. And think of the health benefits."

"There are no health benefits to being poisoned!"

"A fiver says you can't finish everything on your plate." Knutsen carried on eating, immune to the potency of the spices.

"A fiver is a fiver. Wager accepted." Sign carried on eating, his mouth on fire, his lungs feeling like they had locked up, and his shirt now a sodden mess. He gasped for air when he finished. He put his plate on the side table. "Next time I'm going to order from the restaurant. You can't be trusted."

Knutsen handed him a five pound note. "You better get showered and changed. I'll clear up while you're doing that."

Ten minutes later, Sign was back in his chair, slowly sipping his cider. He felt like his stomach lining had been attacked by bullet ants. But, at least he was no longer sweating and was in clean clothes.

Knutsen returned to his seat. "There's a bit left over. I might have it for breakfast."

"You really are beyond redemption."

Knutsen watched him. "Sometimes it takes an unexpected shock to the mind and body to kick start a train of thought."

"And you thought your curry trick would be just the tonic?! Foolish boy!"

Knutsen laughed again. "Look at it from my point of view. There's nothing on TV tonight apart from bloody dumb quiz shows and documentaries about farmers and their new born fluffy baby lambs. It was far more fun to watch you suffer."

Sign breathed in deeply. The internal attack on his body had abated. And Knutsen was right about one thing – the intensity of the meal was a cleansing process of sorts. That still didn't mean he'd trust him with food choices ever again. He finished his cider, walked to the drinks cabinet, and poured two glasses of brandy. As he returned to his seat, he told Knutsen about the call he'd received from Archer. "We must be in suits tomorrow."

All sense of hilarity was now gone from Knutsen. "I've never been to a foreign agent meeting before. It's above my paygrade."

Sign had a dismissive expression. "Your paygrade is the same as mine. But, I concede that it is a delicate and intricate process to win over an agent during a first meeting. Tomorrow, and in the presence of Natalia, I will ask you to do something. Don't, under any circumstances, be offended by my instruction. It will be directed for tactical reasons."

"Wouldn't it be better if I wasn't at the meeting?"

"No." Sign sipped his brandy. "Bring your handgun."

"What?!"

"Please."

Knutsen leaned forward, his brandy cupped in both hands, and sighed. "Look. I trust you. And I know you like to keep your cards close to your chest."

"Because often I don't know what the cards are until they reveal themselves to me."

"I realise that. But is a gun in a London hotel the right decision?"

"It shall be a prop. Do make sure it's loaded, though."

Knutsen leaned back and looked at the fireplace. It was now the beginning of autumn. The fire would need to be lit soon. It occurred to him that he'd have to call Dave, who supplied them with wood and coal. He didn't know why that thought had just entered his head. Maybe it was because it was a normal thing to think about. "Do you have a strategy for dealing with Natalia? Do you have a theory on what happened to Susan and if so how you can prove that theory to be fact?"

Sign looked at the fireplace. "You're thinking about calling Dave, aren't you?"

"Stop reading my mind and answer my questions."

Sign swirled brandy in his mouth. The spirit was a bad idea. It exacerbated the inferno atop his tongue. "I have an idea about Natalia and how to find out what happened to Susan. It may work, or it may fail. That isn't what's troubling me."

Knutsen was silent as he looked at Sign.

Sign placed his brandy down. "Call Dave. We need to stock up before every Tom, Dick, and Harry buys his logs." He looked serious as he addressed his business partner. "There's something that's worrying me about this case. It is based on the usual."

"One of your hypotheses."

"Yes. It is a nagging thought. When I get the nags, I don't ignore them. I do hope I'm wrong. I must prove myself wrong."

"What's the nag?"

Sign smiled. "Dear fellow: sometimes in life we must hold the upper hand until we are exposed as fools. You tried to trick me with your curry. I bettered you. But, I could have failed. The nag pertains to an issue that may go well beyond the current issues we're presented with. If so, we have a major situation. And if, as I hope, I'm wrong then I have my reputation to uphold. I don't want to tell you what's on my mind and make myself look stupid when it turns out to be a load of codswallop."

Knutsen nodded. "I understand. But I've yet to see you achieve anything other than the complete opposite of codswallop. Hold on to your nag. I'll stand by you."

Sign smiled. "You are indeed the finest friend. Now: let us drink our drinks. I'll put the coffee on in a moment. And I'll spray the lounge and kitchen with air freshener. This place smells like the back-end of a balmy Bombay."

CHAPTER 3

At two forty five PM the following day, Archer was sitting in an armchair in a room within the five star Langham Hotel, Portland Place, Regent Street. The room was far larger than the one she'd visited in Duke's Hotel,. Indeed, the whole hotel was huge by comparison to the bespoke but luxurious Mayfair hotel. She'd paid for the room using a credit card that was in the name of a non-existent French woman. Her attire was smart, but casual. The room contained four chairs, a stationary desk, a bed that was covered with expensive linen, a bathroom with complimentary designer soaps, and a minibar stocked with fine wines, mineral water, chocolates, and spirits.

Archer waited.

At precisely three PM there was a knock on her room's door. She answered. Natalia was there. Natalia gave the slightest of nods and entered. Archer shut the door, locked the entrance, opened the minibar cabinet, withdrew two bottles of water, and handed one to the Russian.

When both women were seated, Archer said, "I've been reflecting on your decision to put our work together on hold."

Natalia looked angry. "Not put on hold. I've made it clear – I'm not doing this anymore, full stop."

Archer calmly replied, "That's not acceptable. The job's not complete. You've come too far to quit now."

"Are you threatening me?! If I don't keep working for you then you'll throw me to the dogs?"

Archer shook her head. "Of course not. I don't work that way. You've done a brilliant job for my service thus far. That will always be remembered. But imagine the kudos you'll get if you hang in there a bit longer and give us the rest of the Russian spies. You will be rewarded – money, asylum in Britain, a new identity, a new life."

Natalia huffed. "There's no such thing as a new life where Russia's concerned. They'll find me and kill me. It may take weeks, months, or years. It doesn't matter. Their memories are long. My murder will be a message to others in the SVR, FSB, and GRU ranks that betraying the motherland only ever results in the death sentence. The SVR has a long reach. It can go anywhere. You could house me on the remotest Scottish island and they'd get to me. They wouldn't make it look like an accident or suicide. They'd want to hammer home to Russians that this was cold-blooded murder. Publicly they'd deny to Britain and other western countries that Russia had any involvement. But, Russians would know. My country is held together by fear of the state. My death would make many people think twice about working for the likes of you guys."

"That is true. But, you underestimate us. We can make Natalia Asina vanish and give birth to a new young woman. The Russian Intelligence agencies may be more brutal than us, but they are not as sophisticated. If MI6 helped you, the SVR would never find you."

"Mrs. Banks." Katy Banks was the alias Archer used with Natalia. The Russian spy didn't know her real name. "I believe that you believe in what you're saying. But you are not me. Should I gamble my life on the basis that you may be ninety nine percent right and one percent wrong?"

Archer sighed. "What your brother advise you, if he were still alive?"

"Don't try that one on me! He took his life because he was riddled with demons. I wanted his death to be revenged. I've done that."

"No you haven't. Not yet, anyway. Are you religious, Natalia?"

Natalia shrugged. "Not practicing. But I guess I have faith."

"Do you believe in the afterlife?"

The hostility was back in Natalia's expression. "I can see where this is leading!"

"I'm sure you can. So, to use the percentage ratio you used a moment ago, what if there was a ninety nine percent chance that the afterlife didn't exist, but a one percent chance it did? Would you risk shaming your brother's memory if the one percent turned out to be true? He'd be watching you. And he'd be sad that his little sister didn't have the courage to see matters through to their natural conclusion. He deeply admires you. I suspect that he believes that you have greater mental fortitude than he did at his end. He would be disappointed if his analysis of you turned out to be inaccurate."

"Stop it with the mind games!" Natalia stood.

"Sit down." Archer decided to change the subject. In a soothing voice she said, "I've ordered some tea and cake. It's your afternoon off and I know you like cake. Room service should be here any minute."

Natalia sat back down. "No more reference to Petrov."

"Agreed." Archer leaned forward. "I don't want you to be put in prison or killed. But, I do want you to work for me for a few more months. Russia is on a covert war-footing. We've had cyber attacks, meddling in the British and American leadership elections, assassinations, land grabs in the Crimea, indiscriminate bombings in Syria and Iraq, veto after veto in the United Nations Security Council, flagrant abuse of sovereign nations' air and sea space by Russian military craft, sleeper cells spread across the West, constant lies and misinformation, and ultimately the diplomatic relations between Russia and the West are the worst they've been since the height of the Cold War. If we're not careful, there'll be a flashpoint that will lead us to war. The flashpoint won't come from Russia. It will either happen somewhere that Russia, Britain, and its allies didn't expect; or, it will be the brainchild of Russia and in a place that Russia knows will matter to people like me. Either way, Russia is playing a very dangerous game. It thinks it knows how to play chess. But right now it has all the competency of an eight year old learning the game for the first time and going for broke. People like you and me must keep the child in check but resist going for checkmate. Containment is the right course of action in the current climate. We must protect Russia from itself. The alternative would be catastrophic. Western military action against Russia would result in the decimation of Russia as we know it. We don't want that. Instead, we want to play the long game. One day, we hope to see a Russia that has evolved into a democratic and less paranoid nation. You and I are taking steps to help that happen. Don't underestimate how important your work is to MI6. I know you love your country and hate the regime. So, let's get rid of the latter and focus on the former."

Natalia looked sarcastic as she smiled. "That's a pretty speech. But I might not be alive to see this new wonderful Russia you speak of."

"Maybe both of us will be long dead by then. But I like to think we'd have died of natural causes, with smiles on our faces because we knew that we'd influenced history." There was a knock on the door. "Thank goodness! Room service has arrived." Archer walked to the door and opened it.

Sign and Knutsen walked in.

Natalia stood, eyes wide, mouth open, shock evident across her face. "What the hell's going on?!

Archer went to her, but Natalia pushed her aside, grabbed her handbag, and tried to get past Sign and Knutsen.

Knutsen grabbed her and forced her back into her chair. "Stay there. You are not in danger."

Natalia was breathing fast. Her eyes were venomous as she glared at Archer. "I trusted you!"

Archer replied, "It's because you trust me that I've asked these men to be here. They're friends of mine. Do not be alarmed."

"Who are they?" Natalia looked at Sign. "He's MI6; senior; maybe your boss." She looked at Knutsen. "He's the hired gun; the man that protects people like you." She stared back at Archer. "You knew I wouldn't agree to meet anyone else from MI6, so you bounced me with this. You lied to me!"

"Natalia, we're just worried about you. And I don't think I can help you now." Archer pointed at Sign and Knutsen. "These men work for British Intelligence, but they they're employed in different circles to mine. They're independent. And they're untouchable. You can trust them as much as you trust me."

"Right now that trust is at a low point!"

Sign sat in one of the seats, crossed his legs, and clasped his hands. "My name is Ben. My colleague is Tom. They are our real first names. We will not be supplying you with real or fake surnames." He pointed at Knutsen. "Tom's job is to protect you. He won't hesitate to jump in the way of a bullet that's intended for your head. Tom – open your jacket and show Miss Asina what's attached to your waist."

Knutsen did so, revealing his pistol and holster, before closing his jacket.

Sign kept his eyes on Natalia. "Tom – be a good fellow and go into the corridor. Stay there until Natalia leaves. Shoot anyone who tries to disturb our meeting. Katy – leave now. I wish to speak to Miss Asina alone."

The instructions shocked Archer. She said, "Natalia's my agent. You have no authority to…"

"Yes, yes. Just get out and have a gin and tonic or latte downstairs, or go and see a movie, or do anything else other than being here."

"You arrogant…"

"Stop there, your tongue is equipped with a masterful command of English. Don't corrupt it by the use of expletives. Leave now. I'm in command now."

Jayne shook her head. "This wasn't the deal."

"Leave now!"

Archer's face was flushed red as she stormed out of the room. Knutsen winked at Sign and also exited.

When they were gone, Sign said to Natalia, "I do apologise for our unexpected arrival. Would you prefer to converse in Russian or English?"

She replied in English. "Who says I want to converse with you?"

"I did. You are in a pickle. I'm here to sort out matters."

"Against my will."

"You'll reconsider that stance." Sign scrutinised her, his gaze cold. "I've not read your file. I don't want to. I prefer to make my own judgements on people. MI6 and SVR files are usually filled with lies and guess work. I like to start afresh, because I never lie to myself." He picked a peanut out of an adjacent bowl and tossed it into his mouth. "You are refusing to continue working for MI6 because you are scared. That's understandable."

Natalia shouted, "And you think you can change my mind?"

"Actually, I don't want to change your mind. It's your brain. Why would I tinker with it?"

"Because it's what people like you do!"

"And people like you. But why don't we get off to a good start and agree not to do any tinkering. What say you?"

Natalia frowned. "What do you want?"

"Katy Banks has been hard on you, has she not?"

"She's just doing her job."

"Yes, but her job is a high wire balancing act. Have you heard of Phillippe Petit?"

"Should I have?"

Sign grabbed a handful of nuts and held them cupped in his palm. "He was an impeccably brave and crazy adventurer, specialising in tightrope walks. He decided to be the first man to do a tightrope walk between the Twin Towers. It was 1974. The towers had just been built, though were not quite completed and ready for occupancy. Petit enlisted the help of some friends. He and they devised a devious yet highly risky plan to infiltrate one of the towers, set up the tightrope, and allow Petit to do one of the most death-defying ventures of the last century. Of course, the whole thing was completely illegal. That didn't stop Petit. And absolutely nothing was going to stop him getting on the wire. His successful transition from one tower to the other is well documented, and was caught on video camera. It was breath taking and brought lower Manhattan to a standstill as people one thousand three hundred and sixty eight feet below him couldn't believe what their eyes were seeing above the streets. But here's the thing – what if it had gone wrong? What if halfway across the tightrope, Petit started losing his balance and knew he was going to fall? If that had happened, there would have only been one outcome: death. There could have been a way out. He could have used every muscle and instinct in his body and mind to correct his balance. He couldn't turn around, because the task would have been impossible. His only hope would have been to keep walking to the other side."

Natalia was quiet for a moment. "You think I'm on that tightrope?"

"Yes. Katy Banks is watching you. If you fall left, it's because you've given up on yourself. If you fall right it's because your treachery has been discovered. You're damned either way. So, Katy imagines herself on that tightrope with you. She can only make one decision. And it's the toughest decision."

"I must keep walking the tightrope if I'm to survive."

"Correct. You see, when you're walking a steel wire that is barely two inches thick, only you can finish the journey. Katy and I can shout instructions at you from our safe positions at your start point, but that's not going to help you. I don't want to change your mind or tinker with your brain. To do so would be catastrophic to your circumstance."

Natalia's demeanour mellowed; her tone of voice softened. "Keep spying or fall to the devil or the deep blue sea?"

"That's one way of looking at it."

"And the other?"

Sign rubbed his hands to get rid of peanut dust. "Petit couldn't resist high wire acts. It was in his DNA. And when the Twin Towers were constructed, he knew he was facing his Everest. Every neuron in his body was yearning to be up there. But, was he ready? That was the question. He practised for years; had successes in the incredible Notre Dame act; and failures on low slung wires. A wire is a wire, whether it is one foot above the ground or one thousand feet high. So, on the day he embarked on the Twin Towers escapade, the thought going through his mind was did he now possess all the skills to avoid death? He did. If he'd done the crossing a year or so before, he'd have probably died." Sign pointed at Natalia. "The problem you have is that you were put on the wire before you were ready. I'm here to safely take you off, dust you down, give you more training, and wait to see if you're ready to put one foot in front of the other on the tightrope."

Natalia was confused. "I thought Katy brought you in to bully me into doing my job for MI6."

Sign waved his hand while looking at the ceiling. "Well, there might have been an element of that in her thought process. The problem is that I never do what I'm told." He looked straight at her. "Slap whatever labels you wish to on me: guardian angel, mentor, manipulator, scoundrel, knight, barbarian, contrarian, doctor. It doesn't matter to me and it does matter to you. All that's relevant is I want you off the high wire."

Natalia rubbed her forehead. "Who are you really?"

Sign dabbed his handkerchief against his lips. "If you wish to choose one label, think of me as your consigliere – the person who advises you."

Natalia shook her head. "That's Sicilian mafia shit. And a consigliere isn't the boss. Are you saying I'm the boss who you're advising?"

"Let's work on that assumption, until it proves true or false."

Natalia's eyes narrowed. "You don't strike me as someone who has a boss." She sighed. "It doesn't matter who you really are. You obviously have power over Katy. Will I continue to meet her?"

"Yes. She will wish to check on your welfare. And she will continue to try to persuade you to spy for her. You will also separately meet me. Any attempts by Katy to force you to reveal more Russian spy names must be firmly but gently rebutted by you. Only I can judge when you are ready to recommence work, if indeed you will ever be ready."

"What is this? Some good cop, bad cop routine between you and Katy?"

Sign smiled. "No. Katy and I are not professional partners. And you'll find out that I'm nothing like a *good cop*." He reached into his pocket. "I've bought you a gift." He handed her a small box. "Katy said you were a fan of vaporisers, though normally prefer cigarettes. In the box are one hundred hand rolled cigarettes that I procured from the Balkans. You won't source finer tobacco anywhere else in the world."

Natalia opened the box.

"I'm not a smoker. But, I've been told that it's recommended to smoke one of them after partaking of a rich meal containing red meat. These are not fags to puff on while you're having a morning coffee. Savour them for special occasions. The box is hermetically sealed. The cigarettes should last several months."

Natalia placed the box in her handbag. "Thank you."

Sign checked his watch. "You are off duty tomorrow. I'd like to meet you for lunch. I've already taken the liberty of booking a table for two for one PM at Simpson's In The Strand. One PM, tomorrow. You'll be there."

Natalia looked horrified. "Meet you in a public place? You must be crazy!"

"You'll be there. This is all part of your training. Plus, Simpson's does a lovely roast on Sunday. It's extremely satiating. You won't need to worry about cooking your supper tomorrow evening. The table will be booked in the name of John Scott. Obviously, it's an alias name."

"Why do we need to meet? I may have plans tomorrow."

"You don't. I suspect you hide when you're not working, afraid of open spaces. And we need to meet because you may be able to help me." He stood and extended his hand. "Good day to you Miss Asina. I will leave now. Wait ten minutes before you depart. Katy has paid for the room. You just grab your bag and leave."

Natalia shook his hand. "Do my colleagues know who you are?"

Sign's only response was, "I don't exist." He left the room.

Before heading home, Sign went to a butcher's shop in east London. The place was established in eighteen seventy six, was close to a warehouse which once housed sheep which were slaughtered in the Victorian era by being pushed off ledges so that their front legs were broken and they could easily be dispatched, and was thirty yards from where Jack the Ripper killed one of his victims. Now the establishment was run by a burly cockney who'd spent time in Parkhurst Prison for dissecting a dead gangster who'd tried to extort money from him, had tripped on pigs' blood while holding a gun at the butcher's head, and had accidentally blown his own brains out. The butcher had tried to dispose of the body the best way he knew how. Unfortunately, forensics technology got the better of him. Police found cremated body parts in the furnaces of local hospitals. And they had CCTV footage of the gangster's last whereabouts before he went missing. The butcher went down for contamination of a crime scene and mutilation of a corpse. He was a simple fellow. But he knew his meat and was utterly loyal to those who stood by him. Sign had helped him get his business back when he was released from jail. He told the butcher that his motive for doing so was that he needed a wise and skilled artisan in the neighbourhood who understood fine cuts of flesh. It was a white lie. In truth, Sign knew the butcher was on his uppers and needed a helping hand. That's why he'd stepped in to help him.

"Hello Brian."

Brian smiled. "Mr. Sign, sir. What a pleasure." Brian was behind the counter in his shop, wearing a bloody apron, preparing his produce for the following morning. On the nearby work surface were a brace of hares, partridge, chicken, lamb cutlets, shanks of beef, and an array of offal. Once preparations had been completed, all of the meat would be refrigerated overnight, before being displayed the next day.

Sign asked, "Do you have my order?"

"Of course." He went into the rear room that was kept at two degrees Celsius, walked past carcases that were hanging from the ceiling, unhooked what he needed, and re-entered the shop. "Here we go, sir. She's a mighty fine specimen." He laid the muntjac deer on a slab, underneath which was a large sheet of brown oven-proof paper. "It took me a while to source her. This one came from the north. Do you want me to butcher her for you?"

"I'll do that." Sign walked behind the counter and examined the beast. Like all muntjacs, it was small; approximately two feet long. "I like to do my own butchering, because I want to respect the food I eat."

"Quite right, sir. I wish all of my customers were as discerning and skilled as you. But you won't stop me from packaging her up." Brian rolled the paper around the carcass and bound the parcel with hemp twine. "Job done." He handed the deer to Sign.

"How much do I owe you?"

"Twenty quid."

"The meat is worth at least five times that amount."

"Twenty quid and just promise me you'll come back here when you need some nice bangers, or a beautiful rib-eye steak. I'll be charging you full price then."

Sign smiled, paid him the money, and placed the deer on his shoulder. He walked back towards West Square. He must have looked odd, wearing a suit and lugging an unusual package on his shoulder. The sun was going down as he reached the Thames embankment. People were still out, though not as many as in the height of summer. Sign adored this part of London. And he loved the different light, smell, and temperature of autumn. Particularly in London, for him summer was two or three months of enduring life in a cauldron. Now, the air was crisp and had the first hints of a bite. It felt like he could breathe again. On the other side of the Thames were the Houses of Parliament; nearby to it, the headquarters of MI5. When he was in MI6 he'd visited both buildings many times – briefing ministers and high ranking counterparts in the Security Service. He was glad those days were behind him.

A woman was walking towards him – tall, pretty, late thirties, wearing jeans and a white blouse, and with long brunette hair that was entwined in layers so that it was raised over her shoulders. Her name was Ruth. She'd once worked with Sign in MI6. He'd heard she'd recently left the service and was now employed as lecturer at University College London. At first she didn't notice him; her eyes were fixed on the Thames and she had headphones on. But when she did see him, she smiled. Ruth was the only woman who Sign had wondered about having a relationship with after his wife was murdered. They'd gone out on a date of sorts to a cinema viewing of The English Patient. He'd held her hand. But back then he knew in his heart that he was still an emotional mess. It wouldn't have worked. They were different times. But, as he saw her now he felt different.

She walked up to him. "Ben! What a lovely surprise." She kissed him on the cheek. "How have you been?"

"Good. How about you? I haven't seen you for at least four years."

"I'm fine, thank you. You may have heard that I've quit the cloak and dagger stuff. Now, I'm earning peanuts teaching bored students." She laughed. "But it beats killing time at three AM in the departure lounge of an international airport, before boarding a plane to some hellhole. What have you got on your shoulder?"

"A dead deer."

Ruth leaned against the wall by the Thames, in fits of giggles. "Of course you have. I'd expect nothing less from you." She composed herself. "What are you doing these days?" A cloud shifted and exposed the sun to her face.

Sign was for the briefest of moments lost for words. "Private consultancy. I'm still in West Square. I've got a lodger who's also my business partner."

Ruth raised an eyebrow. "*Just* your business partner?"

Sign smiled. "It's a he, and he is not of that orientation and nor am I. We work cases."

"So, you're private detectives? Philip Marlowe, Sam Spade, Sherlock Holmes types?" She laughed again.

"More like Inspector Clouseau." Sign took a step closer to her. "You… you look good Ruth. Life outside of the madhouse must be the right tonic."

Ruth smiled. "And you look like you haven't aged since I last saw you. Is there a Mrs. Sign in your life, keeping you on the straight and narrow?"

"Alas, no. I work, I solve problems, I cook. Talking of which, I'm cooking up a storm tonight. Unless you're busy you're welcome to come over to dinner." He patted the deer. "I have to do something with this thing. It's enough to feed the five thousand."

Ruth averted his eyes. "I… sadly I can't."

"You have other plans. I understand."

Ruth pushed herself off the wall and went right up to him. She touched his cheek. "It's not that. I'm getting married. It would be appropriate for me to go to any man's house for dinner, providing I didn't fancy the pants off the man."

Sign nodded. In a quiet and tender tone of voice, he said, "I missed my chance."

"It wasn't your fault. The timing was awful for you." She kissed him on the lips. "Goodbye, Ben. I still remember when you held my hand. I can feel it now. It felt like you were transferring your enormous energy to me. It was the most romantic and extraordinary experience I've ever had." She walked away, her back to him, one hand rubbing her face.

Sign watched her until she was out of view. He sighed and continued his walk to his home.

Thirty minutes later he slammed the deer onto his kitchen chopping board, grabbed a meat cleaver, and expertly hacked at the carcass until it was in different joints.

Knutsen wandered into the kitchen, opened the fridge, and took out a can of beer. "What the fuck are you doing?"

Sign removed three knives from the wall mounted magnetic strip. The knives were of different weights. "I'm making dinner. And I'm going to freeze everything I don't use in separate bags. The deer must be respected and butchered now. It will feed us for many meals."

"Oh okay." Knutsen went into the lounge and put on the TV, while opening his beer can. He flicked through channels before exclaiming in a loud voice, "Cocking Christ. There's bugger all on TV!"

It took Sign thirty minutes to finish the job of boning and filleting the deer. He laid two immaculate fillets on the board and packaged the rest up for use on other days. He made a cranberry jus, infused with lemon, heather, pepper, and whiskey, peeled potatoes, made clapshot - boiled and mashed suede with added chives, and placed kale into a saucepan of cold water, ready to be boiled ten minutes before they wanted to eat. He walked into the lounge. "Tonight we are Scottish." He poured himself a single malt whiskey and sat in his armchair.

Knutsen asked, "Is everything alright? Looks like something's on your mind."

Sign wasn't going to tell his friend about his encounter with Ruth. "Sometimes we forget there are other things in life," was all he said.

Knutsen knew Sign was withholding something from him, but he wasn't going to press him further. It was obvious it was a personal matter. "How did you get on with Natalia?"

Sign made a conscious effort to change his mood. It was time for him to get his business head back on, he told himself. But the image of Ruth's face bathed in sunlight remained with him. What a fool he'd been for not wooing her when he had the chance, he concluded. He breathed in deeply. "Natalia is an egg shell that has cracked but has not yet bled yolk."

"Because if she cracks further, all the king's horses and all the king's men couldn't put Natalia together again."

"Correct, if a tad flippant." Sign sipped his whiskey. "There is a problem."

The downstairs doorbell rang.

Knutsen exclaimed, "Who's coming here at this hour?"

Sign sighed. "Stand by your beds. We're about to endure the company of a vitriolic woman."

"Archer? You invited her?"

"No. But I know it's her."

He was right. One minute later Archer was in the lounge. "What the hell were you thinking, ordering me to leave the hotel room?!"

Sign asked with resignation, "Would you like a drink?"

"No!"

"To take a seat?"

"I'll stand!"

"Would you like to dine with us? I've procured muntjac deer. The deer are native to Asia though have been introduced to Britain. The one I bought was raised in Northumbria. They're delicious to eat."

"I'm not hungry!"

Sign chuckled. Then his expression turned icy cold as he looked at Archer. "Then what are you and what do you want? My patience right now is cigarette paper thin."

Archer hesitated, uncertainty on her face. In a softer tone she said, "I want to know what you were playing at, kicking me out of the room."

Sign kept his eyes on Archer, unblinking, his clipped tone of voice like a precise hydraulic hammer. "There was no *play* to be had today. You needed to be out of the hotel room so that I could curve Natalia's way of thinking. If you'd have been present, Natalia would have been conflicted. The two of you have history. I was the unknown quantity in the mix of an established handler-agent relationship. She'd have been confused – looking at you, wondering what she should do; looking at me, wondering whether I'm right or you're right. You had to be away from her proximity in order for me to do my job. And I do not care one jot if that's put your nose out of joint." He placed his fingers together, and closed his eyes.

"I wanted you to give me a second opinion! Not... not push me out of my job!"

"I have my methods. They are sound."

"Not when they result in my agent thinking I've been demoted!"

"Boring."

Archer's anger was at its zenith. "This is anything but boring!"

"Still boring."

Archer's face was flushed as she looked at Knutsen, then back at Sign. "I need to get Natalia back on track. She trusts me. She doesn't know you."

Sign smiled. "She no longer trusts you. I made sure of that."

Archer's mouth opened wide. "What?!"

Sign drummed the tips of his fingers together. "Don't worry. It's all for a reason." He opened his eyes and looked at her. "I have also demoted myself to the role of advisor. It is deliberate. You and I need Natalia back in the saddle. I don't care if my ego is dented in the process. It seems, however, that you very much care about your status and prestige. We both know that is the road to hell. We must be dominant when we have matters under control; subservient when we don't. What's more important to you – Natalia or your pride?"

Archer sat in the spare armchair. She said to Knutsen, "Get me a drink."

Knutsen smiled. "Get it yourself. I'm sure you're capable of doing so."

Archer cursed, got a drink, and sat back down in her chair. She addressed Sign. "I want your assessment."

"I'm sure you do." Sign's tone of voice was deliberately patronising. He leaned forward, his demeanour serious. "Natalia respects you. There is no doubt in my mind that the information she's given you about Russian spies in the UK and elsewhere is one hundred percent accurate. Nor do I doubt her motivation to spy on Russia. But she is withholding a secret from me and you; of that I'm certain."

"What secret?"

"I have a theory, but no evidence. Nor do I want to coax the secret out of her. Not yet, anyway. Think of her as a virgin bride on her wedding night. Foreplay is required. Every move must be delicate and with her consent. Matters must not be rushed until she's ready."

Archer rubbed her face. "I don't have much time to placate the blushing bride! In three months, Natalia is going to be posted back to Moscow. When that happens she's of no use to the service because she will have lost her access to the names in Europe."

"Then I must move with the patience and tunnel vision of a fly fisherman stalking a trout on the River Itchen." Sign looked at Knutsen. "What do you think of Miss Archer's indignation about my approach?"

Archer threw her arms up in despair. "Knutsen's not a trained intelligence officer! His opinion is worthless. No offence intended, Mr. Knutsen."

"None taken," replied Knutsen.

Sign kept his eyes on Archer. "Mr. Knutsen is a highly experienced undercover operative who'd had years of experience navigating the nuances of different agendas within those around him. And he's highly intelligent. Last night he tried to poison me with tampered curry. It was an emboldened and mischievous thing to do. Mr. Knutsen – what do you think about my approach with Natalia versus Miss Archer's indignation?"

Knutsen looked at Archer. "I trust Ben. I don't know you. Sometimes when running sources, or agents as you call them, one needs to know when to ease off the gas. You brought Ben in to solve Natalia's stage fright. Going at her like a bull in a china shop will achieve the opposite of what you want. My opinion? Wind your neck in and let him do his job."

Archer had never been spoken to like that before. Thankfully, her intellect overpowered her anger at the comment. She smiled. "*Wind your neck in*? It's a bit of a robust comment but it hits the target." She addressed Sign. "Are you confident your methods will work?"

"You can take a horse to water but you can't make it drink. I'm confident I can get the horse to the water, but after that all of my confidence evaporates because only Natalia can decide whether to sup from the lake." Sign decided to drop his icy demeanour. "It must have been hard for you to bring me in on this case. I respect that. I will try my best to make this work for you, because I know that you are the best case officer for Natalia. I can't replace you. I'm just a sticking plaster. All I'm here for is to patch her up and hand her back to you. But, I know what I'm doing. Please, Jayne, let me help you and Natalia."

Archer stared at her drink. "Alright. I understand that you have your methods and I have mine." She looked at Sign. "What about Susan?"

"I have a strategy. It's in play, though only at stage one." Sign went silent.

Archer nodded. "Very well." She looked at Knutsen. "No more rudeness. Get this woman another damn drink."

Knutsen laughed, stood, and took her glass to the drinks cabinet.

CHAPTER 4

At nine AM the following morning, Knutsen was on foot in London. It was the first time in a while that he'd had to wear a coat. Rain was pounding the city and the umbrella he was holding, cars had their headlights on because the sky was filled with black clouds and there was reduced visibility, very few people were walking in the area he was in because it was too early on a Sunday and because of the weather. And those that were out were dashing to tube or mainline stations or bolting to then warm refuge of coffee shops. By comparison, Knutsen walked steadily along the embankment, crossed the Thames into Charing Cross, and stopped by the tube station there. He looked around. Here it was busier than on the south bank. There were newspaper vendors, miserable-looking groups of tourists who'd been dropped here by coach and told to have fun until they were collected at five PM, buses and cars, honking their horns, the occasional police car racing to the scenes of nearby vehicle accidents, and shops that were opening up for business despite it being a Sunday. Having worked in London all of his adult life, his current surroundings and activities with were so familiar to him. He could never work out whether he loved or loathed the capital. There was immense energy here, history, diversity, pride, manifold activities, big green spaces that were protected by Royal Charters, brilliant restaurants, pubs that looked the same way they did in the days of Shakespeare and latterly the Kray Twins, buildings constructed in the seventeen hundreds that were nestled alongside ugly 1950s properties that had been made a few years after the World War Two blitz, cathedrals, street performers, theatres where every self-respecting actor desired to work, and music halls. But, there was also crime, poverty, grime, tension, an urgency that raised the blood pressure of every commuter passing through the capital, and thanks to terrorism these days London was an armed police state. What glued the city together, in Knutsen's view, was the mighty Thames. But he never thought of the river as glue; rather it seemed to him to be a massive serpent, slithering through the metropolis, not caring that it's belly was gliding over the bones of murdered men, women, children and babies who'd been disposed of in the river over the centuries. The river carried so many secrets. It didn't care. It was older than humanity. And when humanity became extinct, the serpent would still be here.

Knutsen looked down the Strand. He walked, counting his steps. He passed theatres and shops. He also passed an alleyway where a drunken and unfaithful woman had been strangled to death by her lover, a shop where he'd spent a bitterly cold winter's day prone on its rooftop with a pair of binoculars while watching a transit van that was illegally parked up and contained enough plastic explosives to destroy half of the Strand, a café where a man had entered and slit a man's throat because the victim owed him a fiver, a pub which a woman had tried unsuccessfully to burn down and instead had accidentally set fire to herself, prompting her to run down the road engulfed in flames, and the location outside a tobacconist where Knutsen had rushed at an armed robber who was holding a sawn-off shotgun, had taken a blast of pellets to his body armour, had fallen to the ground, and fired two shots from his pistol into the criminal's head.

Knutsen stopped outside Simpson's In The Strand. He turned around. From Charing Cross tube station to here, he'd taken exactly four hundred and seventy two steps.

He looked up. The sky was still black; the weather showing no signs of abating. He walked back to West Square.

When he arrived home, he shook his umbrella free of rain water, removed his coat, and entered the lounge. Sign was in the kitchen, cooking bacon, eggs, and toast.

Knutsen said, "I did what you asked."

"Excellent, dear chap.!" He brought Knutsen a plate of food. "I'm not partaking, given I have a big lunch ahead of me. But you most certainly will need this after your excursion in the inclement weather this morning. It will be your last meal until supper."

Knutsen devoured the food. "It's busy on the Strand. The rain's helping, though. Natalia will minimize walking distances. She'll either take the tube to Embankment or Charing Cross and walk the rest, or she'll get a cab to the restaurant from her home."

"She'd be wise not to get a cab. They are notoriously unhelpful when it comes to trying to spot a trail. Natalia's smart and she's been trained. My bet is that she'll walk from Embankment tube station."

"I'll do my best to spot her but it's not going to be easy. I've no idea what time she's going to arrive, plus, every sane person out there has got an umbrella covering their faces."

Sign went back into the kitchen and returned with two mugs of black coffee, one of which he handed to his colleague. "You'll spot her. She'll walk slowly – slower than you. Last night or this morning, she'll have done what you've just done. The difference being she did so to research an anti-surveillance route. You, however, are on counter-surveillance duty."

Anti-surveillance was the technique deployed by intelligence officers to see if they were being followed. If they spotted a tail, the trick was not to let the hostile surveillance team know that you know they're there. By comparison, counter-surveillance was used when anti-surveillance was impossible or likely to be inconclusive. It usually required a team of intelligence officers stuck reasonably close to a colleague who was going to an agent meeting. Their job was to spot whether he or she was being followed , communicate that to the IO, and then disrupt, by any means, the hostile team following him or her. Today, Knutsen was going to be a counter-surveillance team of one.

He placed his plate in the kitchen sink, returned to his armchair, and drank his coffee. "Do you think she's in danger?"

"No. But I want you to get used to this procedure. Based on today's lunch, I dearly hope that you and I will shortly be going to a place of significant danger." Sign smiled. "Therefore it's best that you dust down your skills here, before we go there."

Knutsen looked resigned as he sarcastically said, "Fucking fantastic. It's always a rollercoaster with you." He swallowed the dregs of his coffee. And checked his watch. "I'm going to clean my pistol and then get back out there. Good luck. And given we haven't got military or police-grade comms, make sure you've got your mobile fully charged up. It's the only way I can get your attention short of running down the Strand firing shots in the air."

When Knutsen had left the flat, Sign brushed his teeth, shaved with a cutthroat razor, showered, applied eau de toilette, and got dressed into a tailored charcoal grey suit, immaculately pressed expensive double-cuff white shirt with a cutaway collar, gleaming black leather Church's shoes, blue silk tie which he bound in a schoolboy knot, and fitted gold cufflinks that had been given to him as a gift by an Indian tea plantation owner who was being hassled by rogues who wanted him to diversify and harvest vast quantities of drugs. He placed his mobile phone in one of the inner pockets of his jacket, and three hundred pounds cash in the other pocket. He examined himself in a full length mirror, straightened the knot on his tie, grabbed his house keys and an umbrella, and departed his home. Outside West Square he hailed a cab. "Simpson's In The Strand, if you please," he said to the driver. As he sat in the car as it took him towards his destination, he looked out of the window and wondered how Knutsen was faring in the god-awful weather. He'd be on or close to the Strand now; just waiting; trying to blend in, as opposed to looking like an armed killer.

Sign paid for the cab and entered the restaurant. He was ten minutes early and hoped that Natalia wasn't already here. After giving his false name to the reception desk, he was ushered to one of the oak-panelled booths that lined the right side of the restaurant. Thankfully, it was empty. The remainder of the large room contained open-plan tables that were not suitable for discreet conversations. So far, the restaurant was three quarters full. During the week the venue was a favourite for politicians, high-ranking military officers, Whitehall Mandarins, and famous Shakespearian actors who liked to fortify themselves with a hearty lunch before their matinee performances in the nearby theatres. Today, the mix of clientele was more eclectic. There were middle and old-aged, well-dressed, American, British, and Australian tourists, London residents who'd opted for the restaurant's refinement over getting a roast lunch in a pub, and a pair of respected food critics who were compiling a *100 Best Restaurants In London* feature for Time Out magazine. Customers were drawn to the venue because it was steeped in history and refused to move with the times. It was a throwback to an age of civility and manners, served thoroughly British food, and not one restaurant in the capital cooked better cuts of meat. Having been established in eighteen twenty eight as a smoking room, it was also once a coffee house and a national chess venue, until it was transformed into a fine dining establishment. During its history, it was a favourite of Sir Arthur Conan Doyle, Oscar Wilde, many other famous authors, playwrights, prime ministers, and royalty. P.G. Wodehouse called it *a restful temple of food.*

Sign had switched his mobile phone to silent and vibrate, before entering the restaurant. His phone vibrated It was a text message from Knutsen.

Spotted her. On foot from Embankment tube. Nothing to report. ETA 10 mins.

Sign waited, thinking through the conversation he was going to have, considering her possible responses, how he would reply to her answers, and ultimately how he could help her. Perhaps it was because he was in such an esteemed chess venue that his mind was thinking this way, establishing how the game of chess is going to proceed before the game has even started. But, like all great chess masters, Sign possessed the ability to rip up the rule book and change pre-determined tactics if the lay of the board required him to do so.

Natalia was shown to his table. She was wearing a box-cut lilac jacket, a silk scarf around her throat, black suede trousers, and ankle-length boots. The clothes looked expensive, but in all probability she'd bought them in one of the markets that specialised in selling cheap replicas. Still, she looked at home here as much as she would do having a glass of wine in a Chelsea bar, or perusing the boutique shops in Bond Street that sold designer brands, fine jewellery, and arts and antiquities. She sat opposite him, looked around, before returning her gaze to Sign. "So it seems you are a *dyed in the wool* Englishman who harks back to the good old days of Great Britain's empire."

Sign laughed as he placed his starched white napkin on his lap. "I've also eaten sheep's testicles in a Bedouin tent in the Yemen. I adapt, depending on my circumstances. Would you like a glass of wine?"

"Yes. White. You choose. My knowledge of wine isn't good."

Sign gestured to a waiter, who came to the table. "A bottle of Maximin Grunhaus, please. And would you send the carving trolley over."

The waiter replied, "Of course, sir."

When the waiter was gone, Sign said to Natalia, "I would like us to enjoy lunch and avoid business as much as possible. There is a small matter I'd like to discuss with you, but we can leave that for when we have our coffee. Are you hungry?"

Natalia nodded.

"Are you averse to large cuts of meat?"

"I'm Russian. What do you think?"

Sign smiled. "Then we are indeed sitting in exactly the place you and I should be."

Another waiter wheeled the craving trolley to their booth. On its surface was a razor sharp carving knife and two huge joints of meat.

Sign asked, "What do you have for us today?"

The waiter replied, "Twenty eight day dry-aged roast rib of Scottish beef and Daphne's Welsh lamb."

"Excellent. I'll have the beef." He glanced at Natalia.

"The same."

Sign rubbed his hands together, his expression enthusiastic. "And could we have a selection of sides – roast spuds, veg, the usual."

The waiter expertly carved the beef. From the middle section of the trolley she withdrew bowls containing vegetables and served them onto the plate. She asked, "Gravy?"

Sign grinned. "It would be a crime not to. And a healthy dollop of horseradish sauce for me."

"Me to," said Natalia.

After they were served their food the waiter wheeled the trolley to attend to other customers. Their wine was delivered and poured, Sign raised his glass, "I took the liberty of ordering German wine. So, here's to Germany. We have to mix things up in this place otherwise we Brits really will start thinking that we rule the world."

Natalia smiled and chinked her glass against his. "It's the same in my country."

"Empires come and go." He started eating his food. "Empires are like children in sweet shops – they overindulge, get sick, and have to go home." He sipped his wine. "Do you have other siblings?"

"No."

"Parents?"

"They died a few years ago." Natalia cut into her beef.

"I'm sorry to hear that. Which part of the motherland do you hark from?"

"Saint Petersburg."

Sign nodded. "A beautiful city. I've been there many times."

"As a tourist?"

"No. As a man who was being hunted by people you may know."

"I see." Natalia ate a mouthful of her food and washed it down with some wine. "I have an uncle and an aunt. They live in Moscow. They're poor. Good people. They're all that remains of my family." She delicately cut her vegetables. "Who are you really?"

"I've told you. I'm Ben."

"You know that's not what I'm asking."

Sign said nothing for a few seconds. "I understand that your brother was a ghost. I too am a ghost. But your brother and I are different. He had a chain of command. I only answer to my conscience."

"You don't have a boss?"

"No."

"How do you have this freedom?"

Sign was about to take another mouthful of food but stopped, staring at his plate. "I emancipated myself."

"Because you wanted to or because you needed to?"

"Both." Sign's tone of voice was subdued as he added, "I had a wife. She was all I needed. She was an NGO worker. She was murdered in South America. After that things changed for me. For a long time I thought life didn't make sense. I knew I was spiralling. Probably, I still am. But I have control mechanisms. One of the most important of them was for me to recognise what I could deal with while I was grieving and what I couldn't deal with. I made choices. I could no longer bear being in a hierarchy. I don't like being in large groups of people unless no one knows me. So, I try to restrict my professional and personal life to one-to-one encounters." He waved his hand toward the rest of the restaurant. "Like men used to do here. They found peace by sitting opposite each other with a chess table between them. They were loners; so too the brilliant scholars and artists who frequented this place. They were gregarious on the page, but when they weren't working they only needed the company of one person."

"So, you are shutting yourself off from the world."

"No. I'm creating a world of my choosing." Sign finished his food. "You know what that's like."

The observation struck home. She said, "It's not just grief that does that. It's a number of things. I like to think of it as dodging bullets. Love, hate, anger, awkwardness, regrets, hope, failure, sadness, happiness that's dashed – who wants any of that?"

Sign frowned. "You're a very young woman; old and young enough to be my daughter. You have your whole life ahead of you. Don't be like me until you have to be."

Natalia smiled, though looked sad. "Maybe.

Sign said, "There's something I need you to do for me. I'd like you to go back to Russia for a week. Tell your boss that it's a family emergency to do with your uncle and aunt. They have health issues. Something like that. Your boss won't be suspicious because it's a trip to your homeland. Say you'll only be gone a week and will check in every day at the SVR headquarters in Moscow."

"Why do you want me to do that?"

Sign handed her a slip of paper. "Memorise this and destroy it. A woman called Susan Archer was born in the medical centre in Moscow listed on the paper. She's English. She was born fifty years ago. The precise date is on the note. She has a twin. The twin returned to England with her parents. But Susan vanished in Moscow. Obviously this was back in the Soviet Union era. I wondered if you could do some research to see if you could find out what happened to her."

Natalia looked at the paper. "Is this important?"

"It has some importance, though not to our line of work. It is not a dangerous enquiry."

Natalia shrugged. "I don't see why not. In any case, I'm due some leave, given I haven't had a holiday for two years. But you'll have to pay for my flight."

"Of course. The sooner you can fly the better. Let Katy know when you have the dates. She'll arrange to get the money to you. But don't tell her about the Susan Archer enquiry. It's a matter that's personal to me." Sign paid cash for the bill. When they were alone, he said, "I must confess there is another reason I want you to go back to Russia. I want you to have a change of scenery. It will do you the world of good."

It was late afternoon when Sign returned to West Square. Despite the weather, he'd walked from Simpson's in order to aid his digestion and burn off calories. He called Archer. "I had lunch today with Natalia. I've asked her to go to Russia ASAP, for a week. She'll be flying economy class, for obvious reasons. I need you to pay for her ticket."

"Why did you ask her to do that?"

"It's based on a gut instinct. She's been living for too long in a pressure cooker – both at work and at home. I want to release the steam in a place she feels largely safe, but partly scared. And most importantly I want her to check in to her Moscow headquarters so that she's reminded why she hates the place and the politicians who run it."

"That makes sense. Yes, it's a good idea."

Sign said, "Knutsen and I will also travel to Moscow. We need to keep an eye on Natalia. But, the main purpose of our trip will be to investigate what happened to Susan. I have an alias passport with a Russian visa. Knutsen doesn't. Can you use the service's fast track system to get him the necessary documentation? I doubt Natalia will be able to travel until Tuesday at the earliest. But that's still a tight turnaround. Knutsen and I need to be flying on the same day as Natalia, though on a different flight."

"It's tight, but can be done. I'll need his passport photos. Get him to bring them to me this evening." She paused. "Actually, why don't you both come over to my house. I'll rustle up some food." She gave him her home address in Putney. "Let's say seven o'clock."

"We'd be delighted." Sign rubbed his belly. "Though don't cook anything elaborate or too filling. After the lunch I've had, s small plate of beans on toast would suffice." He ended the call and called out, "Knutsen! Are you having a nap?"

Knutsen emerged from his bedroom, looking bleary eyed. "Might have been."

"Nap time's over. Do you have any passport photos?"

"No."

Sign checked his watch. "We have an appointment at seven PM in Putney. That only gives us less than two hours to be where we need to be. There's a photo booth on Waterloo Station. Go there now, get the photos done – they must be passport standard – and while you're at it pick up a bottle of wine from the off license there. Do it as quickly as possible, get back here, shower, shave, and get changed into casual attire. We're going to see Jayne this evening. She's going to help us travel into the mouth of the beast."

Knutsen rubbed his face. "Okay. Do I need to bring my gun this evening?"

"No. Jayne's unarmed and is highly unlikely to kill us by other means." He smiled and pointed at his suit. "I need to get out of this work clobber. If we move quickly, we can get this done. We'll hail a cab at six thirty. That's our deadline."

When Knutsen was gone, Sign poured himself a small whiskey and drank it while having a bath. He tried to relax but his mind was racing. He thought about Natalia and Susan. Natalia was Russian; if Susan was still alive, in all probability she might as well have been Russian. But, his brain didn't just focus on the two women. He was thinking about moving parts, like a Swiss watchmaker who was trying to engineer a highly complex timepiece and get everything to sync together. Different variables raced through his brain. One stuck, and he didn't like that moving part one bit.

He got out of the bath, dried himself, dressed into smart but casual attire, and made himself a green tea. He placed a record onto his player and relaxed in his armchair as he listened to Bach's Toccata in d minor. He finished his tea and shivered. Shortly he'd have to put the flat's heating on, light the fire, or both. Summer was gone; autumn was upon Londoners. That was good. West Square was magical in the colder months. Residents draped tasteful white lights on the trees in the square. It transformed the place into a fairy tale setting. Sign's brain transcended most ascetically beautiful things in the world. But he was a sucker for the lead up to Christmas. Probably that's because he remembered his deceased father giving a five year old Sign a pen knife that was contained in a brown paper bag, while the two of them were sat by the Christmas tree in their modest home, while Sign's mother was cooking a lovely roast on Christmas Day. Sign's father – back then a merchant marine officer – had said to him, "Don't tell your mother I gave you this. I got it off the captain of my ship who'd tried to defend himself from a polar bear in the Arctic. The captain was dead by the time I and other sailors got to him. I followed the bear for hours, with the intention of killing him or her. I had a rifle. Finally, I had the bear in my sights. It was approaching its cubs. I couldn't take the shot. It just seemed wrong to do so. The cubs ran up to the bear. Before they reached it, the bear collapsed to the ground. You see, the captain had used the small knife you're holding to penetrate the bear's throat. The bear simply ran out of breath. It starved of oxygen. This knife is a bear killer." Sign still had the knife. It was in a drawer in his bedroom and was as sharp today as it was when the captain thrust its blade into the bear's gullet while the bear mauled him and subsequently tossed him onto ice like a rag doll.

Knutsen returned. "What are you listening to this shit for?"

"It's Bach. He was a genius. Do I need to educate you further?"

"No thanks. And by the way, people who describe other people as geniuses do so because their mental faculties are severely restricted."

"An astute observation." Sign got out of his chair, removed the record and placed another on.

Knutsen was wide eyed. "Where the hell did you get this from?"

Sign shrugged. "After lunch I perused a delightful record stall outside the Royal Festival Hall. The owner of the stall specialised in your kind of music. He educated me and recommended I buy this."

Knutsen was stunned "You bought this for me?"

"I bought it to prove a point." Sign smiled. "The point being is it's never too late to challenge one's senses. Actually, this band is rather good."

The record was an album by the band Groove Armada, a two-man English electronic act who collaborated with well-known rap, soul, rock, hip-hop, and jazz artists. The track playing was *Superstylin'*, a thumping upbeat house track, with influences from dub, speed garage, reggae, and dancehall.

Knutsen shook his head. "I went to see Groove Armada play live in Brixton Academy. I was with some mates of mine who were big-time drug dealers. They were nice blokes, though I'd infiltrated their gang to bust them when the time was right. The concert was amazing." He hesitated as he stood outside the bathroom. With an earnest tone, he said, "You never fail to surprise me." He entered the bathroom and turned on the shower.

Fifteen minutes later, Knutsen was shaved, refreshed, and wearing jeans and a T-shirt. He entered the lounge.

Sign said, "You're wearing that? Strong move."

Knutsen shrugged. "I don't have to get dressed up for Her Nibs."

"Quite right." Sign checked his watch. "We have ten minutes before we need to leave. That gives us just enough time for a sharpener." He poured two glasses of Calvados. Both men sat in their armchairs.

Knutsen took a gulp of his drink. "Why do I need passport photos?"

"Because I'm going to turn you into a spy. In the next few days you and I will travel to Moscow. Jayne is going to get you a passport and visa. The passport won't be in your name. We have to decide what to call you."

Knutsen blew on his lips, making them vibrate. "John Smith will do."

"Too obvious."

Knutsen giggled. "Something like Engelbert Humperdinck."

"In that vein. What about Ernst Stavro Blofeld?"

"You want to send me to Russia with the name of a Bond villain?!"

"It's just a thought."

Knutsen knew that Sign was being silly. He liked it when he was in this mood. "Harry Palmer?"

Sign smiled. "Though I loved Michael Caine's portrayal of the anti-hero spy in the Ipcress File, I fear the name may be a little bland. What about Red Adair?"

"Jon Bon Jovi?"

"What?"

"Never mind. Plácido Domingo?"

"You don't speak Spanish. What about Jack The Hat? In a parallel universe you'd have been a London east end criminal."

With sarcasm, Knutsen said, "Yeah, that would really work when I'm trying to get through immigration."

"I won't be standing next to you. I'll be okay."

Knutsen chuckled. "I like the theme though. How about Ronald Kray?"

"Spot on. Alas I already have an alias passport. It would have been perfect if I could have travelled as Reggie Kray." Sign checked his watch. "Time to move. Grab a coat, or umbrella. It doesn't look like the weather's giving in today."

Thirty minutes later they arrived at Archer's house in Putney. It was a town house, in a quiet cul-de-sac, overlooking the Thames.

Knutsen said, "Blimey. This area's a bit posh." There were six other detached properties in the immediate vicinity. "How much do you reckon it costs to buy one of these gaffs?"

"*Gaffs*? Are you getting into Kray Twins character?"

"Actually the term gaff originated in Ireland and was adopted by 1950s working class Londoners."

Sign looked at the Thames. There were rowing teams on there, despite the weather. "I would estimate that each house around us costs at least a million to buy. That's a lot of money for a three bedroom place. Come on. Let's get this over with." He rang the doorbell.

Archer let them in. "I can't move far from the kitchen because I've got a Chinese stir fry on the go. Can you do me a favour? I've got two heavy boxes at the base of the stairs. They need lifting up to the first floor. Dump them wherever you can. They contain equipment for a stair lift for my mother."

Sign and Knutsen obliged. It took both of them to carry each box. When the job was done, Knutsen looked around. The house was pristine, modern, and quite functional. Quietly, he said, "I'd say this place needs a woman's touch, but obviously that hasn't worked so far."

Sign replied, "She's a busy person and doesn't spend much time here."

"How did she afford this place?"

"Back in the eighties her parents were quite the academic celebrities. They wrote some non-fiction bestsellers about Russia, were also put on a lucrative lecture circuit and were engaged as after dinner speakers. It earned them a lot of money – enough for them to buy a house in Oxford and to put a sizeable deposit down on this place for Jayne. Jayne picked up the slack of mortgage payments. She must have paid for the house by now. And bear in mind, back in the eighties this place would have been at least half the price of its current value."

They went back downstairs. Knutsen put the bottle of red wine he'd bought on the kitchen counter. He asked Archer, "Would you like me to open this?"

Archer was busy frying strips of beef. "Absolutely. And be a darling and pour three glasses. Corkscrew's in the top drawer. Glasses are in the cupboard above." She was wearing jeans, socks, a jumper, and had no makeup on. Knutsen didn't blame her. It was Sunday; she could look however she damn well liked.

Knutsen said, "I've put my photos in the lounge. I'd like to be called Ronald Kray."

"Don't be ridiculous." Archer added spices into the wok, stirred the meat for a few seconds, and added soy sauce. "You'll be called Thomas Peterson." She briefly glanced at him. "Russia is no joke. Thomas is important because it is an elongation of your real forename. Peterson is sufficiently different from your real surname but it also has origins in Scandinavia. When constructing an alias, it's always important to bring an identity as close to your true identity, without the alias betraying who you really are. Least ways, that's important when you're an amateur. As you become more experienced, you can be more elaborate with your identities." She added finely chopped spring onions, tomatoes, zest of lime, and a splash of orange juice into the pan, before turning the mixture down to simmer.

Knutsen poured the wine, while looking at the vegetables on the chopping board. "Are these for dinner?"

"Yes, but they need to be added to the pan five minutes from serving."

"Would you like me to chop them for you? I'm not as good at cooking as Ben, but I'm a dab hand with a knife."

Archer smiled. "Be my guest. That's very gracious of you." She walked into the lounge, holding two glasses of wine. Sign was in there, sitting on the sofa with his feet up on a foot rest. She handed him one of the glasses. "I do think it's a clever idea to send Natalia to Moscow for a week. But, are you sure it's wise for you to go to Russia? Last time you were there you were tortured."

Sign smiled. "Torture's overrated."

"And Knutsen? He's not trained for this."

"If he can infiltrate the seedy side of London, he can work in Moscow. Same cities; different languages."

Archer sat in a chair. "You know it's not that simple."

"Do you remember the first time you were deployed after our training? I certainly remember the first time I was sent overseas. Was I ready? Not in a million years. But, I knew it was an extension of our training. It was the chance for me to go it alone and to achieve nothing, great success, or slip up and fail. Those first forays into the jungle are tests. And they're essential. Remember: on day one of training we were told we would never be wrapped in cotton wool. The service always knows that at some point it must deploy us and keep its fingers crossed. Knutsen will be fine, I'm sure of that. Correction, I will make sure of that."

"So long as he knows the risks."

"He knows risk as well as you and I. After all, he's lived most of his adult life fearing execution by thugs,"

Quietly, Archer asked, "Is everything alright? You don't look or sound like your normal self."

Sign shrugged. "It's nothing untoward aside from I bumped into someone today who meant something to me but is untouchable. The encounter reminded me that I keep the world at bay, but wish for slivers of hope, only for those slivers to be dashed. There is nothing worse than false hope."

With a sympathetic tone, Archer replied, "Hang on in there. One day you'll meet the right woman. You'd make a splendid husband." She smiled. "Women like challenges. You're brilliant, irascible, good looking, non-conformist, polite, a good cook, clean, and a pain in the arse. Were it not for the fact that I'm off the market, I'd shag you."

"Charming." Sign sipped his drink. "Are you mentally prepared for the strong possibility that Susan's dead?"

Archer hesitated before replying. "As you rightly say, sometimes it's better not to have hope. Part of me wishes my mother never told me about Susan. But, the cat's out of the bag. I grew up in a loving household. My parents were a bit eccentric and were certainly very demanding in terms of what they expected from me academically. They put me under a lot of pressure. I often wondered what it would have been like if I'd had a brother or sister. I doubt I'd have been under my parents' microscope as much. Now, decades on, that doesn't feature in my thinking. Instead, the two overwhelming drivers I have are fear and curiosity. If Susan's alive I worry about what kind of life she's having. If she's dead I will have to grieve for her. But how do you grieve for someone you've never met?"

"We will need to cross bridges when we get answers."

Archer asked, "How will you go about making enquiries on Susan?"

Sign replied, "I have contacts and resources and they must remain private, even from you. But, my findings will be handed to you on a plate. At that point, you alone will be entitled to judge my success or failure."

Archer nodded. Quietly, she said, "I won't blame you if you can't trace Susan. It was so long ago. In all probability, all traces of her have vanished. And if you discover she's dead, at least I can relay that to my mother and hopefully give her closure. You won't have wasted your or my time."

Knutsen entered the lounge, sat down, and sipped his wine. "Right. Chillies, peppers, ginger, and coriander are chopped. I also tasted the sauce. It was okay, but needed peppercorns, star anise, lemon juice, a teaspoon of sugar, bamboo shoots, and water chestnuts. I had a rummage through your cupboards and found most of what I wanted. The meat sauce is now much better." He smiled. "So, what are you two old spooks yarning about?"

Archer replied. "We were talking about the case, and we were also talking about you and whether you're ready to go to Russia."

Knutsen placed his glass onto a side table. His expression was serious though his tone of voice flippant as he quickly said, "See, here's the thing *love*. I had a mate of mine – his name was Phil - who was a complete scumbag. He was a geezer and would make your guts ache with laughter if you went out for a few pints with him. Popular guy. Always carried a gun or blade, or both. Would take a bullet for any of his pals. Phil thought I was a safecracker. He needed me because he was about to do a bank job. He'd done many in the past, until his previous safecracker got shot by SCO19. So, that's when I came in. The Met wanted to stop him in his tracks, not just because he was robbing banks but also 'cause he had no qualms about gunning down civilians when he was on a job. Trouble was, we had no evidence. So I was sent in by the Met as the *get the evidence man*. He was suspicious of me at first. Put a gun against my head. Asked me all sorts of questions. Punched me. Checked me out by getting his foot soldiers to make enquiries around my fake home address. Asked me which school I'd been to and the names of my teachers. Spoke to the teachers. And on and on and on it went. He was smart. For five weeks he raked over every detail of my false identity, and during that time he kept me locked in a room. No windows, Just a bed and a pan for me to shit and piss in. My alias identity held up. He let me out of the room, took me to his tailor in Battersea and bought me a suit, shirt, tie, pair of shoes, and then took me to a lovely brasserie in Covent Garden where we had lobster for lunch. After that, I was part of the family. Before that, it was a living hell – sleep deprivation; buckets of cold water thrown over me; beaten day and night; tested on cracking safes; constantly questioned about previous jobs I allegedly had done; asked if I was an undercover cop; fed little; and overall treated like a piece of trash. I knew it was an initiation test of sorts, to get into the gang. I didn't blink. No way was I going to let those cunts get to the real me. It paid off. They took me on the bank job. It was a place in Norwich. I wasn't just there to open safes. I had to disable cameras, blow up thick tempered glass screens, and I was a shooter. There were three of us in the bank. Outside there was a driver and further away from him were two spotters. The job had been planned to the inch. The trouble was, my mate did his usual nut job thing and was going to execute the manager unless he let us in to the vault. It was a bit of a shit situation. Cops were on their way but couldn't enter until cash was nicked. We had to have that evidence. So, I had to make a decision on my own. Phil was holding his gun against the manager's head, while screaming at the other bank staff. He had that look in his eyes. I knew he didn't give a shit. He got off on killing more than he did on money. Split second decision. I shot him and his two colleagues. Clean shots. They were dead before they hit the ground. Then I ran out and shot the driver. The spotters were a fair distance away, but I managed to wing them. They didn't get far when they tried to escape. SWAT picked them off." He grinned as he picked up his wine and looked at the floor. He raised his head and stared at Archer. His voice was icy as he said, "I could give you a dozen or so other examples of what I've done, Miss Archer. You think you're special? Try seeing and doing what I've seen and done." He nodded at Sign while keeping his eyes locked on Archer. "I know he's done similar and has been put through the meat grinder. Like me, Ben kept to the script and never cracked. I don't know whether you've properly been tested. Maybe you have, maybe you haven't. But, when you discuss me out of earshot while I'm rescuing your pathetic excuse for a meal, always remember that you're talking about a fucking grown up who's spent his entire adult life expecting a bullet in the back of his brain." Knutsen smiled. "That reminds me. I need to turn the sauce down and put a pan of water on to boil. Enjoy your Jason Bourne conversations about how great you are and how naive I am." He went into the kitchen.

Archer looked at Sign. "I can see why you chose him to be your business partner."

Sign smiled. "Mr. Knutsen is a man of many hidden depths. And I never underestimate him." With sincerity he added, "He is also a gentleman who wishes to be respected. Go into the kitchen, talk to him, help him with the meal. You don't need to apologise – he'd feel awkward. Just ask him about his life."

CHAPTER 5

Two days later Sign got a call from Archer. She said, "The passport's ready for collection. Get Tom to meet me on Vauxhall Bridge at eleven o'clock this morning. I've seen Natalia and given her cash. She flies tomorrow on an 0845hrs British Airways flight. That means you're on. Book your flight now. Tomorrow it's time to visit Russia. Natalia's going to meet you at sixty thirty this evening in The Coal Hole pub on the Strand. You can discuss in-country logistics with her then. Do you need anything else from me?"

"No. I'll take over from here." When the call ended Sign stood in the centre of the lounge, deep in thought.

Knutsen was in the kitchen, brewing coffee. "All okay?"

"Yes. We fly tomorrow." He gave him details of what Archer had said.

Knutsen handed him a mug of steaming black coffee. "Are you sure about this?"

"Why wouldn't I be. Natalia is our only hope of discovering what happened to Natalia. And in doing so, we're putting Natalia back in the saddle."

"Killing two birds with one stone."

"Something like that."

Knutsen was earnest as he said, "When I asked if you were sure about this I wasn't talking about Natalia and Susan."

"I know, dear chap. You were talking about me. Don't worry. I've been tortured and threatened with death in other countries as well. That doesn't stop me going back to the places. We put one foot in front of the other."

Knutsen sighed. "Come on Ben. It's never as simple as that. When we go to Moscow you might get flashbacks or trauma or both."

Sign blew on his coffee. He was quiet for a moment before saying, "I do not for one moment underestimate the devastating consequences of trauma. I've seen men, stronger than me, who've achieved so much in their lives and have finally cracked. When it happens, it's often a fairly minor thing that breaks them down. A trigger, as I call them. There was one chap who'd served with me in Afghanistan, Iraq, Russia, China, and Colombia. We'd witnessed a lot of appalling behaviour – beheadings, massacres, the results of artillery strikes, mutilations of children, rape, hangings, and so on. We also dealt out our punishments – assassinations, drone strikes, tricks that persuaded war lords to get in a vulnerable position so we could put bullets into their head. It would take me a long time to tell you even ten percent of what went on. But, the chap I served with lost his mind when he saw a car accident in Swindon. He was just standing on the side of the road. The car hit a boy on a bike and smashed him. That was the trigger. A random event that dug up the worst recesses of my colleague's memories. But, despite everything I've gone through, not least in Russia, I don't have those trigger points. I know why. There is nothing that could be done to me, or I could see or do, that in any way comes close to the grief I have for my murdered wife. I carry the relentless burden of grief. Others carry the horror of trauma."

Knutsen nodded. "Grief makes you bullet proof."

"I would gladly relinquish that armour in a nanosecond if it would give me my wife back."

"I bet you would, mate." Knutsen didn't want to press Sign any further. His colleague had a thousand yard stare. His thoughts were not in the room. They were elsewhere. Knutsen said, "I've got to do the Cold War shit and meet Her Nibs on a bridge, we've got to book a flight, need to pack, and you've got to brief a girl who's lost her nerve. We've got our work cut out today."

Sign looked at him. "We have indeed, sir." He looked at his watch. "I'll make the flight bookings. From memory there's a 1040hrs Aeroflot flight out of Heathrow. Aside from the carrier Natalia's travelling on, there's another early morning British Airways flight, but we must avoid BA. I will also source accommodation close to Moscow."

"A hotel or B&B?"

"No. The place I have in mind will be free of charge."

"Do you have access to weapons in Russia?"

Sign nodded. "Yes. But bear this in mind – if you have to use a gun it will be because Natalia's in danger from her own people. Any assault on FSB or SVR personnel in close proximity to Natalia would mean that Natalia is fully compromised. We would have to grab her and use a covert exfiltration route out of Russia. As a backup, I will arrange for that exfiltration out of St. Petersburg. But the use of guns and my covert get-out-of-Dodge-card must be a last resort. We want Natalia to remain in the SVR and safely fly out of Russia without raising any suspicion from the authorities there." He gulped his coffee. "I don't want to offend your knowledge, but do I need to brief you on how to pack."

Knutsen wasn't offended. "Before I used to go on an undercover job, I'd strip naked, place my bag on my bed, alongside clothes, ID, and cash. I'd check my bag and wallet to make sure there was zero documentation – shopping receipts and stuff – that could be traced to Tom Knutsen. And I'd check every single pocket in my clothes. Only after that was done would I pack."

"Excellent. I do the same. Do you have any tattoos?"

"No."

"Have you ever been arrested?

"Loads of times, but only as a result of undercover work and always in a different name."

"Good. Our cover for flying to Moscow will be simple. We are high school teachers at the Cotswold School. You teach history; I teach languages. We are in Russia because we are, as per UK educational law, required to do a risk assessment analysis prior to a planned school trip to Moscow. We intend to take twenty students to the capital in January next year. But, we can't do so until we've checked the hotel they will be staying in, and looked at all the usual potential risks – fire hazards, transportation, crime, et cetera. We have a Skype call at four PM this afternoon with the head teacher of the Cotswold School. He and I went to university together. I've used him in the past. He will brief us and ensure that we're temporarily on the school list of staff, should anyone in Russia call the school to verify our credentials. Are you happy with that?"

"Makes sense. History was always my strong point. But we're going to have to dot the Is and cross the Ts. Which hotel are the students staying in? Are we staying in the same hotel on tomorrow's trip? What activities are we planning for the kids? And what's currently on the history and languages curriculum?"

"The head teacher will brief us on our role at his school. Regarding the hotel, I have that in hand. We won't step foot in the place. But, I know the concierge. He's Muslim. I saved his daughter after she stupidly went to Syria to join ISIS. As a result, he is utterly loyal to me. He will confirm to anyone who calls the hotel that we are booked in there, are staying there, and have been talking to him about hotel fire evacuation procedures and other mundane emergency protocols. He'll cover for us in every respect."

Knutsen smiled. "Sounds like you've got all angles squared away."

"Let's hope so. But always remember, things rarely go to plan. Now, you need to get ready and go and see Jayne. Please don't tell her that Sunday evening's Chinese meal was only edible because you stepped in to rescue the dish. Oh, and say please and thank you. In other words, don't be yourself."

Knutsen laughed. "I'll try my best." He went to his room to change.

Sign opened his laptop and placed three mobile phones on his desk. He needed to make calls to three people in Russia.

Ninety minutes' later, Knutsen was back in the flat, clutching his passport in the name of Thomas Peterson. Sign was still sitting at his desk. Knutsen asked, "How's it gone?"

Sign closed his laptop. "I've booked our flights, have arranged our accommodation, secured a trawler out of St. Petersburg should the need arise, and have spoken to a criminal who can get you a Makarov pistol and three spare magazines."

"Blimey! You've been a busy bee."

Sign stood and arched his back. "If you have to use the gun, get cornered, and have no way out, kill me and turn the gun on yourself."

Knutsen was stock still. After ten seconds he said in a quiet voice, "I'm sure it won't come to that, Ben."

"One must prepare for every possibility." Sign smiled. "Don't worry, old fella. I'll make sure that we minimize risk to Natalia and ourselves. Okay, you and I need to pack. Make sure you shut your bedroom door. Life is traumatic enough without me seeing you in your birthday suit."

At four PM they had the Skype call with the Cotswold School head teacher. He told them that they were now officially members of his staff, that his reception desk was instructed to forward any enquiries about them to his PA or to him in person, that Sign was teaching Year 11s Russian language and culture, and that Knutsen was teaching Year 10s the history of Russian Tsars. He gave them the names of other key members of staff, thumbnail sketches on their backgrounds and personalities, and details of the school's location in Bourton On The Water and its local amenities and foibles – including pubs, what beers were on draft, what the council was doing to deal with a petition to oust a high street fish and chip shop that had a particularly noisy extractor fan, flooding issues with the River Windrush that ran through the centre of the village, and the fact that the last remaining cash machine in the village had been excavated by criminals who'd nicked a digger lorry from the nearby industrial estate, had dug out the ATM, and driven off with it into the night. He also said that he'd issued a newsletter to parents, advising them that Simon Priest and Thomas Peterson, the false names being used for the Russia trip, were now formally on the staff-roll of the school and had previously worked in remote charity schools in respectively Africa and Nepal.

After the call, Knutsen said to Sign, "He's pulled out the stops for you."

Sign replied, "I have lots of people who pull out the stops for me, primarily because I've pulled out the stops for them. In the case of the head teacher, I saved him from a fall from grace when we were at university. He'd been accepted for teacher training, with the proviso that he had to undergo security vetting to assess his background and suitability to teach minors. The problem was that he was one of the biggest dealers of cannabis to university students. He had a barn in a nearby Oxfordshire village. It was on a farm, owned by his father. But father had dementia and hadn't a clue what his son was up to on his property. In the barn were a third of an acre of lamps and cannabis plants. It was an extremely lucrative cottage industry. I knew about this because the teacher-to-be was my friend. I didn't condone his extra curricula activity, but nor did I do anything about it. I've never taken drugs. People who had a few puffs of his weed seemed very harmless when intoxicated. And they were functioning – attending lectures, getting essays done, zero violence towards others. They weren't like the strung out heroin or meth addicts I'd read about. And my friend was a good chap. Most of the profits he made from dealing were put into his father's health care and upkeep of the farm. His mother didn't feature. Years before she'd run off with an Australian exporter of snakes and other deadly creatures. One day I got summoned to the dean's office. He grilled me on whether I had any evidence about my friend's illegal affairs. He said matters were getting serious, beyond my friend being potentially expelled from our college. Of course, the dean was tipping me off. I went straight to my friend and said that he was going to be busted by the cops. He panicked. I told him I'd help. We went to his farm, removed the lamps which I sold to a very friendly local gypsy called Frank, and we took all of the cannabis pot plants outside of the barn. My friend suggested we burn them. I told him not to be ridiculous – the smell would carry for at least a mile. I had a better plan. At 0500hrs the police drug squad hit our campus. They found nothing. They searched my friend's farm. Again, nothing. No doubt they were extremely frustrated. And I wonder how long it took them to realise that every member of the Thames Valley Police drug squad had one cannabis pot plant in their homes' gardens."

Knutsen was incredulous. "You planted one pot in every drug cop's house?! How the fuck did you do that? How did you even know who the cops were?"

Sign smiled. "There is a reason why I was later recruited into MI6. Anyway, my friend completed his degree, like me got a double first, and he successfully entered the teaching profession. And now he's helping us with our cover story to enter Russia."

"Jesus! You've led an odd life."

"I prefer the word *unusual*. A rich tapestry of life is never cluttered with swathes of dullness. You know me well enough to understand that I do not tolerate chapters of mundanity." Sign grabbed his wallet and keys. "So, now I'm off to see a Russian spy. Do me a favour while I'm out. I've ordered a hare from my butcher in east London. Would you mind collecting it, bringing it home, and skinning the hare?"

"Er, no problems. The only thing is I've never skinned an animal before."

"Use one of my sharp, thin blade, knives to make an incision in the fur from throat to anus. Then simply peel the skin off the flesh. It's easy. Oh, and you'd be a champion if you could get dinner on the go while I'm seeing Natalia. Chop the hare's head off, gut the animal, pan fry the head, liver and kidneys in butter, add white wine, mustard and mixed herbs, gently simmer the sauce, remove and discard the meat after about an hour, take the sauce off the heat, braise the whole hare on a high heat with equal measures of rapeseed oil and butter, in a separate pan gently sweat chopped shallots and garlic, place sauce, hare and onions into a casserole dish, add one tin of tomatoes, and place the casserole into the oven on seventy degrees heat. Do you think you could do that?"

Knutsen rubbed his face and said with resignation, "I thought I was your business partner, not your sous chef."

"We must all aspire to have more strings to our bow. By the way, when you walk to the butcher's shop, stop off at the independent record stall I mentioned, outside The Royal Festival Hall. I've pre-ordered a vinyl album for you and it's ready for collection. The stall doesn't close until five thirty. It's a very limited edition of early Jane's Addiction. I've paid for the record. Just give the proprietor my name. He's expecting you."

Knutsen screwed his eyes shut and shook his head. "How... how the hell do you know about Jane's Addiction? And, Jesus, the record must have cost you a packet."

Sign stood by the door. "The stall owner is a very knowledgeable chap. He was once a roadie for Nirvana, whoever they are. He's educating me. I like turning my tastes on their head. He also let slip to me that he spent five years in Wandsworth Prison for smashing an electric guitar over a rather rude audience member at a Faithless gig. He's quite a character. Alas, the audience member is now a quadriplegic as a result of his head trauma."

Knutsen opened his eyes. "You bought the record as a gift?"

Sign smiled. "No. I bought it as bribe to get you to cook tonight. When I'm gone and you've returned home in possession of the hare and the record, put the music on loud, cook while you have a couple of beers, put your feet up with a glass of calvados, and enjoy the fact that you've got a couple of hours of escape from my nonsense." He winked at him. "Adieu Monsieur Knutsen." He left the flat.

Fifty minutes later, Sign was in The Coal Hole pub. The establishment was a tasteful yet traditional London boozer, with a rich history. Once it was the place where coal was stored for use in the nearby Savoy Hotel; actors from Shakespeare's day frequented the place when it was converted into a hostelry; Gilbert and Sullivan performed there; and the late actor Richard Harris used it as his local pub after he'd made a mint from selling the rights of his West End play and had enough money to have a permanent room in the Savoy. Over the centuries, it hadn't changed much. It was medium sized, but not spacious; instead it had nooks and crannies where people could talk in private, as well as an upstairs and downstairs bar. The place was clean, but embedded within the old walls was the smell of long ago hops, tobacco smoke, smog, and fossil fuel.

Natalia was standing at the bar.

Sign stood next to her and ordered a pint of pale ale. After he was served and the barman moved away to attend to other customers, Sign spoke without looking at Natalia. Instead he stared at the bar. "In the bag by my feet is a mobile phone and charger. The only person who has the phone's number is me and Tom. Keep it with you at all times during your trip. I've stored my number in there. It is listed as *House Repair Man*. I've also enclosed five hundred dollars and the location of a dead letter box in Moscow. Memorise the location and destroy the note before you travel. If you have anything of interest to communicate but are worried about using the phone, use the DLB and text me saying you've just paid the invoice for the repair to your boiler."

Natalia took a sip of her wine and smiled. Like Sign she was staring forwards. "Did you put a suicide pill in the bag as well?"

"No, because there's no need for that." He drank some of his beer. "Tom and I will be on a different flight tomorrow. We'll be in country late afternoon. I truly hope we don't have to see you during your trip."

"So do I." Natalia finished her wine, picked up the bag, and left.

CHAPTER 6

The following morning Archer was summoned to the office belonging to the chief of MI6. She was feeling nervous, but not because she was seeing her boss. Natalia had flown out of London an hour ago. For one week the young woman was a free agent. Sign was right to send her to Russia. From what Sign had told Archer, Natalia had nothing to do when she was in the motherland, but just her presence there would reinforce in her mind why she spied against her country. And it would give her a much needed break. She was getting claustrophobic and paranoid in London. Hopefully, a break would get her judgement and courage back on track. Still, the fact that, for a few days, she couldn't be protected by Archer made the MI6 officer anxious.

She entered the room adjacent to the chief's office. It contained two secretaries and one mid-ranking intelligence officer. The IO beamed as he saw Archer, stood up behind his desk, and said, "Lovely to see you Jayne. How are you settling in to your new job?"

"Good thank you."

"Excellent." He nodded toward the door that led to the chief's room. "He's waiting for you."

She opened the door, without knocking, closed it behind her, and said, "Sir, you wanted to see me."

The chief was standing by his desk, flicking through a file that was marked Top Secret, Your Eyes Only. He closed the file and looked at Archer. "Take a seat."

The large room had no windows, walls were adorned with framed photos of every previous chief since the service's creation in 1909, artificial flowers were in pots on the floor, and the only furniture in the room were the chief's desk and chair and four armchairs. The chief sat in an armchair, opposite Archer. He was medium height, early fifties, had receding dark hair, a slight paunch, and was wearing a shirt, tie and pressed trousers. His suit jacket was on the back of his desk chair. Aside from his glistening eyes, that right now were peering at Archer over the top of his spectacles, he looked like an unremarkable middle aged civil servant who wouldn't stand out of place in the Department for Transport or the Department for Work & Pensions. And yet, he'd led a remarkable life. His father was a catholic priest and his mother was a Church of England vicar. While trying to feed and shelter Bosnian Muslims during the siege of Sarajevo, both died from Serbian sniper fire. He was in his early twenties at the time and was climbing Everest, while serving as a lieutenant in the Household Cavalry. When he got to the summit, he radioed base camp news of his successful ascent. The radio operator there said that a friend had been trying to get hold of him – a chap that the chief had gone to university with at Harvard and had momentarily been a lover before both young men decided they weren't gay. His friend was now a paratrooper and part of the peacekeeping force in the Former Yugoslavia. The operator patched his friend through to the chief's radio. He learned about his parents' deaths while sitting on the summit and overlooking the world. He descended the mountain in treacherous conditions. The siege of Sarajevo was still raging – it was the longest siege of any city in modern warfare. The chief passed selection for the SAS. Via Bosnian Serb propaganda video footage, facial recognition technology, and various contacts, he ascertained the identities of the four Serb snipers who were on duty the day his parents died. When he was granted a few days' leave, he paid them a visit in Serbia, armed with a handgun. Their dead bodies were never found. Three years later he joined MI6. Since then he'd served in nearly every continent and was regarded as one of the brightest spies of his generation. He was a tough man, but wise.

He said to Archer, "I wish to have an update on Natalia Asina."

Archer kept her eyes fixed on the chief's penetrating stare. "I am making progress, but I'm not there yet. Baby steps, nudge her thinking, get her back in the saddle when she's ready."

"We don't have time! We need a download of her brain before she's shipped back to Russia for good."

"I know. And that's why she's my number one priority."

The chief look bothered. "I'm getting pressure from the Americans, French, Germans, Austrians, and others. They all want to know two things: who is our source and when will our source give us the names of the high ranking SVR and GRU spies in their countries. I can deal with the pressure. But, there are other wheels in motion. *Political* wheels. The Yanks think our relationship with them is diabolical and at an all-time low."

"They're right. We can't trust them while they have a lunatic dictator as president."

The chief didn't respond to the comment. "The Europeans are in a chaotic frenzy as a result of Brexit. They're turning on each other. The only sane partners we have now are Canada, Australia, and New Zealand. The PM wants me to build bridges. I've told her that the best way we can do that is to give gold dust to our foreign intelligence counterparts." He was silent for a few moments. "Natalia's knowledge is the gold dust. You must get her to continue to spy for us."

"She spies for me, not you, sir."

"Yes, yes! I know how it works." He looked away, irritated. "What steps are you taking?"

"I've been meeting her regularly, counselling her, and today she's on a plane to Moscow so she can get a breath of fresh air outside of London. She'll be back in a week."

"Alright." The chief asked, "Are you up to this job?"

"Which job? Running the Russia Department or running Natalia?"

"Both."

"I am. You shouldn't need to ask me."

The chief sighed. "These are trying times. Sometimes I wonder whether I'm up to my job. I meant no malice when I posed the question to you. We're all floundering amid shifting sands."

"I know, sir. I don't envy you." Archer asked, "Would you like me to make you a cup of tea? I could murder a cuppa right now."

The chief smiled. "That would be extremely gracious of you, Jayne. Once it's poured, let's sit down and talk about anything other than Russian spies and politics. In fact, I'll tell you about the time, twenty years ago, when I was in a bare knuckle fight in a wasteland in Algeria and lost because one of the members of the gambling audience stabbed me in the back with a three inch blade."

Four hours' later Archer visited her mother in her retirement home in Godalming. The grounds were still wet from rain the day before, but now the sky was clear and there was no wind. She decided it would be nice to take Elizabeth out into the beautiful grounds. She pushed her mother in her wheelchair, along one of the many footpaths that ran between manicured grass, sensationally sculptured medium-sized trees and hedges, flower beds, and vegetable plots that were wired off to protect the crops from being eaten by hedgehogs. The air was rich with the scent of the moist grass, pine, rhododendron, bay, and burning logs of birch that had been cut, stored and dried since last winter, and were fuelling an exterior stone fireplace. She looked at the beautiful house that contained the residents. Smoke was billowing from three of its chimneys. Inside the house, lights were on, making the windows look amber, as yellow light mixed and reflected off the gorgeous heavy and currently parted crimson curtains. Patients were in there, some playing cards or board games, others reading or watching TV. Though Godalming was a small town, the care home was sufficiently far from the centre to be completely untroubled by the hurly burly of everyday life. It was, Archer always thought, a refined and magical oasis. She stopped by a small pond that contained frogs, carp, newts, and other aquatic life. Two ducks, a male and female, were on its surface. They'd lived here for two years. The residents called them Bonnie and Clyde, due to their proclivity to nick stuff out of people's hands or pockets.

From her handbag, Archer withdrew bread and a bag of raisons which she handed to her mother.

Elizabeth said, "Raisons?"

"I've researched it. Apparently ducks shouldn't eat bread. It swells up in their throat, plus is difficult to digest. The bread's for the greedy carp."

Elizabeth smiled and started tossing the food. "I'm hoping to see the old fella today." She kept her eyes on the pond as the ducks chased after the bread and ignored the raisins. "There he is! Do give me a hand."

Archer helped her mother out of her chair, fully supporting her weight, and assisted her to get on her knees. Elizabeth handed *the old fella* chunks of bread. He was a thirty pound carp who was often shy and other times brazen and greedy. Today he had no fear and sucked the bread from Elizabeth's fingers. Archer lifted her mother back into her wheel chair.

Elizabeth shivered, despite wearing a shawl. "Autumn's upon us."

"Are you cold, mum?"

"No. Shivering's a good reflex. It shakes off fear." She patted her daughter's hand. "The estate is beautiful at this time of year. I know I must leave soon, after all the tests are complete, but even this ancient been-around-the-block gal can get the collywobbles when change is afoot." She looked at Archer. "I'm looking forward to moving in to your house. It will be lovely to spend time with you and see the Thames again. But, I will miss the old fella, Bonnie and Clyde, and the bonkers residents." She laughed. "They are a crazy bunch." She pointed at the house. "But, all of them in there would make an obituary writer have a wet dream. They have so many stories to tell about their lives."

"You can visit them, mum."

"True. I have their mobile numbers in a black leather-clad notebook that your father gave me because he wanted to stop me forgetting stuff when I went to the shops. I never used it for shopping lists. Now, I've used it for listing who, one by one, will die."

Archer said in a curt tone, "Don't get maudlin. We've spoken about this before."

Elizabeth replied in a matter-of-fact tone, "I'm not being maudlin. It is what it is. Try being my age and thinking that you're going to live forever. Sorry to disappoint you." She tossed more bread. "We all get buried or incinerated. I don't worry about that. What worries me is, in a year's time, I'll be ringing up my friends in the estate, to see if they'd like to join me for a gin and tonic or a trip to the flicks, and I'll have forgotten they're dead. I'll have to cross their numbers out in my notebook. I have no bucket list. Instead I have an imminent dead list."

Archer pushed her mother onwards, passing sycamore, and a rabbit warren that drove the groundsmen crazy as much as the mole hills. "I'm trying to find out what happened to Susan."

Elizabeth smiled. "That's kind. You know that I don't mourn her. It happened so long ago. I was a wreck at the time. But I had to bring you up. I had to function. So, I kept telling myself that someone kind was raising Susan, even though I was conscious that I was telling myself a lie. I don't believe in mothers' instinct and all that nonsense. I believe in facts. But, sometimes we have to fib to trick our brains. Now that you're head of the Russia desk, do you think you've got the power to get to the bottom of what happened to Susan?"

"I don't think power's the right word. What I do now have is significant autonomy and access to expert resources. That said, I wish you'd told me about Susan before."

"Don't be angry with me. I was protecting you. And you weren't in the Russia Department. You wouldn't have been able to do anything." Elizabeth looked up. "Clouds are coming in. We'd better turn back before it rains."

"It might not rain."

"It will, according to my phone's weather app. It's predicting a downpour this afternoon." Elizabeth breathed in deeply. "Let's just wait here for a minute. If it does start raining I want to feel the droplets on my face. It'll make me feel alive. And anyway, my skin's waterproof." She ran a finger over Archer's hand. "It's a weird thing – you're all I have now, and yet you may not be all I have. Your father and I spent fifty years trying to find Susan. I know Russia, I speak Russian, I have contacts there, though all of them are now old and retired, or dead. I persisted, but got nowhere. Susan vanished on the day she was born." Tears ran down her face. "It's… well, it's…"

Archer wrapped her arm around her mother's back. "Mum — you've carried this burden for too long."

"So did your father. It broke him in the end, I'm sure of that." Elizabeth rubbed away her tears. "It's just I'm not a smart academic anymore, and I don't want to be. I want to be a soppy old lady who looks back on her life and takes pleasure from my memories. That's hard to do when one of the memories is a mystery; a very *painful* mystery." She looked at her daughter. "It's a fool's hope, I know, but I keep having this image of you me, and Susan together in your house. It's stupid of me, I guess. But, it is what it is."

Archer pushed her mum back to the care home. "When I was a teenager I used to fantasise about marrying the actor Jeremy Irons. I loved his voice and his elegant mannerisms. The fantasy put a smile on my face. It might have been a foolish thought but most certainly it wasn't a wasted dream."

Sign and Knutsen arrived in Sheremetyevo International Airport, one of Moscow's largest transportation hubs. It was the first time Knutsen had been to Russia. As he stood in the queue for passport control, he yawned — not because he was tired, instead because he wanted to look bored and unsuspicious. Sign was behind him, ten people back. He couldn't help Knutsen now. Knutsen was on his own.

The queue was moving at a snail's pace. Passengers on the Aeroflot flight in to Moscow had been warned by the plane's captain that there might be delays getting through immigration and security due to increased analysis of passengers by airport authorities. The captain didn't need to elaborate why that was the case. Passengers knew that everyone entering and leaving Russia were treated as potential terrorists or spies.

It took Knutsen thirty minutes to reach passport control. He handed over his false passport. The man behind the desk scrutinised the passport and repeatedly looked at Knutsen. He asked in English, "What is the purpose of your visit?"

Knutsen yawned again. "I'm a teacher. I'm bringing some of my school children to Moscow early next year. I'm travelling with a colleague. We have to make sure it's safe to bring them here."

The official frowned. "Why would it not be safe?"

Knutsen put on his strongest London drawl. "It's not that mate. It's a pain in the arse. We have to do the same thing if we take them on a day trip to Madame Tussauds or the London Eye." He screwed up his face and sucked in air, as if he was trying to stifle another yawn. "It's the bloody law. We have to check everything, down to is it safe to cross the road, can we get gluten-free food, are there minibars in their hotel room that they can raid? You know – that kind of stuff. So, the teachers have to come here in advance and check it out. Have you got kids?"

The man nodded.

"Then you know what it's like. Eyes in the back of your head all the time." Knutsen smiled. "There's only one advantage on these bloody risk assessment trips – we get to have a few bevvies."

"Bevvies?"

"Booze, drinks." Knutrsen winked at him. "I've heard you Russians have got some brilliant Polish vodka in Moscow."

For a moment the official looked stunned. Then he laughed. "British sense of humour. I get it. Only Russian vodka here. Polish vodka is rubbish." He handed the passport back to Knutsen. "Enjoy your stay. Before you travel with your school children check the website of The Ministry of Foreign Affairs of the Russian Federation. It's in English. It will tell you if there are any security threats in the area where you will be staying."

Knutsen put his passport in his coat pocket. "Nice one, mate." He grabbed the handle of his trolley bag. "By the way – do the bars stay open late here?"

"Da. Of course." The official waved his hand.

Knutsen walked onwards.

Twenty four minutes later Sign joined Knutsen outside the terminal they'd arrived in. They walked together to the taxi rank. Sign peered into the window of the taxi at the front of the rank and said in fluent Russian, "The Ritz-Carlton hotel, please."

When they were on the move, Knutsen asked Sign, "We're staying at the Carlton?"

"It's a smashing five star hotel, in the centre of the city."

This didn't make any sense to Knutsen. Sign had told him that their accommodation in Russia was free. However, it was highly likely that Sign knew the manager of the hotel and had cut a deal with him or her. Knutsen kept his mouth shut.

As usual, traffic into the city was horrendous. While Knutsen stared out of the window, Sign was jabbering to the driver about anything that came into his mind – questions about the Russian world cup; weather; restaurant recommendations; how long the driver had worked his cab; roadworks; and a raft of other local matters.

When the taxi dropped them off outside the hotel, Sign placed his hand on Knutsen's shoulder and quietly said, "This is not the end of our journey. Keep an eye on my case." He walked to the porter standing beneath the regal hotel's entrance and asked him to hail a cab, adding that they needed to work this evening before checking in. Five minutes' later they were on the road again. After travelling five hundred yards in the dark and almost gridlocked traffic, they were dropped off outside the beautiful St. Regis Moscow Nikolskaya hotel.

Sign said to his colleague, "Walk with me."

They pulled their trolley bags down the road and turned into a side street.

"Now we wait." Sign checked his watch. "Timings are never precise in Moscow." The street was only illuminated by lamps. Sign and Knutsen were in the shadows. Sign stared at his phone. It pinged. "ETA five minutes."

Knutsen was certain that they were being picked up by one of Sign's assets. However, he had no idea where they were headed. All Sign had told him before they'd departed London was that it was best if he didn't know where their accommodation was until they reached the place. That comment had really annoyed Knutsen. But he also was highly cognisant that Sign had his methods. And it had also occurred to Knutsen that this may well have been the first time that Sign had deployed overseas with a British colleague. During his MI6 career, Sign worked alone. Now, Sign was figuratively having to hand-hold Knutsen, letting him witness his spy tradecraft while at the same time not telling him what was happening until they were in a safe place.

Sign's phone pinged again. A car approached. Sign moved quickly to one of the street lamps. The car slowed, then stopped.

Sign grabbed his bag and said, "Quickly now!" He got into the back of the car. Knutsen followed. The car pulled away.

The driver was a male, in his late twenties, short haircut, but that was pretty much all that Knutsen could discern about the man from his angle in the back passenger seat. The driver was silent as he drove north. One hour later they were out of the city. They continued north on the A104. Either side of them was black, the only illumination coming from vehicles' headlights. The further they drove, the fewer cars they encountered. The driver turned off the main road, onto a gravel track. Now there were no cars or any signs of life whatsoever. Six miles later he stopped.

Ahead of them was an isolated and stunning large wooden house, on the banks of a lake. It had illuminated oil lamps hanging on the porch's canopy, strings of solar-powered white-light bulbs draped over fences that were either side of the property, two chimneys emitting smoke, and windows that were a golden glow due to interior lights.

The driver turned off the engine and got out.

Sign nodded at Knutsen. "So here we are dear fellow. Our journey has ended." He smiled and got out of the car.

When out of the vehicle, Knutsen arched his aching back. The travel to Moscow had cramped the tall man's muscles. He breathed in deeply, inhaling a multitude of smells including the fresh breeze that was gently wafting over rippling lake water, burning logs, and aromatic aromas from trees that were shedding their leaves in the cool autumn air.

Sign walked up to the driver. "Yuri – how the devil are you young sir?" He embraced him.

Yuri grinned and replied in Russian, "It's so good to see you my friend." He pointed at Knutsen. "Should we trust him or pretend we trust him?"

Sign laughed. "We trust him. Come on, let's get inside and say hello to your dad. I hope he's preparing a nice meal."

They entered the property. It was a four bedroom house. Downstairs was a big lounge that was open plan with a kitchen. The lounge had a fire blazing, four fishing roads resting on struts in the wall, other fishing equipment beneath the rods, a stuffed twenty pound trout in a glass cabinet on an antique mahogany cabinet, lit candles, mismatching armchairs and sofa, photos of Yuri's dad, Yuri, and his deceased mother, a battered balalaika that had once belonged to a White Cossack warrior and was leaning in the corner of the room, hermetically sealed copper jars of tobacco from Asia and America, bottles of wine and vodka stored in buckets, coils of rope and twine scattered on wooden furniture surfaces, books haphazardly piled on the floor, paintings of the rural landscape adjacent to the property, small TV that was manufactured in 1987 and only worked intermittently, oak bowl on a coffee table that contained six briar pipes, gun rack of rifles, and a rug in front of the fire. Lenin was lying on the rug. He was a two year old huge Eurasian wolf, and had been rescued by its owner from a farmer who'd tried to kill the animal when he was a cub.

The kitchen had a long, waist-height, work bench that acted as the only partial barrier to the lounge. Behind it was a stove, cupboards, microwave, refrigerator, chest freezer, mugs that were hanging on hooks under one of the units, pots and pans hanging from other hooks in the ceiling, sink, two wooden baskets containing an array of berries and vegetables, pots of herbs, string of garlic bulbs draped over a window ledge that overlooked the lake, vine of tomatoes that were attached to the door handle of one of the cupboards, and spot lamps in the ceiling that cast a golden glow over the room. On the stove was a large metal pot. Flames were underneath it, and whatever was in the pot was producing a delicious aroma.

Yuri's father, Gregor, was standing behind the workbench, holding a knife. On a chopping board in front of him was a fourteen inch chunk of meat. Gregor was in his early sixties, medium height, built like a wrestler, had a black beard, bald head, and a scar that ran from one eye to his jaw. He was wearing waterproof trousers, boots, and a jumper reminiscent of the type worn by submariners when on deck. The sleeves of the jumper were rolled up, displaying his massive muscular arms and tattoos. When he spotted Sign he put down the knife, smiled, and walked into the lounge, his arms outstretched. "Ben! My friend! Part of me was hoping you'd get arrested by the secret police in Moscow." He hugged Sign, then took a step back while keeping his hands on Sign's arms. "The other part of me didn't want my food to go to waste." He turned to Knutsen and switched to English. "And you are Thomas. It won't be your real name, or it might be close to your real name. I don't need to know your surname because it will be false." His smile remained. "I will think of you as Thomas The Tank Engine – full of steam; always up to mischief; strong as a herd of oxen." He laughed. "Yuri used to watch Thomas The Tank Engine when he was a boy."

"Shut up, dad." Yuri was pouring four large glasses of neat vodka.

Gregor laughed louder and shook Knutsen's hand. "Welcome Thomas."

Knutsen felt like he was in the presence of an unstoppable force of nature. He pointed at Lenin. "Erm, is that a wolf?"

Gregor nodded. "His bite is ten times stronger than a dog's bite."

Knutsen eyed the wolf. "I thought you'd say something like that. Is he dangerous?"

"Only if he wants to feed. Don't worry – I fed him before you arrived. You should be safe for a few hours."

Knutsen kept his eye on the animal. "It's just that I get uneasy around dogs and… things like that, ever since I was attacked by pit bull when I was a kid. Wolves are a step up."

Gregor put his arm around Knutsen and stroked Lenin. "But now you are a man. You and Lenin will become great friends. You're taking him for a walk now. He needs to do a shit and piss."

"What?! A walk?"

"Follow the shore for half a mile, then bring him back. Keep him on the lead. There are rumours that there's a female wolf nearby. Lenin will bite your head off and escape if he gets her scent. Be firm with him. Show him who's boss. And talk to him. He's calmer that way. Well, usually it keeps him calm."

Yuri handed Knutsen a lead and a torch. "Don't touch his tail, or his rear legs. In fact, don't touch him at all unless things go wrong. If he does get aggressive, pin him down by his neck and hold him for ten minutes. Be *very* strong. Don't let his jaws get anywhere near you. He should be fine after that."

Knutsen breathed in deeply. His heart was racing. To himself he said, "Okay, let's do this." To the wolf he said, "Lenin – if you pull any crap I'll cut your dick off. You got that mate?" He attached the lead and walked Lenin out of the house.

Gregor and Yuri were sniggering when Knutsen was gone.

Sign smiled. "You are naughty."

"Is there a better way to be?" Gregor patted his son on his shoulder. "Glasses on a tray, bottle next to them, put them on the rear balcony. I need a moment alone with my friend."

"Sure, dad."

When Gregor and Sign were alone, Gregor said in Russian, "Come with me into the kitchen." He pointed at the vat on the stove. "I've sweated down onions, ceps, garlic, and added water, tomatoes, herbs, a deseeded chilli, two cloves, beer, and broiled pig's snout. Once the reduction is complete I'll strain it off, discard all but the liquid, and use the sauce as a gravy." He spun around. Alongside the chopping board with the joint of meat were two other chopping boards. One of them had potatoes. The other had vegetables. "I'm thinking boiled cabbage that's then caramelised in butter and pickled in vinegar, shredded and fried potatoes, and cold cucumbers coated in a lovely vodka and lemon sauce. I brewed the vodka last winter. All of the vegetables are either grown by me or foraged by me and Yuri from the woods." He slapped the meat. "And here's the masterpiece. It's cut from the side of an Elk, meaning it will be tender. There's a friend of mine twenty miles up the lake. He rears a lot of animals, and has a wooded and enclosed thirty hectare plot containing elks. Occasionally he lets me take Lenin in there so that I can give him the freedom to remember how to hunt. It's important because I'm hoping to release my dear friend back into the wild when he's five. But he must know how to survive. Lenin killed this elk. Some of it I gave to him; the rest of it is in the freezer. I paid my friend for the meat. I will roast the joint. Yuri will take care of everything else while you, me, and Thomas have a drink by the lake." Gregor looked satisfied with everything around him. "What do you think of this evening's meal?"

Sign gently punched his fist against Gregor's arm. "Thomas and I have just arrived at the finest restaurant in Russia."

"You have." Gregor oiled a roasting pan, placed the meat into the dish, put the pan in the oven, dipped a finger into the vat's sauce and placed it in his mouth, nodded with approval, and rubbed his hands together. "Keep your fleece on. It will be cold outside." He walked out of the house and onto the long rear balcony facing the vast lake. He said to Yuri, "Thank you, son. Over to you. Grab yourself a vodka and get on point in the kitchen. It's my turn to cook tomorrow. Usual drill. Divide and conquer."

Gregor and Sign sat on wooden chairs. There were two other chairs on the balcony, but they were brought from the lounge this evening. Gregor and Yuri lived here alone; they didn't have many visitors since Gregor's wife died in her sleep on the balcony. When she passed away she was in a third chair that matched the two that Gregor and Sign were in. For a while, Gregor and Yuri kept the third chair until they could no longer look at it, due to their grief. They burned the chair on the lake shore and said a prayer for the woman they so dearly missed. That was ten years ago. Gregor and Yuri had muddled through ever since.

The balcony was twenty yards long and contained handmade flaming torches that were fixed in plant pots on the rail that separated the balcony from the lake. Water was beneath them, lapping the struts that supported the exterior seating area. The torches illuminated glimpses of the lake; aside from that it was impossible to see anything beyond the rear of the house.

Gregor handed Sign a glass, took one for himself, and raised his glass. "To that crazy escape we did in Belarus."

"Amen to that." Sign chinked his glass.

Both men swigged their vodka.

Gregor said, "Tell me about Thomas."

Sign looked at the lake. "He's an ex-cop; single; killed the man who murdered the woman he wanted to marry; is sometimes quiet, other times has a mouth like a sewer; highly intelligent, but not worldly wise; and is one of the finest fellows I've met."

Gregor nodded. "I like him. Except the cop bit."

Sign smiled. "Don't worry. He never liked being in the police."

"He's a rule-breaker?"

"Most certainly. But, his moral compass is pointing in the right direction."

Gregor poured them another drink. "So, why are you here? I don't need specifics."

Sign replied in a quiet voice, "It's a babysitting job. I have an asset in Moscow. The asset's lost her nerve. I've given her a task that shouldn't ruffle her fear. It's the first step to getting her back on to the road to recovery. Thomas and I are here in case she needs us. Then we fly home."

Gregor nodded, his expression sombre. "She's in the very best hands. But take care, my friend. The old guard in Russia is being replaced. Trust no one except Thomas, me, and Yuri." He laughed. "Remember that crazy guy Anatoly Shkuro?"

"How could I forget? He put a bullet in his head a day after I asked him to plant a bomb under an ambassador's car. I should have known that Shkuro had cracked."

"There was no way you could have known. It was bad luck. You gave your instruction to him a few hours before his nerves went into meltdown. Before that he was fearless and mental." Gregor shook his head. "You were with me when we watched him through the sights of our sniper rifles as he walked up that mountain in Afghanistan, entered a Taliban village, strangled the leader, and jogged out of the village. He *was* mental, or an adrenalin junkie, or both. I guess it takes its toll on the mind and body in the end." He gripped Sign's arm. "You did nothing wrong. You saved his crazy arse so many times. The point is that men like you can control people's minds ninety nine percent of the time. But, then there's always that damn one percent."

"Yes. I hate the one percent."

Gregor looked left. "Mr. Tank Engine! You have returned! And Lenin hasn't killed you! This is a good evening! Join us for drinks."

Knutsen sat next to them. Lenin was with him, attached to his leash. The wolf laid down at Knutsen's feet. Knutsen stroked him. "That was interesting - walking something that might want you for dinner."

Gregor roared with laughter. "But look at you now. No fear of silly little pit bulls. And you've made friends with a wolf. Lenin doesn't let anybody but me or Yuri walk him. You must have something special in you. I thought that might be the case. But, I wasn't sure. It was my test. If Lenin tried to kill you, it meant he was suspicious of you. Therefore I'd be suspicious of you. But, he has accepted you. Therefore I accept you."

Sign leaned over and held his fist in front of Lenin's mouth. Then he stroked him. "Gregor – you do talk nonsense."

"Always." Gregor poured Knutsen a glass of vodka. "I must check on dinner. I hope you're both hungry." He walked into the house.

Knutsen asked Sign, "Alright – what's the deal with Gregor?"

Sign watched bats swoop near the torches. "I met him in Butyrka prison, Moscow. He and I shared a cell together for three weeks. I was being held on suspicion of espionage. Gregor was in there pending trial for mass manslaughter. He was a highly decorated submarine captain. While sailing his vessel in the Bering Sea his submarine snagged on a fishing net, careered off course and walloped into a huge subterranean rock. It was a catastrophe. The vessel was very badly damaged and took on water. Its engines cut out and the submarine sunk to the sea bed. Sailors drowned. Gregor tried to save the rest but it was a hopeless cause. Nevertheless he worked tirelessly for over forty eight hours, in freezing water, swimming back and forth with no light, trying to resuscitate his men and drag them to the few remaining areas where there was air. It was a herculean task. But, the Russian navy did nothing. It knew where the submarine was, yet took the decision that its crew should die. They didn't want bad publicity. So, they kept the incident secret, with the intention of salvaging the vessel without the world's media knowing what had happened. Eventually, all of Gregor's crew were dead. It broke his heart to do so, but he had to leave them in their watery grave. He escaped the tomb via a torpedo tube and swam fifty yards to the surface. His lungs were bursting and he was suffering the bends. But, he was lucky. A Russian naval ship was static, over the scene of the incident. He was pulled on board and given medical care. And when he was brought back to shore he was arrested by military police for dereliction of duty. When we were in prison together we spoke. He couldn't forgive the Russian authorities for not coming to his crew's rescue. I told him that he might be of use to me and that we should stay in touch."

"How did you both get out of prison?"

Sign shrugged. "For me it was easy. Britain's Special Branch was holding a GRU spy. Our government said it would hand over the spy in exchange for me. The exchange was done and I was released. When I got back to England, I sent a note to the head of the FSB. The note contained the exact grid coordinates of the submarine accident and simply said *I shared a cell with the captain. If you lay a finger on him and keep him in jail for another day I will tell every Russian, American, British, French, German, Japanese, and Chinese media outlet that the Russian navy is run by a bunch of spineless fools*. I didn't need to say anything else. Gregor was released."

"isn't the FSB suspicious that he may be working for MI6?"

Sign shook his head. "That was the beauty of my demand. The Russian navy was severely embarrassed. In a private ceremony, Gregor was awarded Russia's highest medal. And quite rightly so, even though Gregor knew it was given to him to shut him up. What it did do, however, was grant him freedom and infinite respect. No one watches Gregor and no one in this country dares touch him. He's invincible. And he works for me on odd occasions. We've done a lot of jobs in various parts of the world. He's useful to me because he's very precise."

"Precise?"

Sign didn't elaborate.

Gregor walked on to the balcony, with a huge grin on his face. "Dinner's nearly ready. Are you two swapping war stories? What is it you Brits say? Something like *pull up a sandbag and swing the lantern*?" He rubbed his hands together and sat next to them. "Time for one more drink before we eat. Now, tell me Mr. Tank Engine – how did you kill your girlfriend's murderer?"

Natalia was sitting on her room's bed, within a cheap hotel in central Moscow. She'd checked in to the hotel two hours ago, had called Sign to say she'd arrived safely in Russia, and had done little else since aside from purchasing a burger from a nearby street vendor. The room was clean, small, and functional. She'd tried watching TV, but couldn't concentrate. The journey had been tiring and she felt uneasy being in her country's capital. Her stomach was cramping and her mind was giddy. She knew that had to stop. The temptation to get under her bed's duvet was almost overwhelming, but she told herself that to do so would be submitting to fear. She had to spend the next hour or two in a state of calm meditation. After that, she'd sleep. And tomorrow, she hoped, she'd be relaxed and confident. So, she sat on her bed, her hands placed together in front of her face, as if in prayer, her eyes closed, her breathing deliberately deep and slow. She silently repeated the line that Sign had said to her when he asked her to briefly visit Moscow.

It is not a dangerous enquiry.

Her cover for staying in the hotel was sound. Though she was ostensibly in Moscow to see her aunt and uncle, they lived in a one bedroom high rise apartment. They didn't have room to accommodate her. Also, they lived in the outskirts of Moscow. Natalia wanted to be near to the SVR headquarters in case she needed to work. Tomorrow evening she'd visit her family. Sign's suggestion that the purpose of her trip was due to a medical emergency was apt. Her uncle had been a chain smoker all his life. He now had emphysema. Her aunt needed MRI and CT scans after suffering from blackouts during the last few months. Natalia had previously spoken to them on the phone from London, suggesting that they move to the house that her brother had bought near St. Petersburg. But they'd rightly refused the kind offer, given it was too far away from medical facilities and they didn't drive. Natalia had a bit of savings, not much, but she hoped she could help them with their health care costs. It deeply saddened her. If they died she'd have no one left aside from the woman who called herself Katy. Ben and Tom wouldn't feature for much longer in her life. They were hired help, she could tell. Soon they'd move on to another project. And even Katy might vanish from her life if Natalia couldn't get her act together and prove her value to MI6.

She stopped meditating and walked to the only window in the room. She was four stories up from the road below Cars were bumper-to-bumper in the evening traffic, producing a river of neon headlights. Either side of the vehicles were low-rise shops and office buildings. In the distance were taller buildings. The city was buzzing and aglow with a multitude of illuminations. Tourists would have thought it looked cool. But Natalia didn't think of it that way. She knew that underneath the veneer of the cosmopolitan, post-Soviet, hip metropolis was the same old dogma of corruption, cruelty, and disregard for life. Russians understood that; most tourists didn't. Everyone who lived here were acutely aware that they were ants that could be squashed without a second thought by the government. They were disposable. To the governments and previous tsars, that mind set made sense. Who wants to run the biggest country in the world if it's getting overpopulated? And how can one stop the country fragmenting into smaller countries without holding the motherland together with the use of a rod of iron and brutal punishments on its populous? It's why Natalia and so many other Russians hated their homeland – they knew there was no feasible alternative to how rulers governed such a vast chunk of the world. It left Russians with two choices: leave or accept how matters have always been conducted for centuries. Natalia had chosen to leave, but she'd done so as a Russian spy. Her career choice now seemed utterly ridiculous..

She changed into her bedtime attire, drank some water, and got into bed. She thought she'd fall straight to sleep. She didn't. She thought about Petrov and how, at the end, he looked so utterly alone in the world; her parents and how exhausted they were with life, and her own lonely and unusual life. Sign had been right in his comment to her when they'd dined. She was young. Ordinarily she shouldn't be ready in life to resignedly accept her plight and the realities of her day-to-day existence. Most women her age were dating, going out in the evening with friends, communicating with pals on social media, going on holidays, dreaming about the future and joyous events, sometimes laughing, other times sad. She had none of those things, not even sadness. Her life was all about survival.

She turned off the bedside light. Her eyes remained open. After thirty minutes, she closed them. Before sleeping she decided she had two choices: die you as an emotional and physical wreck; or get a new life in Britain. But to get the latter she'd have to complete her work for Katy. And before that she'd have to do her best to find answers to Susan Archer's disappearance.

CHAPTER 7

Early the following morning Knutsen was woken by the sound of squealing. Bleary eyed, he put his clothes and boots on and went downstairs. He couldn't see anyone in the house, though lights were on and the kettle was boiling. But the squealing was louder and he could hear men shouting from outside. He opened the front door and walked outside. Gregor and Sign were chasing a mid-sized pig that was bolting along the lake's shoreline. Yuri was standing nearby, holding Lenin on a leash.

Gregor was apoplectic, shouting in Russian, "Stop, you little fucker!"

Sign ran ahead of the pig, stopped, turned to face the swine, and held out his arms. The action confused the pig. It slowed sufficient for Gregor to catch up with it and attach a lasso to its neck. He dragged the beast back towards the house and placed it in a nearby pen. As he walked past Yuri he muttered, "I told you to bolt the door! The others in there might be docile but this one's a lively bastard. If you hadn't grabbed Lenin he'd have ripped the pig apart." He smiled as he walked to Knutsen. In English he said, "Good morning Thomas. Unless absolutely necessary I would advise you never to keep animals and wayward sons. I'm going to make a pot of coffee for us all, but take your time. It will stay warm on the stove." He went into his house.

Knutsen wandered over to Sign. For the first time, he could properly take in the surroundings of the house. Aside from the small wooden barn containing the pigs, there was a chicken coop, small outhouse for smoking and drying fish, pond that was fed by a tributary from the lake and contained a fish trap at its entrance, two horses and one pony in a paddock with a large shelter, garages, large gas unit that supplied the house, tractor, and an assortment of other farm equipment – some of it in good condition, others rusting and cannibalised for spare parts. The land was also farmed for crops, though most of the plots were bare at this time of year. It was hard to tell how much land Gregor owned. Aside from the two hundred yard fence that stretched from the house and followed the lake's shore, there were no discernible man-made boundaries. The only natural boundaries were the lake and a forest that was either side of the track into the property and four hundred yards away. On the vast lake, a rowing boat was tethered to a post, fitted into the slim beach. On the far side of the lake was another forest that stretched for as far as the eye could see. Knutsen estimated it would take at least three hours to row to the other side. And goodness knows how long the lake was. It was impossible to see where it began and ended; at the very least it was a mile long, probably considerably longer. One thing was clear – there were no visible dwellings near Gregor's farmstead.

Sign was checking the rowing boat.

Knutsen asked him, "Sleep okay?"

"Like a hibernating bear." Sign walked towards the house. "Let's get a brew down our necks. Then you and I need to fetch some breakfast."

Knutsen followed him. "Breakfast? How far is the nearest shop?"

"Too far." Sign entered the house.

The fire was lit. Lenin was curled up in front of it, having become fatigued after his five mile walk with Yuri this morning. In the kitchen, Yuri was pouring freshly brewed coffee. Gregor was sitting in the lounge, smoking his pipe and reading a week-old newspaper.

Gregor flicked the paper, and tossed it onto the fire. "The world has gone mad." He gestured to the spare armchairs. "Sit and have a drink. Then you must work for your supper."

The comment didn't seem to faze Sign, who slumped into a chair. By comparison, Knutsen had no idea what was going on.

Yuri served them mugs of coffee and said, "I need to check the chicken wire. We've got a family of foxes nearby." He left.

Gregor put his hands around his mug. "Have you heard from your asset?"

Sign nodded. "Today she's going into SVR headquarters. It'll make or break her. All we can do is wait here, unless there's an emergency."

"Da, I know. Do you have a back-up plan if the wheel comes off?"

"Yes. But, I'm not going to tell you what it is." Sign winked at Gregor. "Officially you are a Hero of the Russian Federation. You're the last person I should be speaking to."

Gregor chuckled. *Hero of the Russian Federation.* What a joke." His expression turned serious. "My men drowned in a steel coffin."

"You tried to save every one of them. Your efforts were nothing short of spectacular." Sign sipped his coffee. "You have survivor guilt. That's all. We discussed this a few years ago. And look at what you and I subsequently did to the identify and neutralise the butcher in Myanmar, our heist of dirty bank money in Bahrain, the trick we played on the CIA in Venezuela, that bloody long trek through the jungles of Borneo to catch the man who slit Jacob's throat, and that incredible two mile shot you took on the side of K2 to knock off the head of the man who wanted to set fire to the world. There are so many other examples." Sign smiled. "Not bad for a sailor."

Gregor waved his hand. "That was then and this is now." He stood and took two guns off the rack. "Mr. Thomas. I presume you can shoot." He handed Knutsen one of the guns. "You and I are going hunting in the forest now for this household's dinner. Meanwhile Ben is going on to the lake to catch our breakfast."

Natalia entered the headquarters of the Sluzhba Vneshney Razvedki, in the Yasenevo district in southwest Moscow. She approached the security desk, showed her passport, and was told by the guard behind the desk to wait. He made an internal telephone call and told her to wait. Five minutes later a man swiped his SVR on an electronic recognition pad on the inside of the rigid clear plastic barriers in the lobby, came through the gate, and smiled when he saw Natalia.

He approached and said, "Good to see you." He nodded at the security guard. "She is who she says she is. Give her a temporary pass." When Natalia was issued the pass, the man said to her, "Come with me."

She followed him through the gates and into the huge building.

As the man led her along corridors with offices either side, up lifts, and along more corridors, he jabbered. "It's the busiest here that I've known it for years. We've got all this terrorist shit to deal with, organising missions in Syria that look like we're targeting ISIS whereas instead we're wiping out the rebels who want to oust that psychopath president who our politicians support, cyber attacks against the West – and my goodness, you should see the size of the cyber team now, I bet it's four times the size since you were last here, bolstering the Crimea, monitoring North Korea and China, alongside the FSB dealing with the usual internal shit within Russia, and having fun and games with Brexit, Europe in general, Britain, and America." He stopped by an office. "And we're clearing out the rotten apples. What we did to the Skripals in Salisbury is a drop in the ocean. We're going after every single defector, no matter where they are, and we'll send them to Hell." He knocked on the door and entered.

A fifty three year old man was sitting behind his desk. He was slim, wore glasses, had silver hair, and was wearing a suit. He stood when he saw Natalia, and walked into the centre of the oak panelled room. "Natalia. Take a seat." To the man who'd escorted her to the room, he said, "Leave us now." When they were alone, he sat behind his desk. He was the head of the SVR's Britain Department and had served in the foreign intelligence service for thirty one years. During his career he'd been posted to Tokyo, Islamabad, Kabul, Kiev, Munich, Washington D.C., and three times in London. Some SVR officers thought he was destined to be the next director of the service; others thought not because he loathed politics and wanted to stick to what he did best. His name was Alexander Surikov.

Surikov asked, "How was your flight?"

Natalia replied, "We need a better national airline."

Surikov smiled. "Technically, Aeroflot is semi-privatised. Where are you staying?"

"You know the answer to that."

"I do. Does the hotel serve your needs?"

"I've slept in worse places."

Surikov nodded. "We do what we have to do. How are your aunt and uncle?"

"I'm seeing them this evening. Things are not looking good."

"Your aunt should get her scans as soon as possible. Regrettably your uncle may be beyond repair."

Natalia hadn't told anyone in the service about her relatives' medical condition. She said, "I just need to check on them and see what I can do to help. But, I can't stay long. We're really stretched in the London office."

"I'm sure you are. How are you finding it there?"

Natalia replied with part lies and part truths. "London looks like it's under martial law. There are cops everywhere, armed with Heckler & Koch submachine guns, and wearing body armour. Every inch of the city is monitored by CCTV. There's brilliant food to be had, and the cinemas and theatres are great. But I don't go out much. Actually, I don't go out at all when I'm not working. It's a scary place. We work really long hours in the London office. When I get home I just want to sleep. And I don't feel that I belong in London. It feels so alien to me."

"You are young and this is your first posting. You'll get used to operating in strange places. Are you planning to do any work while you're here?"

Natalia replied, "I'd like to decompress as much as possible, alongside my family duties."

"Quite right. I was going to suggest the same."

She added, "But I would like to do some research. Can I have access to our archives section?"

"For what purpose?"

"I'd like to look into an old case. It's to do with the disappearance of Sergey Peskov in nineteen sixty eight." Peskov was a KGB officer, based in London, who'd gone to meet a British asset in Manchester and had never been seen since. His disappearance was a mystery to the Soviet Union. "I have a contact who has told me that she knew Peskov. My contact thinks he was assassinated by British authorities. I don't know much about the Peskov case. My understanding is that it was assumed by us that he'd defected and his identity had been changed. If that's true, he'd be an old man by now, or dead. However, I imagine in the current climate it would be good if we could prove he was killed by the British. They might stop finger pointing at us about the Salisbury thing if we confront them with some home truths."

"Good thinking. Who's your contact?"

"It's delicate. She's not yet fully recruited by me. If I'm successful in getting her on board I'll happily tell you her name. For now I have to tread carefully."

Surikov pondered the statement. "I understand." He smiled. "You are putting your field training to use. Don't worry – one day soon I will give you the freedom to get away from your analyst desk job. Enjoy it while it lasts." He slapped his desk. "When you get to my age you soon find yourself back behind one of these damn things. Yes, you can have access to the archives and investigate the Peskov case. You are right – it would be good to have some dirt on the Brits. The UK, America, NATO, the whole bunch of them, are rattling their sabres at us." He stood and held out his hand. "Good work Natalia. But, make sure you have some time for yourself as well. You look tired. I don't want you to burn out."

Natalia shook his hand. "Thank you sir." She left his office.

While Gregor and Knutsen were stalking through the nearby woods, Sign was in the lake, sitting on Gregor's rowing boat, casting the line from a fly fishing rod. Due to the depth of the lake he'd opted to use a reel loaded with a sinking line. On the tippet was a gold head nymph and two droppers containing pheasant tail flies. After the line was extended he silently counted to fifteen before beginning the retrieve using a figure of eight hand technique. There were no strikes. He cast the line into a different spot and counted ten before retrieving. Still nothing. This didn't perturb Sign. He was used to the complexities of fly fishing and the odd temperament of the trout he was targeting. He looked at the lake. Five hundred yards away was a ripple on the surface. This was good. It meant that it was less likely the trout would see him and it gave them extra courage to chase after aquatic life. He rowed there, let his boat gently drift, and cast again. His line pulled tight. He'd had a strike. He raised the rod to twelve o'clock and played the fish, sometimes pulling it in, other times letting in run in case it snapped the tippet line. The process lasted ten minutes before he was able to net the trout and despatch the fish using a wooden priest. The trout was at least three pounds. He placed it in the hull of the boat and cast again. Forty minutes' later he rowed to shore, tethered the boat, and walked to Gregor's house, his rod and other kit in one hand, the two trout he'd caught dangling by their gills in the other. As he neared the property, Gregor and Knutsen emerged from the forest. Gregor had two ducks lashed on a piece of rope and slung over his back. Knutsen was carrying a goose that he'd shot while it was flying close to the lake. Both men had smiles on their faces. They'd caught dinner and like all respectful hunters they'd only killed what they needed for the cooking pot.

When the men were inside, Sign set about cleaning the fish, pan frying them, and cutting slices of bread. It was a simple yet hearty breakfast. He served up the plates of food on the dining table. Yuri came into the house, washed his hands, and sat with them at the table. For the most part, the four men ate in silence.

When they'd finished, Gregor rubbed his stomach and had an approving look on his face. "All days should start this way. Yuri and I have some jobs to do on the farm today. After that we'll prepare the birds. Do you have plans today? If the answer's yes you may borrow one of my cars. If the answer's no I have a tree that needs felling and turning into logs."

Sign gathered up the plates and placed them in the kitchen. "Thomas and I have to see someone today. Thank you for the offer – yes we'd be grateful to use your car. We'll be back before dinner."

Lenin walked up to Knutsen and nuzzled his ferocious jaw in his lap. Knutsen stroked him.

Gregor beamed. "Take the wolf with you if you like. He enjoys car travel. Just make sure you leave one of the car windows a few inches open so he can get the outside smells. Keep him on a lead. And if anyone asks about his pedigree, for the love of God don't say he's a wolf. Tell them he's a huskie or similar breed. And don't let him near dogs, or children, or women, or anyone for that matter that you think he will kill for pleasure or food."

Fifteen minutes later Sign drove out of the farmstead. Knutsen was in the rear passenger seat. Lenin was half-on-half-off his lap, panting as he had his nose stuck out of the window. The wolf's one hundred and seventy pound weight was crushing Knutsen's legs. And Knutsen had to keep pushing his fur away from his mouth.

Sign looked in the rear view mirror and smiled. "I hope you're both sitting comfortably back there."

Knutsen made no effort to hide the irritation in his voice when he said, "This is weird. I should have stayed in the police. When you asked me to come with you to Russia you didn't mention anything about looking after a wolf, staying at a mad submariner's house, and having to catch my dinner."

"Ah, but dear fellow we must always strive to enrichen our lives with periods of the unusual."

"I'd like to see how you'd get on with a monster sitting on your lap. I can hardly breathe!"

"The drive isn't long. I'd say about ninety minutes."

"Ninety minutes! Oh, that's just bloody fantastic!"

Sign headed north on a road that followed the lake for six miles before veering northwest. All around them was countryside. Very few cars were on the road. At one point a car overtook them. In the rear seat was a young girl. She waved at Lenin and Knutsen. Knutsen gritted his teeth, put on a fake smile, and waved back. When the car was gone he said, "When we get back to London you're going to take me to a pub and buy me as many beers as I want."

"I'll do better than that, old boy. I'll take you to my club in St. James's. They do a lovely beef and ale pie and have an excellent cellar of wines and port."

Thirty minutes later, Lenin started retching. Knutsen screamed, "Pull over!"

But it was too late. Lenin vomited on the window, door, and Knutsen.

Sign tried to suppress laughter as he stopped the car on the side of the deserted road. "The poor fella needs some air. Take him out for a few minutes."

"He needs some fucking air?! God, you're going to pay me back big time for this." He took Lenin onto a grass bank, walked him back and forth, stopped to allow the wolf to have a pee, and brought him back into the car. "Right – wherever we're going let's get there fucking quick!"

Sign drove on. Twenty minutes later he turned the car into a layby and stopped. "We walk from here." He got out of the car. "Bring Lenin."

Knutsen couldn't work out who was more relieved to exit the vehicle – him or the wolf. He tried to wipe vomit off his fleece with blades of grass, but it only resulted in smearing the bile and slime further into his coat. Cursing, he followed Sign while holding Lenin on his lead. They trudged over rough, uneven, open ground, through a copse, and down an escarpment.

Sign pointed at a house boat that was moored on a river. "We reach our destination."

"A boat?"

"Yes, a boat and the man who lives inside the vessel." Sign strode onwards, then stopped sixty yards from the river, spun around to face Knutsen, and said in a quiet voice, "Listen. The man in there is friendly enough, but don't let that fool you. He was a mercenary in Africa in the seventies and eighties. People who worked with him gave him the nickname Mad Dog. You can imagine some of the things he did. None of them were pleasant or pardonable. He's retired now, but still retains contacts in his old world and dabbles in arms smuggling. He thinks I run a private military contractor company. Can you put on a German accent?"

"What?"

"A German accent. You're ex-GSG9 – the elite German police counterterrorism unit. Now you live in London and work for my company, though you're freelance. Make up the rest, if he asks you questions."

"I can't..."

"You're learning to be a spy and that means you have to think on your feet. Don't worry, I'll step in and pick up the slack if I sense you're faltering. One other thing – don't tell Gregor that we've been here. He hates the man after a job Gregor and I did in Sierra Leone a few years ago. To my knowledge, Gregor doesn't know he lives here. Regardless, let's tread carefully." He walked to the boat.

Knutsen was stock still for a moment. He sighed and said, "Come on Lenin. This can't be any worse than you puking on me."

Sign called out, "Knock knock! I'm looking for a crazy Russian guy who owes me money after he crashed my jeep in the Congo."

A man in his mid-sixties looked through one of the boat's windows, grinned, and walked out onto the vessel's gangplank. He was medium height, had a handlebar black moustache, long silver hair that was tied in a ponytail, and the physique of a soldier – slim and athletic. He was wearing camouflage army trousers, desert boots, and a green jumper. Wrapped around his forehead was a thin green bandana that he told people he wore to prevent sweat getting into his eyes, wherein the truth was he used it to hide the results of being branded by a red hot iron after he'd pissed off a tribe of Hutus. "Ben! My friend!" He held up his palm as he swaggered to Sign.

Sign slapped his palm and embraced him. "Good to see you, Anton. It's been a while" He pointed at Knutsen. "This is Thomas. He's German and doesn't speak Russian. He's an associate. Like I said to you on the phone, we're in Russia to do a rather tricky business transaction."

Anton switched in to English. "Nice to meet you, Thomas. Come aboard. What is that?" He pointed at Lenin.

Knutsen replied in an accent that he borrowed from the movie The Great Escape. "It's a Siberian husky."

"He looks like a wolf. Doesn't matter. Bring him in." Anton walked inside his boat. Sign, Knutsen, and Lenin followed.

The interior was narrow, cramped, but not cluttered. There was a tiny kitchenette midway in the boat, a single bed that folded up into the starboard, cupboards, fireproof metal containers of fuel strapped to the floor, a steering wheel and controls at the helm, and a triangular seating area that was permanently fixed to the rear of the boat.

Anton gestured towards the only place to sit. "Make yourself comfortable. The dog-thing can sit on the floor. I'm making tea with a dash of rum." As he prepared the drinks, he asked, "Thomas – how did you come to work with Ben?"

Knutsen replied, "He wants me to test weapons, to see if they're combat ready."

"Small arms?"

"That is correct."

Anton poured boiling water into a pot. "The types needed by special forces and mercenaries in unusual circumstances?"

Knutsen glanced at Sign. Sign nodded.

"Yes."

Anton stirred the tea leaves in the pot. "You are ex-military?"

"No. Police. I served in GSG9. Then I went freelance."

"Did you see action in GSG9?"

"In Germany. I've seen action elsewhere since I left."

Anton poured the tea and added a glug of rum to each mug. "Where is GSG9 headquartered?"

Sign held up his hand. "We all know its garrison is in Sankt Augustin-Hangelar, near Bonn. This is Thomas's first trip with me to Russia. It's a delicate situation for him, and for me for that matter. I want Thomas to keep a low profile, for reasons I'd rather not go in to. It wouldn't serve me or him if he was grilled by trusted friends like you."

"Alright. Keep your hair on." Anton smiled, brought the mugs over, and sat with them after carefully avoiding the huge wolf.

Lenin looked at Anton and growled. Knutsen stroked his head to calm him.

Anton addressed Sign. "Last time I saw you we were hightailing it out of Zambia. That was hectic shit. You really screwed over that South African mine owner. Can't remember his name. Hendrik, or something. Doesn't matter. He put the hounds on us. We'd be dead if you hadn't evaded those ex-Legionnaires by heading into the jungle. Also, it helped enormously that you managed to get the herd of elephants to stampede toward the Legionnaires. I still don't know how you did that."

Sign waved his hand dismissively. "I speak elephant and told the beasts that the men were coming to kill them."

Anton laughed. "Always the storyteller." His expression turned serious. "How can I help you?"

Sign sipped his tea. The taste reminded him of the time his parents had taken him on holiday to France and they'd gone to a bar-tabac at seven AM to get breakfast. Farmers were propping up the bar, taking a break from their four AM start, before heading back to work an all-day shift. Sign had marvelled at the sight of them having a nip of rum in their tea, so early in the morning. His father explained that it fortified them. Much to his wife's consternation, the father bought tea and rum for Sign to taste. Sign looked at Anton. "Thomas and I are shortly due to meet rather unsavoury customers. We will be discussing terms of a trade. They will likely get agitated and unpredictable. Guns will be involved. Therefore we need a gun; specifically a highly reliable pistol. I wondered if you could help us."

Anton looked at Knutsen. "To my knowledge, Ben no longer uses guns. So, I presume the pistol is for you. Are you right or left handed?"

"Right."

"Are you scared of recoil?"

"No, but I prefer precision over power, though ideally I like to opt for a combination of the two."

Anton nodded. "Because you don't want a shot man to have a few moments to shoot back. Yes, I can help you. Come with me." He walked onto the exterior bow of his boat, lifted a hatch, and withdrew a silk bag from a storage area. "This should do the job." He walked off the boat and into the copse. "Whose dog or wolf is it?"

Knutsen replied, "It's on loan. Ben and I are taking it to the meeting in the rural outskirts of Moscow. There will be six men there. We have intelligence that three of them are petrified of wolves. So, we got a dog that looks like a wolf, just to have a bit of leverage."

"Clever." From the bag Anton withdrew a MP-443 Grach Yarygin Pistol. He handed it to Knutsen. "What is this?"

Knutsen weighed the pistol in his hand. "It's an MP-443. It's a very good gun = accurate, reliable, packs a punch, and easy to strip down and clean. It's been issued to some Spetsnaz units but is not yet in service in the police."

"Very good, Thomas. You can see I've inserted targets of men in the forest. Most of them are only partially visible. I'll pick a target and you shoot."

Knutsen handed Lenin's leash to Sign. "Take him close to the boat. I don't want him getting jumpy when he hears the shots."

Sign walked off with the wolf, calling out, "If the gun's any good you can deduct its price off what you owe me."

Anton inserted ear defenders and quietly said, "Target two o'clock."

Knutsen crouched and put two bullets into the target."

"Excellent. Fast and accurate. That person's dead. Eleven o'clock."

Knutsen pointed his gun left and fired two more rounds.

"Perfect. Six o'clock."

Knutsen spun around and shot.

"That GSG9 training has obviously paid off."

They continued until all of the targets were shot. Then they walked back to the river boat. Anton said to Sign, "He is highly proficient. The gun is his, plus I've thrown in three spare magazines and a cleaning kit. Will you stay for lunch?"

Sign shook his head. "That's an extremely kind offer but we must get on the road." He shook Anton's hand. "Until next time, my friend."

"Ah, there might not be a next time. My adventures are catching up on me." He tapped his head. "A bullet I took in the shoulder in Chad is heading up towards my brain. Doctors can't remove it. Still, at least I know what I'm going to die from." He laughed. "When we face the devil we are no longer scared of the devil."

Sign nodded. "What was that music you hated so much when we were in Mauritania? One of the mercs kept playing it on his CD player."

Anton scratched his head. "It came from your country. Four girl singers." He smiled. "The Spice Girls, that was it."

"You're right." Sign placed his hands on Anton's arms. "When you're dead and before they close your coffin and put you in the ground, I'm going to put a record of the Spice Girls on your chest. They'll be with you forever."

Anton laughed. "Outstanding. But if you die first I'll put a jar of mayonnaise on your chest. I know you hate that crap."

"I would expect nothing less. Adios Anton." Sign walked off and handed Knutsen Lenin's lead.

When they were in the car and heading back to Gregor's place, once again Lenin was on Knutsen's lap. Lenin was licking Knutsen's face. Knutsen said, "Why oh why does the wolf like me?"

"Because you're like him."

"I might weigh pretty much the same as him but that's where the similarities end." Knutsen continued to let Lenin lick him, even though it prompted the ex-cop to wince. "I don't bite people, only have two legs, buy my food from the supermarket – though that's changing since I've been out here, am not looking for a mate, and I certainly don't sit on people's laps and lick them."

"Small details." Sign turned on to the main highway south.

"You seem to get on well with Anton."

"He was fine after I stopped him killing me in Kenya. We did a few jobs together after that. But throughout I knew all about his history. He and his men once got into a firefight with a Congolese army. Anton and his men were significantly outnumbered for days and besieged in their camp. It was hopeless. One night Anton crept out at night and entered the enemy's village, grabbed the army commander's six year old son, and dragged him back to his tiny base. The next day more fighting ensued. Finally, Anton wandered out across the grasslands, holding a white flag. The Congolese leader met him half way, expecting Anton to surrender. Anton shook his hand, tossed a hemp sack on to the ground, and told the commander that he and his men were facing a small unit of unspeakable creatures. Anton returned to his base. The Congolese commander opened the sack. His son's severed head was inside. Anton's men then mortared the bejesus out of the commander's army and opened fire with everything they had. They slaughtered the Congolese army."

"How the fuck can you be friends with someone like that?"

"*Friends*? How can Lenin be friends with you? He likes you now but if he's starving he'll kill you without a second thought. I used Anton for my own benefit. In my world we work in the dark side of morality and pray our souls remain intact."

Natalia entered the basement archive section of the SVR headquarters. It was a vast room that stretched the length and width of the building. Files of current and former cases were housed in tall shelves that were fifty yards long and eight feet apart. There were forty shelves in the archive. The room was illuminated by strip lights in the ceiling, some of which needed replacing because they flickered when electricity oscillated over the poor contact between light fittings and energy source. The place resembled a museum's vault of historical documents. One man worked in the archive. His name was Osip Delvig. He'd worked here for eleven years and prior to that he'd conducted various administrative jobs in the SVR and KGB. He was a wizened man, in his early seventies, widower, had arthritis in his nicotine stained hands, and liked the archive job because it meant he could work from nine until five and then lock up his room for the night and go home for a few cigarettes and drinks. Natalia had met him many times and they'd formed a connection because they both liked reading works by the brilliant literary novelist Franz Kafka and the Philip Marlowe crime stories by American author Raymond Chandler.

She smiled with genuine warmth as she saw him behind his desk that contained an antiquated computer, ink pens, paper, a packet of cigarettes that he wasn't permitted to smoke in the room, gold lighter given to him by his wife, and a deck of cards that he used to play solitaire to while away the time in what had to be one of the SVR's most boring and inactive jobs.

Osip looked up and removed his reading glasses. "Natalia my dear. This is an unexpected surprise. What brings you to the realm of secrets?" He liked to think of himself as the gatekeeper to some of Russia's darkest, hidden memories. His eyes twinkled as he asked, "Have you come to see me?"

Natalia sat on the edge of his desk. "Of course. You're the only sane person in this building."

As ever, Osip was wearing his favourite cardigan – brown wool, leather elbow patches, stinking of tobacco. "Are you married yet? Have children?"

Natalia shook her head. "No one will have me."

"More fool them. A young woman such as yourself should have a queue of men wanting to take you dancing. I regret to say that I am too old to join that queue."

Natalia kissed him on the cheek. "But, you can still dream. Did you finish the Marlowe books I leant you?"

"Long ago. If you come back tomorrow I'll return them to you."

Natalia stood. "I'm only in Moscow for a few days and I'm travelling light. Keep them until I return to HQ fulltime."

"As you wish. I've kept them in pristine condition. How can I help you?"

"I'm doing some research into the Sergey Peskov case in 1968. I'd like to have access to the files. I have security clearance."

"I know you do. Your boss called me before you came down here." He placed a finger against the side of his nose. "But I'd have let you have a peak anyway. Old files don't change the world. They simply remind dinosaurs like me that once upon a time we had a ball." He typed on his computer keyboard. "Peskov, Peskov, Peskov. Where are you? There we go." He walked along the shelves and entered one of the corridors between them. Two minutes later he returned and handed her three files. "Use the reading room. It's the usual drill. I'm not cleared to know the content of," he swept his hand toward the library, "my babies. Just return the files when you're done."

The reading room was a small annex, behind clear glass and subdivided into cubicles containing chairs and desks. Natalia sat in one of the cubicles. She had zero interest in the Peskov case. She didn't bother unbinding the elastic clasp that held the file closed. She just sat there, waiting. Two hours' later she walked back to Osip's desk and handed him the files. "These are interesting. They may help us on a current matter. There is an intriguing reference in one of the files. It refers to a Susan Archer. Can you check to see if there's a file on her?"

"Why is she important?"

"Nice try, Osip. Just see if we've got anything on her."

He checked his computer logs. "Yes. She appears on the system. The reference dates to 1968 – same year as your Peskov case. But we don't have her file. Her file's buried in the FSB archive."

Though this was annoying, it did make sense. The FSB was responsible for national state security and was the successor to the KGB. It rarely operated overseas, deferring that responsibility to the SVR and GRU. If there was something suspicious about Susan Archer's disappearance after birth in Moscow, it would have been recorded in Russian police files. But, if there was anything about her disappearance that touched Soviet and Russian national security it would be a matter for the KGB and its successor. The problem was that FSB officers rarely liked working with their counterparts in other Russian agencies. Nevertheless, the fact that Archer's name was in the KGB archive inherited by the FSB made her an interesting subject.

Natalia asked, "How do I get to look at the file?"

Osip pulled out a cigarette from his pack, twirled it, and put it back in. "You don't. You know what those bastards in the Lubyanka are like."

The Lubyanka was a large neo-Baroque building designed by Alexander V. Ivanov in 1897 and situated in Lubyanka Square in Meshchansky District of Moscow. In its history it had been the headquarters of various secret police organisations and a prison for dissidents, many of whom were tortured and executed in the building. The mere name *Lubyanka* sent shivers down the spines of Russians. And nothing within the beautiful yellow brick building had changed. It housed the FSB, state police, and a prison. It was business as usual.

Natalia played it cool. "Not to worry. It was just a thought. Hey – can you recommend a good restaurant I can eat in tonight?"

"There are plenty of good places to eat. You know that."

"I do but here's the thing – I'm going to be on my own and I don't want jerks hitting on me. I'm not in the mood for that stuff. So, I'm thinking somewhere discreet."

Osip pondered the question. "There is nothing more pitiful than a lonely, transient woman, dining alone. Come over to my place at eight." He scribbled his address on a slip of paper. "I will cook beef stroganoff and rice. It won't be fancy. You're safe with me." He laughed. "I haven't been able to get it up for a very long time. Nor do I have the inclination on such matters."

Natalia patted his hand. "It will be good to have dinner with a true friend. I never worry about you. I worry about myself." She smiled. "See you at eight. I don't like my beef rare." She walked out of the room. When she was out of the building and sufficiently far away from the place she texted Sign.

Sign, Knutsen, and Lenin arrived back at Gregor's house. Knutsen's gun was under his belt, his spare bullets and equipment secreted in his jacket. Gregor and Yuri were in the kitchen. On the chopping boards were the two ducks and goose; all plucked and trussed. Gregor was wiping a brush dipped in a soy sauce and marmalade marinade over the ducks' skin. Yuri was jabbing a knife into the goose and inserting a peeled onion, lemon, and a handful of herbs into its cavity.

Gregor's face lit up when he saw Sign and Knutsen. "Tonight we have a banquet, yes? I have unearthed potatoes that have been growing since last autumn, picked four mushrooms the size of saucers, boiled beans and left them to rest in a jar of bacon powder and brine after which they will be drained and flash fried in butter, and I have this beauty." He held up a red cabbage. "Half of it will be used as a coleslaw, the other half as a stir fry with sliced radishes, gherkins, pepper, spices, and slithers of fresh orange. I have also made a red wine gravy. Not bad, eh?" He put down the brush. "We will have a drink now on the lake balcony." He picked up a bottle of vodka and three glasses. "Mr. Tank Engine – after our drink Lenin will need some further training. This will be your responsibility while you're my guest."

They sat on the balcony. As Gregor poured the drinks, Sign said, "My asset needs to get access to the Lubyanka. It won't be easy."

"But she's working on it?" Gregor handed them drinks.

"Yes." Sign stared at the lake. "Whether she'll be successful is another matter."

"Was it your instruction that she must infiltrate the godawful place?" Gregor sat and followed Sign's gaze of the lake.

"No. She's following her own leads."

"Then this is good! She is mustering her own courage without anyone telling her she must become stronger." He chuckled. "That said, it was your clever idea to put her on the battlefield to see if she would fight or flee."

"True, but I've always hated this part. You counsel someone to go over the trenches and when they've summoned the strength to do so your heart's in your mouth because you know you've persuaded the person to die."

"Come on, friend. You told me this is a routine job. She'll be fine. I presume she's a Russian intelligence officer."

Sign looked at him and made the slightest of nods.

"She's doing the right thing. I just wish I could be of service to you these days. But, I'm getting old. Still, it would be nice to have one last crack at this ridiculous regime."

"You are of service. You've been gracious enough to give Thomas and I a safe house. Plus your cooking is nearly as good as mine."

"Nearly as good?!" Gregor swigged his vodka. "Everything you eat here is fresh from the fields and lake. You cook produce from markets."

Sign smiled. A gentle rain was sprinkling over the lake. The sound of the droplets hitting the surface was like that of a drummer making the most delicate and rapid taps on a cymbal. It was a beautiful sound and soothing. He walked to the wooden rail that separated the covered balcony from the lake. "You have a beautiful place here, Gregor. You deserve it after everything you've done for your country and for me."

Gregor wasn't going to allow Sign to get deep and meaningful. In a mischievous tone he replied, "I only worked with you because I didn't know anyone else in MI6. For all I know I could have got a much better partner."

Sign turned to face him, Knutsen, and Lenin, while leaning against the fence. "Do you think we've made a difference, over the years? Have all the things we've done made an iota of change?"

Gregor pondered the question. "We are caretakers who clean our buildings. But we always know they will get dirty again. So, we clean them again, and we keep reliving the cycle of cleanliness versus dirt. And we do so knowing, all the time, that we can't change the structure of the building. Instead we tart it up." Gregor laughed. "That's what we are – a bunch of tarts."

"I hear you." Sign grabbed his drink and sat in his chair. "After dinner and when it's dark I will take your sturdiest rod and go fishing again. I suspect there are zander in the lake. They are strong and their teeth are fierce. The zander will be deep in the lake but they will be feeding. If I net one we will have a sublime plate of food tomorrow evening." He stood. "I'll check on your fishing equipment. I'll need some heavy weights, a wire tippet, and a hooked lure that will imitate something like a frog or a small fish. After that, I'll help Yuri with the rest of the cooking." He walked in to the house.

Gregor felt at peace as he absorbed the vista in front of him.

Knutsen said, "He wants to be alone tonight. Sometimes he gets like this. I don't know if it's him collecting his thoughts about ongoing projects or he wants solitude for solitude's sake."

Gregor drained his drink. In a serious and quiet voice he said, "It's neither. It is his prayer time. He wants to say sorry for his memories. Leave him be when he's like this."

"His memories?"

"He'll be working through the alphabet, or adopting a similar ritual. 'A' is for Anna who he failed to rescue in Budapest. 'B' is Becky who tried to shoot him in Trieste. And on it goes until he reaches 'Z'. Then he restarts the alphabet with new names. And when he's finished it, he restarts it again and again. I'm making this up. I don't know his ritual. And I know less than ten percent of his past. But I know for certain that he needs to process and catalogue his background." Gregor poured himself another drink. "It's not trauma. Not in the strictest sense. Rather it's recognition that one has been thrust into the most unusual situations one can imagine. It catches up with the best of us. And it confuses us. Ben is the most intelligent man I've ever met. No man on Earth is mentally stronger. He fights the confusion and won't give up until he's beaten it at its own game. He'll win... I think."

"That sounds like trauma to me."

Gregor shook his head. "There are matters to attend to that are beyond the human condition and most certainly are beyond trauma. Ben is the warden of a prison of his own demons. He has to be tough with himself and have systems in place. Otherwise, the demons take over the prison." He looked at Knutsen. "Ben and I did many jobs together. One in particular stuck in my mind. We were in Las Vegas, of all places. Ben had constructed the most brilliant plan to entice three Chinese intelligence officers to Nevada. It took him six months to do so and the way he baited them and reeled them in was truly incredible. His objective was to negotiate with them. A thirty year old Chinaman named Sun Xin was imprisoned in a tiny steel cage in Qincheng Prison in China. He was autistic, a brilliant mathematician, had a photographic memory, but had physical limitations due to other disabilities. He was a man-child who should never have been locked up. He was frightened and didn't know what was going on. He worked for the Chinese ministry of defence. In the department's headquarters, video recordings caught him reading blueprints of a new nuclear missile system. The Chinese thought he was memorising the prints with a view to selling the details to the West. In truth he was just curious about the designs. And he wouldn't have had the gumption, knowledge, or desire to contact the West. Nevertheless the Chinese took a different view. They incarcerated him and treated him as a spy. In prison the poor chap was in a dreadful state. Ben didn't want him to defect. He didn't want him to relay what was in his head. He just wanted Sun to be returned to his mum. I was with Ben in a Las Vegas hotel room, with the three Chinese officers. Ben told them what he wanted. The men laughed. Ben pulled out papers and showed them to the men. They were exact copies of the missile blueprints. Ben said that he'd got them six months prior to Sun's arrest. And he added that he got them from a real British spy in the Chinese intelligence service. I suspect he was bluffing and to this day I don't know how he got the blueprints. He said that Sun was innocent and that anything he'd done was of no interest to the West. All that mattered was that he should be released. The Chinese men seemed reasonable. They said they'd return back to their country and tell their bosses that there'd been a mistake. Sun Xin would be released, they promised. They also said they would be investigating the identity of the real spy in their unit. Three months later a letter was received in MI6, addressed to the alias Sign had used when meeting the Chinese men in Nevada.

Sign opened the letter. Inside was a photo. Sun Xin's face was unblemished and easily recognisable. The rest of his body was hacked to pieces. He was dead. It was a message, a warning, to MI6 – the innocents don't matter; don't fuck with us. It devastated Ben. All he wanted to do was the right thing." Gregor looked at the lake. "And that's why Ben wants to fish alone tonight. He wants to hook and reel in a monster. And tomorrow night he wants to eat the thing." Gregor sighed. "Memories, God bless them."

"Why did Ben go out of his way to help Sun?"

"Because of a small, but pertinent matter. Seven months prior to Sun's imprisonment, Ben was on the run in Beijing. Chinese secret police were hunting him. It was a desperate situation. The net was closing in. Ben knocked on a random door in the city. The apartment belonged to Sun's mother. Ben knew nothing about her or her son. He just wanted refuge until the police moved on. He told her that he'd been mugged and was in shock. He asked if he could have a glass of water. I suppose most people would have closed the door in his face. But, she let him in and made him a bowl of chicken soup. It was a Saturday. Sun was at home. Ben speaks passable Mandarin. He spoke to the mother and to Sun. An hour later he told the mother he would repay her for her hospitality – not with cash, that would have been rude. He said that if ever they needed shelter he would ensure they'd get it. And that was all there was to the matter. A brief moment of kindness from Sun's mother meant that Ben had zero qualms about pulling out all the stops to help her son. That's Ben." His tone of voice changed as he said, "Now! You must do your duty and give Lenin some training." He tossed Knutsen a bag. "Take Lenin to the paddock. The horses are not there – they're in their stables for the night. In the bag is a shoulder of beef. I want you to put Lenin on one side of the paddock. Extend your hand in front of your chest. He will sit. Don't speak to him. Back away carefully to the other side of the paddock, keeping your eyes on the wolf at all times. Then pull out the beef and hold it at arm's length. He will charge towards you. Don't flinch. I'm hoping he will accurately grab the meat in his jaws. Don't be surprised if you're bowled over when this happens. The combination of his weight, speed, and aggression will make it feel like you're being hit by a truck."

Knutsen finished his drink and said sarcastically, "Excellent. When you say you're *hoping* he will get the meat and not my arm…"

Gregor laughed. "If he gets your arm it will mean he's not ready to be released into the wild. The loss of your arm will be a small sacrifice in the context of Lenin's rehabilitation. Go to it, Mr. Tank Engine! Dinner will be in one hour."

Natalia visited her aunt and uncle in the outskirts of Moscow. They lived in a high-rise block of flats. Conditions in the building were squalid. The lifts were notoriously temperamental and stank of urine, there was graffiti on the grey stone walls on the ground level, the stairs up the eighteen story building were a place where teenagers hanged out and dealt or took drugs, and the building was surrounded by other tenement blocks of the same height. Despite the champagne swilling and oyster swallowing affluence of other parts of the city, this part of Moscow resembled a throwback to the darkest days of communism. In fact, the buildings had been erected in the 1950s. Ever since, the zone hadn't moved on. It was a place that had been forgotten by the state. Despite the poverty in the area, there was little serious crime. It was a ghetto of sorts. People had to get on with each other to survive. And they were tired. They didn't have the energy to steal from one and other. Plus, there was nothing worth stealing. Wannabe criminals in their midst knew there were far better pickings to be had a few miles south of their location.

And yet, like many of the flats in the area, her aunt and uncle's miniscule one bedroom home was immaculate. Her aunt and uncle were proud people. Her aunt had laid the table; on it were small cakes on her best crockery. She was wearing the dress she wore when attending church. Her uncle had dressed into the only suit he owned and a bow tie before greeting his niece at the door. This evening was a formal occasion, one that the aunt and uncle had been looking forward to for days. Everything had to be right. There'd be no talk of medical problems. No talk of any signs of weakness. All had to be proper and a splendid occasion.

Natalia embraced her uncle and aunt and sat at the table. While her aunt spoke to her, Natalia's uncle disappeared into the kitchen and re-emerged with a smile on his face. In both hands he was cradling a bottle of wine. Natalia had bought it for them last Christmas. It had remained unopened ever since. The uncle said that tonight was as good a time as any to partake of a good drop. He uncorked the wine and sat with the women. As they ate and drank, they spoke about a range of matters – how Natalia was finding London, Russian politics, the nearby dog that kept barking at night, Natalia's love life, British and American politics, and whether Natalia couldn't be persuaded to stay for dinner. Natalia steadfastly refused to capitulate on the latter demand. She had to see Osip. Plus, she knew there'd be no dinner. Or, if there was it would be made from food that would have been allocated for her aunt and uncle's meal tomorrow. She couldn't deprive them of that. She told them that she'd be returning to Moscow fulltime in six months and that she'd visit them regularly. She forced herself to smile as she added that maybe she'd meet a wealthy husband who'd buy them a nice house near the hospital.

After she left she paused on the ground floor of the building and wiped away tears. She walked outside and continued onwards to the nearest underground train station.

Archer met the chief of MI6 in the tea room of Claridge's., in Mayfair. She was exhausted, having barely slept in the night due to her worry about Natalia, and because she'd had to spend all day firefighting a crisis in the Russia Department after one of its assets had been caught by the FSB and allegedly committed suicide in his cell. She sat opposite her boss.

"I've already taken the liberty of ordering," he said. "A pot of earl grey tea, raison scones, and a frangipane tarte."

Archer yawned. "Sounds lovely."

The chief smiled. "You've been burning the candle at both ends. That's why I invited you here. And afterwards I insist that you go home and put your feet up. Don't cook. Order yourself a takeaway pizza. Watch some nonsense on TV. Get an early night."

The food and drink were delivered to the table. When the waiter was gone, Archer said, "It's hard to relax at the moment."

"I know." The chief had to choose his words carefully because their table was too close to other tables and they could easily be overheard by guests. "She will be alright. Trust her. She'll come back safely."

"You can't guarantee that and nor can I." Archer took a bite from one of the scones. She had to force herself to swallow the mouthful, given food was the last thing on her mind these days.

The chief poured tea. "You know the rule. We must accept that we are like parents dropping our children off for their first day at university. We have to let them fly, even though it galls us to do so."

"And at the same time we expect them to get a first class degree."

"Yes. We're fearful for them, and yet we demand significant achievements from them. There is a contradiction within that duality."

"Always the bloody contradictions." Archer blew over film of her tea. "This is make or break for her. Is it make or break for me as well?"

The chief didn't answer her question. "After this posting you should become one of the five directors. You'll be the first woman to achieve that seniority. After that you should consider applying for my job. I'll be long gone by then and there'll be at least one person succeeding me before you reach that point in your career, but it's worth aiming for."

Archer huffed. "That's if I'm good enough, or the right political animal."

"Why shouldn't a woman take my job?"

Archer felt herself getting angry. She wasn't normally like that and she knew it was just down to fatigue. "Come on. It's nothing to do with being a woman. And there's no such thing as the old boys' club. It's down to the logics of the job. A woman can be a minister or prime minister. But those jobs are vastly different to ours. Fifty percent of new entrants to our organisation are women. It's fine for a while. But, some of us gals want to get married and have kids. That's not great if you're constantly being posted overseas. So a few years after joining, we lose a swathe of women. At the mid and senior level it's only spinsters like me who hang on in there. That's okay. We made life choices. But then one has to apply logic. Just because I'm a woman and have stuck the course doesn't make me as good as the ten plus male candidates I'll be up against for a director post and subsequently for the top job. The men have to compete against each other. The best rise to the top. I compete against them as well. But I'm also singled out as the most senior women in the service. That means shit. I become a token. We've always applied the principal that the best person should get the job, regardless of gender, race, creed, or any other bollocks." She rubbed her face. "I'm babbling and that's because I *am* tired."

He stirred his tea while keeping his eyes on her. "In my experience results are all that matters in our company. One can be the most brilliant political animal, super smart, diplomatic as fuck, backstabbing, and sociopathic in ambition, but that means jack. To get to the top one must have at least one major achievement under one's belt. In my case it was that incident with the bomb in Nicosia."

Archer smiled. "We still can't believe what you did when you discovered it adjacent to the embassy – walking down the street with it, depositing on a mountainside, walking back to your station in the British embassy, like it was business as usual. People wanted you dead. You did your stiff upper lip thing. You didn't stop work when you heard the bomb explode. It was as if nothing had happened. The explosion was massive and would have killed hundreds, at least, including you. And there are so many other stories about you."

The chief didn't move. "What did you and your colleagues think when you all heard I was taking the top job?"

Archer didn't have to consider the question. "We thought we had a general who'd proven he can lead from the front."

"Precisely. None of you respected me for how I conducted myself in service boardrooms, Whitehall, Washington, or Paris. That meant nothing to you. What mattered is my track record in the field. There are many that rise to senior management who don't have such a track record. But that's where their career stops." He drank his tea without taking his eyes off Archer. "What you're doing with Natalia is ground breaking. I don't need to tell you how significant her work is and how it will influence geopolitics. Get this one right and you will have walked your bomb onto the mountainside."

"And thus I no longer become the token woman."

"Precisely. It's always results that matter, not what's between your legs."

Archer relaxed and laughed. "Bless you. That's the first time I've laughed in a while." She sliced the frangipane. "I think tonight I will get a pizza, have a nice bath, and watch a movie. Any recommendations on the latter?"

The chief didn't blink. "Genre?"

Archer served him the tarte. "Because I'm not a stereotype, it's not going to be some godawful rom com. I'm thinking war movie. Something where I can see good prevail over evil."

"In which case you could watch a superhero movie."

Archer shook her head. "Too far-fetched. War movie."

"I see. A Bridge Too Far?"

"Seen it."

"We Were Soldiers?"

"Seen it."

"Platoon, Apocalypse Now, Full Metal Jacket, or any other Vietnam War movie?"

"I think I've seen them all."

"In that case you must watch The Siege of Jadotville. It's based on a true story. You will like it." The chief's eyes twinkled. "And for good measure the leading man may well be to your tastes." He touched her hand. "My wife sends her best wishes to you and has asked me to give you an open invitation for a Sunday roast, at your convenience and when work calms down. Have a think about it." He asked a waiter for the bill. "I have to dash. Wretched meeting with an Egyptian billionaire who thinks he can oust the American president."

Natalia arrived at Osip's house. It was a modest bungalow in northeast Moscow, detached, and had a small garden at the rear that had been transformed by Osip, after his wife died, into an allotment that grew root vegetables. Osip guided her in to his home. The air was thick with cigarette smoke and the aroma of beef bourguignon. The home was lovely. Natalia suspected little had changed inside since Osip's wife had passed away. This was not just a man's house. The woman's touch was everywhere – framed photos of Osip's family, artificial flowers, a painting of a female opera singer receiving a bouquet at Carnegie Hall, beautiful drapes, a wooden bowl of fruit on a table, doily clothes on the arm rests of the sofa, scented air humidifiers plugged in to sockets, delicate blue lights strung alongside one wall, and everything was in its place. Osip, Natalia decided, had kept the home as a mausoleum in honour of his dearly departed. The only indication of a man's presence were a baked bean can that was stuffed with fag ends and empty vodka bottles on the floor, awaiting bin recycling day next Tuesday.

Osip poured her a drink. Clearly he'd had a few before she'd arrived. "The beef's in the slow cooker. We can eat whenever we're hungry." He sat in an armchair and lit a cigarette.

Natalia sat in the other armchair. "Thanks for inviting me. I saw my aunt and uncle before coming here. It was tough. They're not well and have no money."

Osip chinked her glass. "We drink to better times."

"We do." She sipped her drink.

By comparison, Osip downed his vodka and poured himself another. "How is London treating you?"

Natalia had to move fast. Osip was already drunk and she doubted he'd be capable of serving up dinner or remembering it was cooking. "London is fine. It's odd being back. I suppose I've grown acclimatised to Britain."

Osip chuckled. "Don't get too comfortable." He blew out a stream of smoke. "When you're back here you'll settle in to the way of things. Once a Russian, always a Russian."

"How are you coping, since Maria died?"

"Routine, booze, cigarettes, routine." Osip smiled, showing off his crooked yellow teeth. "It's all I have left."

Natalia nodded. "I know about loss. My brother killed himself in front of me."

Osip looked serious. "Ah, my precious flower. You should never have seen that." He wiped his mouth. "I was by Maria's side when she passed away from cancer. Her eyes were screwed up due to the pain. All I could think about was how she looked when I first saw her in a ballroom in Vladivostok, forty years ago. She glanced at me but she was keeping options open and checking out other men. It was the most courageous thing I've ever done – going up to her and asking for a dance. We got married a year later. She, or me, couldn't have kids; we never bothered to find out why, because it didn't matter. I wonder if it was my smoking that killed her, or the pollution in Moscow, or the long hours she worked. Who knows? All I know is for some weird reason I'm still here, a cigarette in one hand and a glass in the other. God is cruel."

"Amen to that." Natalia pretended to drink. "You've been doing your current job for a long time."

Osip poured himself another drink. "Over a decade. I'm just filling in the hours, waiting for my pension."

"You must know a lot of secrets."

"I told you – I'm not permitted to read the files in the archives."

"For sure, but you pick up gossip here and there from people who come to your room."

Osip laughed. "Of course. Nothing goes unnoticed."

"And I bet you swap notes with your counterpart in the FSB."

"Yeah. He's like me. Killing time in the archive. Just waiting for the day he can spend all day watching football on the TV."

"You should go out for a beer with him."

Osip shook his head. "We meet up at least once a week. We go to a lovely bar in eastern Moscow. He's like me – widower who drinks too much."

Natalia smiled. "Maybe he'd let us read the Susan Archer file in his archive."

"Now hold on…"

"It won't be a crime. I have clearance. The only problem is it would require an official request from the SVR to the FSB. I don't have time for that. So, shall we have fun and cut some corners?"

"Cut corners?"

Natalia leaned forward. "You and your FSB buddy are in dead end jobs. I'm chained to my desk in London. No one cares about us. But, the three of us might be able to break a big case. I'm not exaggerating when I say that unravelling the mystery of what happened to Sergey Peskov could prevent the West going to war with us. I don't know who Susan Archer is but she's a lead in the Peskov case. Come on – this will be cool and exciting."

Osip thought about what she said. "Technically I wouldn't be breaking rules. I'm permitted to visit the Lubyanka archive to swap notes on their techniques of storage and my techniques. And you have clearance to pursue to Peskov case, wherever it leads. I don't see why not."

"I bet you've got his mobile number. Call him now. He'll be at home."

Osip placed his glass down. "Are you sure this isn't illegal?"

"I wouldn't ask you to do anything illegal. And who knows? If we break the case the three of us might get a nice end of year bonus."

Osip walked to a sideboard, picked up his phone, and staggered back to his chair. He looked at Natalia, nodded, and scrolled through his phone's contacts list. He made the call. Two minutes later he pressed the end button. "He'll let you in to his archive the day after tomorrow. You are not permitted to read anything other than the Susan Archer file. He doesn't want your bosses or his bosses notified about your visit. To do otherwise would bog us down in bureaucracy. I must accompany you. He is satisfied that he's helping mother Russia." He poured himself another drink. "Ten AM on Thursday. Meet me outside the FSB headquarters." He downed his vodka. "I feel tired." He fell asleep.

Natalia placed a blanket over him, turned off the slow cooker, left, and called Sign.

CHAPTER 8

At four PM the following day, Sign walked along the lake adjacent to Gregor's house. He felt restless and hoped that fresh air and exercise would settle his mind. But, he couldn't help thinking about Archer, her sister, and Natalia. He had a theory about all three, and yet it was unfounded and absurd. But, the theory kept bouncing back into the front of his mind. If his theory was correct he would be placed in a dreadful situation. He forced himself to think about other matters. The sun was shining, trout were skimming the lake's surface to feed on flies, in the distance a woodpecker was drilling a hole into a tree, and Knutsen and Lenin were visible in the paddock adjacent to the house. Knutsen's swearing was loud and carried over the water, every time the wolf knocked him over during their training exercises. Sign walked for another three miles, then turned back. He wanted to be in the house before darkness consumed the surroundings, and to help Gregor and Yuri prepare the fifteen pound zander he'd caught in the lake the night before. He smiled as he walked towards the house and the golden glow of its exterior torches and interior lights. The location was idyllic. Gregor deserved nothing less after everything he'd done to help make the world a safer place. Sign was glad his Russian friend was of no use to him now beyond offering a safe refuge. Gregor was always the type of man who would die with his boots on, but he'd do so here, not on a mountainside facing down encroaching hostiles. As he neared the house he could hear music. Gregor was on the lake-facing balcony, strumming his balalaika and singing a song, a glass of vodka by his side. Yuri was carrying logs into the house. Knutsen was on his back in the paddock shouting, "That's the last fucking time, Lenin. Training's over for the day. I thought wolves had good eyesight. Or maybe you're deliberately trying to piss me off." For Sign, everything was perfect in this place this evening – Gregor having a sing song to himself and the lake, the ever energetic Yuri helping his Dad out by doing chores, and Knutsen going twelve rounds with a huge wolf. It was an odd set-up. Sign loved that it was so.

He entered the house. The fire was lit. Yuri was peeling carrots and spuds. A white wine-based sauce, infused with dill, was gently simmering on the stove. Sign asked him, "Do you want me to take over catering duties? You could go outside and have a drink with your father?"

Yuri beamed. "No need. My father and I spend enough time together. Anyway, he likes your company. He doesn't know when he's going to see you again." He lifted the zander by its gills. "I intend to bake this in brown paper, with a few dabs of butter and some cracked pepper. What do you think?"

"Perfect, though a squeeze of lemon wouldn't go amiss. Do you want me to get you a drink?"

Yuri pointed at a glass of wine. "I cook while I drink and I drink while I cook."

Sign smiled and went onto the large balcony. He sat next to Gregor. While Gregor played his balalaika, they sang an old Cossack song together. When finished, Gregor put the instrument down and poured his friend a drink. "War is boredom punctuated by moments of terror. I sense you are in the lull before battle."

Sign took the drink. "You and I rarely had time to be bored. In any case, being here has given me time to think and soak up the free air. It is anything but boring."

Gregor chinked his glass. "To all travellers and adventurers. When we return home we refuel. Then we go out again because we cannot resist doing so. It's in our genetic makeup."

"One hundred percent." The sun was going down. Sign watched swallows dart over the lake. They were grabbing their dinner before the bats came out. "What's retirement like?"

"For me it's like this." He gestured to their surroundings. "But it probably is different for most others. I'm not stupid. I constructed a working farm. So, for me it's not retirement. It's redirection. The thought of me spending all day on a golf course or watching daytime TV fills me with dread. I don't care if I exert myself too much. I get up at four to feed the pigs, horses, and chickens. I tend to the fish in the pond, and periodically clear the pond of weed and mud. In season I nurture and harvest the crops. Off season I work the soil so it's got the perfect balance of nutrients. I help Yuri with logging and house and other repairs. We mend our vehicles. I'm active in the local council to ensure the lake isn't corrupted by human intervention. And I help Yuri to read. He's dyslexic." He filled his pipe and placed a match against its bowl. "The thing is, I might die younger than someone else but I will do so knowing I've put the effort in to life. Say I die at seventy. I guarantee I'll have been awake more than most who die at eighty. What was it Poe said – sleep being slithers of death." He puffed on his pipe. "It's not how long we live. It's whether we've lived at all."

"Quite right." Sign tried to relax.

Gregor looked at him. "The weight of the world on your shoulders? You seem distant."

Sign smiled. "It's the curse of having an overactive imagination. I see things that sometimes aren't there."

"And many times you see things that are there but can't be seen by others until it's too late for them. It's not your fault. Your starting point has always been to consider the near impossible and see if it becomes reality. Most people just take things at face value. You don't." Gregor blew a smoke ring and watched it swirl as it drifted over the balcony fence towards the lake. "You foresee complications?"

"I do. I hope I'm wrong."

"But, if you're right?"

"Lives will be ruined." Sign breathed in deeply. "In our line of work it sometimes pays to be wrong."

Knutsen and Lenin came onto the porch. Lenin was off the lead.

Gregor exclaimed, "He should be on his leash!"

Knutsen sat in a chair. "It's okay. I've cut his dick and balls off. He's not interested in female wolves anymore."

Gregor roared with laughter. "He's been hard work in training? Don't take it personally. It just means he likes playing with you."

Lenin sat next to Knutsen and rested his head on his lap. Knutsen rubbed the wolf's head. "He's alright. But, I just wish he'd stop knocking the hell out of me." He grabbed the vodka bottle and poured himself a drink. From his pocket he withdrew a chunk of meat and let Lenin grab it with his teeth. Knutsen leaned forward and quietly said to the wolf, "Don't worry, fella. I'd never cut off yer crown jewels. But do me a favour pal – don't keep flipping me three sixty when you charge." He placed his face against Lenin's snout. "Mind you, blokes like us aren't designed to be subtle. You crack on. More training tomorrow, if I get a chance." He looked at Sign. "Has she made contact?"

Sign nodded. "Tomorrow morning you and I need to be in central Moscow. Bring your gun."

"Sure thing. Do I need to kill people?"

"I hope not." Sign stretched his legs out. "Gregor and I have been incarcerated in Russia and it's not the only time I've been imprisoned here. It is not a recommended culmination of a trip to the motherland."

Gregor laughed. "The good news is there will be no cops knocking on our door this evening. We must change the topic. Tell me Mr. Tank Engine – why did someone as contrarian as you join the Metropolitan Police?"

Knutsen shrugged. "Why did a rebel join the Russian navy?"

"Touché. I suppose we wanted the adventure but soon realised we didn't like the conformity. In a different life you and I would have been bandits or similar. Still, I don't regret being in the navy and I must have had some skills in order to make it to the rank of captain of a highly classified submarine." He had a look of utter contentment as he added, "History has always shown us that the most brilliant military commanders are those that don't belong in the military." He stood and said in a strident voice, "I want to show you something, Thomas."

"No, I'm fine sitting here, pal. I've got bruises in places you wouldn't want to look at."

Gregor smiled. "You are an excellent guest and an amazing friend to Lenin. The wolf trusts me and Yuri. Now he trusts you. He won't hurt Ben because Ben is kind and firm with him. But, the wolf is wary of Ben because he can sense his intelligence. That doesn't matter. You, me, Yuri, Ben, and Lenin are a pack. Please do come with me. It's only a short walk. After dinner you can have a nice bath to ease your aches and pains."

Knutsen looked at Sign.

Sign nodded.

Knutsen said, "Okay. Lead on."

Gregor and Knutsen, and Lenin walked into the nearby woods. Gregor stopped and pointed at a large hole. "This is a burrow. In there is a family of four badgers. They are sleeping now and won't come out of the burrow until Spring. If you put your head close to the hole you might be able to hear the father snoring. The mother and her two offspring tend to be quieter."

"Gregor – what's the point of this?"

Gregor ignored the question. "Look at Lenin. He knows the badgers are in there, but they don't bother him and he doesn't bother them. They coexist. The adult badgers can bite through your knee cap. Lenin can crush your skull and disembowel you. But none of the animals here will touch us and nor will we hurt them. We are family."

Knutsen leaned towards the hole. His muscles ached as he did so. "I can hear the male."

"He is resting. They gorge themselves on fruit and foliage during the warmer months. It builds fat reserves. Then they hibernate. Ben found the adults when they were kids, one mile from here. They were vulnerable and had got separated from their parents. Ben searched for the parents but couldn't find them. So he bought the children back to my house. We didn't know much about badgers. This was before the days of the Internet where you can Google everything. We gave the baby badgers milk and kept them in the chicken coup. The chickens liked them. I like to think they adopted them, or thought they were odd-shaped chickens. One month later Ben dug this hole – not the entire burrow, the badgers had to complete the task, but he gave them the opportunity. When they were big enough, Ben released them at the entrance of the hole. They made it their home. The next season they mated and made their family. They've stayed with us ever since. Sometimes they bash our front door in the evening. We give them food and they go home."

Knutsen was growing impatient. "What's the point of this story?"

"The point is, Ben did this while recovering from two bullet wounds. He'd fled here after getting into a gunfight in Voronezh. He walked one hundred and fifty miles to my home. Yuri was young then and couldn't help. I pulled the bullets out and cared for him as best as I could. It was touch and go. He was bedridden and feverish for weeks. Then he got out of bed, went for a walk, found the badgers, and carried them back to my house. He had to lay low here for a while before he could leave Russia. So, he kept himself busy – working on the farm, caring for the animals including the badgers, hunting for dinner, and home-schooling Yuri." He looked at Knutsen. "The reason I've shown you the burrow and told you all this is because I want you to know that you made the right decision by not conforming to lesser people's rules. My farm and its surroundings function at the highest level. The humans and animals that live here or visit are their own masters yet respect others with the same mind set as them. You didn't make a wrong decision by joining the police, just as I didn't make a wrong decision by joining the navy. And we both made the right decision to leave our organisations."

"As Ben did – leaving MI6."

"But that's not the end of matters." Gregor pointed at the burrow while stroking Lenin. "It's the beginning. We carve a better future." He turned to face the house and placed his hand on Knutsen's shoulder. "You are blessed. Ben has complete faith in you. That's why I gave you Lenin for the week. If Ben trusts you then I trust you. In turn Lenin views you as a pack leader, just as the hedgehogs believe Ben is their father. We live together and we die together. And we help each other out. No hierarchy. No bullshit. Just life. Come – let's eat."

They walked back to the house, Gregor leading the way while holding a torch. Lenin was ahead of him, his nose to the ground. When inside the house, Gregor laid a vinyl record onto his player, and activated the turntable and stylus. The house was filled with the sounds of the jazz musician Charlie Parker. Gregor stoked the fire and held his hands close to the flames. Lenin laid close to the heat and yawned. Thank Christ for that, thought Knutsen – the wolf's finally tired. Yuri was finishing off preparing dinner. Sign was standing on the porch, staring at the star-filled sky.

Knutsen stood next to him. "I didn't take you for a stargazer."

Sign didn't take his eyes off the sky. "I know nothing about astronomy, and nor do I wish to. But I am intrigued in whether there are patterns of distance and location between the stars. I'm interested in patterns."

"Because that's what you do down here – search for patterns."

"Yes, ones that are imperceptible to the human eye." He looked at Knutsen. "As much as it pains me to say this, I hope we leave Russia the day after tomorrow. It will all depend on whether Natalia gets what we need in the Lubyanka. If she's successful, we'll have business to attend to in England."

The comment made Knutsen sad. He was surprised by his emotional response. When he'd arrived here he'd felt like a fish out of water. But now he felt at home. "We have to follow the paper trail."

"Indeed we do." Sign smiled sympathetically. "Don't worry. We'll come back here another time. Gregor and I keep an eye on each other, just as you and I keep an eye on each other." He looked at the lake. It was glittering with the lights from the stars. In a solemn voice he said, "It's hard to make friends in the secret world. But, on the rare occasions when it happens, it can be heart breaking because friendships should never be born in extreme circumstances."

Natalia went to her hotel room. She withdrew a sandwich from her handbag, sat on her bed, and ate. When she'd finished, she called Osip to remind him about tomorrow's appointment. He sounded relatively lucid, though Natalia knew that would shortly change. She asked him whether he'd arranged cover for his absence from the SVR archive in the morning. He said he'd enrolled a temporary assistant for the morning shift. Natalia suggested he set his alarm for seven AM, giving him enough time to get ready and travel to central Moscow. After she ended the call she laid on the bed, looking at the ceiling. She felt calm, though a muscle in her left cheek was twitching. She told herself that it was as a result of all the previous stress she'd been suffering and was not to do with any current or future stress she was unwittingly hiding from herself. She tried to think about pleasant matters. Where would she live in Britain if she got out of the SVR? City, town, village, or the middle of nowhere? Was she ready for a relationship? Would a relationship happen naturally when she least expected it to occur? What job would she like to do? What hobbies would she take up? Her breathing became fast and she no longer felt calm. All of the dreams seemed so out of reach. She felt trapped. She should never have joined the SVR and she should never have become a traitor. She'd started her adult life in a downward spiral. The only chance she had of clawing her way out of the black pit was to wholly rely on the assistance of Ben and the woman who called herself Katy. But, could they really help? Both of them had agendas. And if she didn't give them what they wanted would they simply walk away and leave her to her fate? One thing she was sure of was that she was out of her depth. In many ways that was a good thing. Ben and Katy seemed so self-assured. And there was no doubting their experience was exponential compared to Natalia's brief stint in Russian intelligence. Maybe it was appropriate that her fate was in their hands. She ran herself a bath and switched on the TV. Her mood was now one of resignation. What would happen would happen. She had no control over her future. Partially, that brought inner peace.

Archer surveyed the interior of her house in Putney. All of the adjustments had been made. The stair lift to the second floor worked; the handrails on the stairs that were previously difficult to grip were now replaced with cylindrical metal rails; the bathroom had been transformed to accommodate a disabled person; there was a wheel chair in the hallway; the two exterior steps to the front door had been replaced with a ramp; a mobility scooter was in the garage; and the spare bedroom had a motorised bed which could be raised to assist getting out of the thing or simply to assist breathing at night. Everything was ready for her mother's arrival. And that could happen tomorrow. Today Elizabeth needed one more batch of medical tests and a nurse from the care home was required by law to visit Archer's London home to do health and safety checks. The nurse also needed to install various medical kit – including an intravenous drip for the administration of medicine and oxygen tank and face mask for use in the night. The nurse would check on her once a week and after six months, providing everything was fine, would reduce her visits to once a month.

Archer poured herself a glass of wine, sat on the sofa, and flicked through a recipe book. She wanted to cook Elizabeth something special and comforting for her first night here. Shepherd's pie, she decided, was the right choice. She placed a piece of paper on the page containing the recipe and shut the book.

Not for the first time, she wondered how she would cope with living with her mother. Consistently, she'd concluded it would work. Elizabeth was a free spirit and hated being needy. She'd spend her days studying, perambulating southwest London, getting to know the neighbours, shopping, and writing letters to The Times about a range of matters including the reasons that had led Russia to become a totalitarian state, politics in the Middle East, why Brexit might lead to the break-up of the United Kingdom, and the socioeconomic factors that had allowed Americans to vote for a sociopathic moron of a president. And she could feed herself. Elizabeth was a good cook. Alongside her standard waist-height cooker, Archer had installed a knee-height oven and a knee height gas hob, fridge-freezer, and work surface with utensils. Elizabeth would be self-sufficient when it came to providing herself sustenance. Once again, Archer decided everything would be fine. In any case, she worked long hours and sometimes had to travel for weeks at a time. She and her mother would be able to live separate lives.

She sipped her wine and thought about her twin sister. Was Susan alive? Dead? And even if she was alive would she have anything in common with Jayne? Maybe it would be better if she was dead. It would close the chapter and end the uncertainty. No, that wasn't right. Jayne Archer wanted her sister to be alive, no matter what the outcome. She'd been ruthless in her career ambition, to the detriment of fleeting relationships with boyfriends, but one thing she was not was callous. If Susan was alive, Archer would do anything to be reunited with her.

CHAPTER 9

The next morning Sign and Knutsen were in a café, drinking coffee. They were two minutes' walk from the Lubyanka. At a sprint, Knutsen estimated he could reach the building in twenty seconds. His handgun was concealed under his fleece jacket. The weapon was needed as a last resort. And even if things went badly wrong for Natalia, the probability of the men being able to help her were slim. Certainly, they couldn't enter the FSB headquarters to extract her. And if an attempt was made to snatch her as she left the building, Sign would have to grab her and run while Knutsen pointed his pistol at anyone who was coming for her. Then they'd have to escape the city and head on foot across country to the exfiltration point. The chances of success would be thousands to one against. It was in their interests that Natalia held her nerve and walked out of the building without having aroused a drop of suspicion.

For the most part, Sign and Knutsen were quiet, though now and again Sign would make a comment in Russian – just in case they were being observed. Knutsen didn't understand what he was saying, but that didn't matter. In Sign's pocket was his mobile phone, set to silent and vibrate. It was his hotline to Natalia.

It was ten AM. In thirty minutes they'd leave the café and watch the main entrance to the Lubyanka, hidden from view from everyone, including Natalia when she left the building. There was nothing they could do now apart from wait.

Natalia and Osip entered the Lubyanka. The interior of the imposing, fortress-like rectangular building, had barely changed since the darkest days of its history. There were some modern touches to the décor but they did nothing to diminish the sense that the walls were and always would be drenched in blood. Natalia thought of the building as a man who hadn't washed for a century and tried to cover up his stench with a bottle of deodorant. So many people had been imprisoned, tortured, and executed in the building. Whether their ghosts remained here or not was down to the eye of the beholder. But, there was no doubting there was a smell that felt wrong. The dead people's blood had been painted over. But the blood remained. It was ingrained in the stone fabric of the Lubyanka.

After they cleared security checks, Osip led her through corridors containing rooms that had once held captive the famous spy Sidney Reilly, the Swedish diplomat Raoul Gustaf Wallenberg who'd saved thousands of Jews in the holocaust, and the Polish-American Jesuit priest Walter Ciszek. There were so many other people who'd been tortured and executed here. A lot of them were innocent of their alleged crimes. All of them deserved a more civilised tenure in the building.

Osip and Natalia went into the archive section of the FSB. It was located in the building's basement and had a similar layout to the SVR's archives – row upon row of files, almost no IT equipment, ceiling fans that helped prevent dust settling on the room's precious papers, spot lights, and a sign at the entrance saying that it was strictly prohibited to remove files without written authorisation to do so. Some of the files in the huge room dated back to the Bolshevik Revolution in 1917. The room was a treasure trove of oppression, pain, insurrection, and misery.

Osip shook hands with the only person in the room. "Alexander. Good to see you, my friend."

The head of the archive looked at Natalia. "The SVR is recruiting youngsters these days."

Osip placed a hand on Natalia's arm. "I can vouch for her. She's not like most of the others in the SVR. She doesn't have a political bone in her body."

"Then she's welcome." Alexander asked Osip, "Are we still on for a few drinks and a game of cards on Friday?"

"Absolutely. But, don't cheat this time." Osip smiled.

Alexander said to Natalia, "You are investigating the Sergey Peskov case, I'm told. And you have a lead relating to a Susan Archer. Why are you interested in her?"

Natalia feigned nonchalance and shrugged. "I've been instructed to look in to Peskov. I don't know why. It's beyond my paygrade. But, I'm pursuing all names referenced in the Peskov SVR file."

"You must have pissed someone off to be tasked with such an old case." Alexander laughed. "Okay. Come with me." He led her to a desk, behind which was a chair. He prodded the file on the desk. "Susan Archer. You're cleared to read it, but you are not permitted to take notes or make copies."

"I understand." Natalia sat on the chair.

"I'll leave you to it. Osip and I have some boring business matters to discuss." He walked away.

Natalia looked at the file. On its cover were uppercase words in red. The words were in Cyrillic. The English translation was *CODENAME SWITCHBLADE*.

She opened the file.

At 1207 hrs Natalia left the FSB headquarters. She was alone and walking fast. Sign and Knutsen followed her – Sign staying close to the woman, Knutsen remaining fifty yards behind his colleague in case FSB people were tailing Natalia and he had to take action. The prearranged drill was for Natalia to call Sign ten minutes after she left the building to let him know she was safe, or to text message him if there was a problem. But thus far she'd made zero contact.

After twenty minutes, Sign knew something was wrong. He called Knutsen. "Join me. My hunch is she's not aroused suspicion. But something's amiss. We'll follow her together."

They stayed close to Natalia. She made no effort to take any form of public transport. Sign assumed she wanted to walk in order to have time to think.

She arrived at her small hotel.

Knutsen spun around. There were too many pedestrians in the area to spot a skilled surveillance team in their midst. He followed Sign into the hotel lobby.

Sign muttered to him, "Move with me now. Put a smile on your face."

Sign and Knutsen walked briskly into the hotel lobby.

Sign came alongside Natalia, a grin on his face, put his arm around her waist, and said in Russian, "My favourite niece. Your aunt can't wait to see you for dinner this evening. Come on – let's help you with your overnight bags and get on the road."

Natalia was too highly trained to show any indications of surprise or resistance. But, inwardly she was flapping.

She forced a smile on her face as they walked past the bored-looking receptionist and took the lift to her room.

When inside, Sign said to her, "Sit down wherever you feel comfortable."

She sat on the bed.

Knutsen stood by the door, his gun in his hand.

Sign sat opposite her on the only chair in the room. "Were you compromised?"

Natalia shook her head, her eyes wide, no attempts now to hide her fear.

"Did the job in the Lubyanka prompt a relapse of anxiety in you?"

Natalia was breathing fast. "Not... not for the reasons you might think."

"It was something you read in the Archer file. Isn't that correct?"

Natalia was trapped in the room. There were bars on the window and there was no possibility of getting past Knutsen, even though he was facing the door. It was clear he was here to stop hostiles entering the room, rather than prevent her from leaving. She asked, "Are you both Russians? SVR? FSB? GRU? Special Forces?"

"If we were, why would we tell you?" Sign was motionless. "The bigger question is why would you ask such a thing?"

"Because I want to know if you're part of this problem!" She placed her head in her hands and rocked back and forth. "I'm dead. Fucking dead!"

Sign sat next to her and held her hand. Quietly he asked, "Were there photos in the file?"

Natalia sucked air through her teeth. It produced a hissing sound. "Three photos. One was of two babies. The other two were of women."

"And the photos have unsettled you."

Natalia pulled her hand out of Sign's hand. "Not just the photos. Everything in the wretched file!"

Sign nodded. "Tom and I are not Russians. We are British. And right now we're working for the United Kingdom's government. But, in doing so we're not representing our state's interests. We're representing you. And first and foremost that means we prioritise your protection. Natalia – this is not a game."

She looked hostile. "People who play games often spout that shit!"

Sign nodded. "You must use your judgement. Rely on your instincts."

Natalia glanced at him, uncertainty in her expression. "If you were Russian, I'd already be dead."

"Yes."

"And it doesn't serve the motherland's interest for me to betray it, unless this is some convoluted chess game."

"Russian spies and politicians are not that adept."

She bowed her head and stopped rocking. Her voice was almost a whisper when she said, "I can't fly out of Russia. Wheels are in motion. I will be arrested at the airport. Then I'll be taken somewhere and made to vanish."

"What wheels?"

Her expression was imploring when she asked, "Do you not know?"

"I have a theory. It is based on facts and supposition. I agree with you – I think you will be dead unless Tom and I do something to prevent that from happening. Will you trust me?"

Natalia looked uncertain.

"Trust is all you have now."

Natalia was utterly exhausted. "You told me I was young enough to be your daughter."

Sign nodded. "My wife and I never had children. She died before that was possible, though she was pregnant when she was murdered. We knew she was carrying our unborn daughter. I often wonder what it would be like to sit and talk to my daughter when she was a young adult. In fact, my life is a series of segments. I imagine changing her nappy and bottle feeding her when she was a baby; laughing with joy when I see her walk for the first time; taking her to a beach in Sussex and a bowling alley in Surrey; seeing her dance in beautiful white dress in my garden; helping her when she hit puberty; talking to her about her studies at GCSE and A levels; being the proudest father when I see her get her graduation certificate from a good university; meeting a boyfriend she's serious about; laughing with her when we watch a silly comedy while eating jalapeno and pepperoni pizzas; and ultimately looking at her and thinking she is similar to me but is entirely her own person." He looked away. "My imagination – it's a curse. I've carved an entire life that never had the chance to exist." He huffed. "It makes me stupid and foolish."

"No it doesn't."

Sign smiled, though the grin was bittersweet. He made a call on his mobile and when the call ended he stood. "Tom – we're taking Natalia to the safe place. I'll pay her hotel bill. You stay here until I'm back. Yuri will collect us. Gun down anyone who comes through the door before I'm back." Before he left the room he held out his hand. "Natalia – I need your personal mobile phone."

She handed it to him.

Sign withdrew the SIM card, snapped it into pieces, took out the battery, and placed the parts and debris into a bag. The bag would be carefully disposed of once they were out of the hotel.

Two hours' later they arrived at Gregor's house. Yuri carried Natalia's luggage to Sign's room, stripped the bed, put fresh linen on, showed her around the property, and told her that he'd be making a round of sandwiches and a pot of coffee for those in the house who were hungry and thirsty. He tossed a blanket on the sofa. That's where Sign wanted to sleep tonight. Gregor was out in the grounds, chopping wood.

Sign walked up to him. "We have a guest. A woman."

"I know." Gregor slammed his axe into the thick tree trunk that served as his chopping board. "Does that mean that while she's here I mustn't swear or break wind?"

Sign looked at the house. "She's in shock. I need to speak to her at length. Change nothing in your behaviour and routine. She must see that your home is filled with normal people who do and say normal things. It will make her feel secure."

"What shit has she gotten herself into?"

"Her potential imprisonment or assassination."

"That sucks. Tell me about her."

Sign gave him her biography.

Gregor arched his back and winced. "Okay. Let me go and say hello." He walked in to the house. Natalia was standing by the fire, shivering. Gregor beamed and strode toward her, his arm outstretched. His voice boomed as he said, "You are most welcome to my humble home. As well as us four ugly men, on site we have pigs, chickens, horses, trout in the lake and pond, a pair of ducks, a family of badgers, and a wolf. The wolf sleeps in here." He patted Lenin. "When he sees you eat with us he will accept you. Be careful though – he's not used to women being around." He laughed. "And you are a Russian spy. Your presence adds to my mad menagerie of misfits and troublemakers."

Natalia shook his hand. "Ben told me about you. You are a Hero of the Russian Federation."

"Nonsense! I'm an old man who eats and drinks too much."

Yuri put a platter of sandwiches and a pot of coffee on the dining table

"Let's get some food down our necks!" Gregor pulled out a chair for Natalia. She sat at the table, alongside the four men.

Gregor spoke while he munched on his sandwich. "I knew a Natalia once. She had beautiful hair, much like yours. I met her at the military academy. She did my washing for me. She wasn't allowed to. The men and women were segregated in different blocks. Some other bitch made a complaint that I'd turned up in the women's quarters with a bag full of my dirty linen. I was hauled in front of the academy's navy commandant. He bollocked me but struggled to keep a smile off his face. He said I was top of my class for a reason – I was unconventional and clever. He told me to fuck off back to my cadet class. There was no written disciplinary action. Secretly I think he admired what I'd done. You see – getting people to help you is a significant part of a captain's job. When we finished our training, I asked Natalia to be my date for the graduation dinner. It was a formal affair. I met her outside of the women's block. She was in a gorgeous black dress. When she walked towards me, the slit in her dress parted to reveal a glimpse of her suspenders." He winked at Natalia. "I thought I was in for a good night. But, she wasn't that kind of girl. I guess she had feelings for me, as I did for her. Trouble is, we then got posted to different parts of Russia. I never saw her again. And these were the days before mobile phones. I often wonder about her." He rubbed crumbs off his fingers. "If only I could turn the clock back and stopped myself from getting into a bloody submarine." He slapped Sign on the back. "What was it Sinatra sang - Regrets, I've had a few. But then again, too few to mention. I did what I had to do. And saw it through without exemption."

Sign smiled. "I've lived a life that's full. I've travelled each and every highway. And more, much more than this, I did it my way."

Gregor held up his hand. "Bang on, brother."

Sign slapped his hand and addressed Natalia. "Gregor and I go way back. We know all about darkness and death. After lunch Gregor and I will take you for a boat ride on the lake."

Uncertainty hit Natalia. "On the lake?"

"There's nothing to fear. It is a place that's brimming with life. Anyway, if one of us has an accident," he gestured to Gregor, "we have a captain who somehow managed to swim in freezing conditions for forty eight hours before making a fifty yard underwater vertical ascent out of his submarine. No Olympian athlete could have done that. We're in the very best hands."

Gregor leaned forward and in a mock solemn tone said to her, "I have gills." He giggled. In an authoritative tone reminiscent of when he was a highly respected naval commander, he said, "Gentlemen, if you please! We now have a lady on deck. Rules must apply. She uses the bathroom before any of us. Understood? If she's in there and you need a piss, you piss outside. If you need a shit, do it on the dung heap – it will be good for the manure. If she doesn't mind us swearing, then we can swear. If she objects to our swearing, we stop." He looked at Natalia and spoke directly to her. "In relation to all other matters, it's business as usual on my submarine. Any questions?"

Natalia shook her head.

"Excellent. Then we sail onwards as per our drills." Gregor rubbed his stomach. "We must think about catching dinner for this evening. But first we will give this lovely lady an opportunity to have some tranquillity. Ben, Natalia, let us depart."

Yuri started clearing up the plates.

When Gregor, Ben, and Natalia were outside, Gregor said, "Just one second." He went back into the house. "Yuri – the dishes will wait until we're back." He looked at Knutsen. "I want both of you to arm yourselves and hide two hundred yards up the lane. Stay there until we get back. If Russians come for us, use maximum force. And work as a team. Watch your angles. Excel in your weapon tactics. If there are dead bodies, leave them where they fall. Take Lenin with you. Like you he must know he's in combat mode. Command him that way. He will understand. To it gentlemen! Do not let me down." His smile was back on his face as he exited the house.

Gregor, Natalia, and Ben walked to the rowing boat, moored on the lakeside. When the three of them were in the vessel, Gregor rowed them out to the centre of the lake. He handed Natalia a rug to keep warm.

Sign said to Natalia, "Tell me everything."

Natalia momentarily glanced at Gregor.

Sign said, "I've trusted Gregor many times with my life, just as he's trusted me with his life. The tranquillity Gregor spoke of is here. It is the epicentre of loyalty and openness."

Natalia bowed her head.

"Head up, Natalia! Now is not the time to be coy."

Natalia looked at Sign. She breathed in deeply. "The woman who calls herself Katy – my MI6 handler... I've always known that Katy wasn't her real name. I now know her real name's Jayne Archer."

Sign was silent while keeping his gaze on her.

"The photos in the file were of Jayne and Susan when they were babies and their current age. Aside from different hair styles, they look nearly identical. The photo of Susan was a professional studio shot. The one of Jayne was a long distance covert shot. I recognise the backdrop – Westminster Bridge."

Sign said, "You are correct. The woman who calls herself Katy is Jayne Archer. Her sister is Susan."

Natalia sighed. "That's just the beginning. It's not the end." She paused.

"Come on Natalia. You can do this."

Natalia summoned her strength. "If I trust you and I'm wrong to do so, you might as well ask Gregor to use a paddle to club me to death out here."

"There'll be no clubbing today, thank you. Proceed."

She responded, "But, it will happen to me, somewhere."

"No it won't. Gregor, Tom, Yuri, and I are soldiers. You are one of us now." He smiled. "And we have a huge wolf to help us."

For the first time since she'd arrived at the farmstead, Natalia smiled. "Soldiers? My brother was a soldier. We're not soldiers. We're more than that, for better or worse."

"But we know how to be the very best combatants."

"You may do. I'm too young to know that stuff." She looked him directly in the eyes. "Jayne Archer is in fact Anna Vichneva. Susan is her twin sister Dina Vichneva. The twins' parents were a brilliant KGB male officer and female physicist. They were murdered by the KGB immediately after the births, because the KGB had a very specific long game strategy to use the twins. Jayne's English parents - Elizabeth and Michael - were not her real parents. They are English KGB/SVR moles. Elizabeth was eight months pregnant with her own child when the twins were born. The KGB instructed Elizabeth to rush to Moscow. They cut the baby out and killed it, with Elizabeth's consent. Jayne was given to Elizabeth and Michael and they were told to pretend they were her real parents. The KGB faked the birth certificate and medical details about the birth. The KGB told Elizabeth and Michael to groom Jayne to reach high office in the UK public sector - preferably MI6, but alternatively some other high security cleared post. The KGB kept Susan. The KGB's hope was that Jayne would be malleable to Elizabeth and Michael's grooming on the basis that Jayne would want to be in a position where she could track Susan in later years. Plus, Jayne would be brainwashed into hating Russia and joining MI6 by her 'parents' throughout her childhood. There was no guarantee this would work, but the KGB was hopeful it would pay off. Meanwhile, Susan/Dina was kept by her fake KGB parents in Russia. Susan's unwitting role was to act as KGB leverage at some point in the future, when the KGB/SVR needed Jayne to betray a UK secret. Susan was and still is innocent throughout. She didn't know her 'parents' were KGB. Nor did she know she had a sister. She grew up and lived an ordinary life in Russia. She got married, but like Jayne she couldn't conceive children. She got divorced and lived alone. Jayne's fake parents Elizabeth and Michael were not tasked to obtain secrets from Jayne. Instead their role was to position Jayne into a powerful government job. Susan's fake parents were tasked to simply raise Susan safely and keep her alive."

Gregor was silent.

Sign asked, "Is Susan still alive?"

"Yes."

"Why are you at risk? I think I know the answer but I want to hear details from you."

Natalia looked around the lake. "It is beautiful here." She returned her attention to Sign. "At the back of the file is a trigger."

"A trigger?"

"A Russian spy file is either of mere historical interest or it's a weapon. The Archer file is a weapon. The trigger was a piece of paper, dated four days' ago. It's very specific. Tomorrow Jayne Archer will be sent a photo of her sister. Alongside the photo will be an instruction. The instruction is: tell us who in the SVR is betraying the names of our officers in Europe and the United States. That person's me. The instruction also says that if she doesn't comply her sister will suffer an agonising death. The SVR knows Jayne is now head of the MI6 Russia Department. They've therefore made their killer blow. Under SVR instruction, her fake mother recently told Jayne about the existence of her twin sister. Jayne will have to decide whether she sacrifices her sister's life or my life. I know she will betray me."

Sign nodded. "She will."

"And there's nothing you can do about it. We've been outplayed by an ingenious Russian long game. It was all about having leverage at some point. That point is now. Jayne's stars and my stars have now aligned. Jayne's promotion and my treachery made the trigger possible." She shook her head. "You suspected all of this might happen."

"It was one of seven possibilities. But, I confess this was the one that kept haunting me."

"What can be done? Can we warn Jayne? Stop her from giving the Russians my name?"

"It's too late. Your name is in Jayne's head. Even if she's arrested in Britain, she'll find a way to speak to the Russians. Plus, she can't be arrested yet because she hasn't done anything. As we speak, Jayne has no idea about her background. All we can do is protect you." Sign nodded at Gregor.

Gregor started rowing to shore.

Sign said to Natalia, "This is what will happen – you and I will have zero contact with Jayne Archer; tomorrow we'll get you out of Russia."

"Tomorrow?!"

"Tomorrow evening. I have to make preparations. Trusted allies of mine will be involved. Even tomorrow will be a tight turnaround but I'm confident it can be achieved. When we reach Britain you will be placed into temporary protective custody. Your identity will be changed. You will then be given a place to live. You will lead an independent life."

"Da. A new life." A tear rolled down her cheek. To herself and quietly she repeated, "A new life."

When they reached land they walked to the house. Gregor whistled three times. Knutsen, Yuri, and Lenin got out of their hiding places and went to the farm. Yuri had a rifle resting on his shoulder. Knutsen was holding his pistol in both hands.

When everyone was inside, Gregor said to Natalia, "Get some rest. You will need it. The rest of us have some jobs to do."

Natalia was grateful. She was mentally and physically exhausted. "I will be safe?"

"Yes."

"I don't mind helping out."

"I know. But, you've done your shift today. Like all good sailors, you work, rest, eat, sleep, and work. Now is the rest part of the day. I've set the boiler's thermostat to permanent. There will be plenty of hot water if you want a bath. But, I must warn you – all we have in the bathroom is an anti-dandruff shampoo and a bar of soap. We weren't expecting female company."

Natalia yawned. "I'm so tired."

"Stress will do that to you." Gregor put his arm on her shoulder and guided her to the stairs. "Make sure you shut your bedroom door. Lenin is a bastard. Given half a chance he'll sleep on our beds. When that happens the sheets smell like something out of the bowels of Hell."

When she was gone, Gregor asked Sign, "Is her exfiltration out of Russia going to be cold?"

"Yes."

Gregor frowned. "She's not equipped for that. All she has is city work clothes."

"You and I had less when we escaped that gang in Kurdistan. And we did so during winter."

"*Less*? We were naked." Gregor was deep in thought. "We must do what we can to clothe her. To a man, a cold sailor who's on watch will tell you that there is no gift on Earth more precious than being given a warm jumper. Yuri – I have a job for you."

Yuri stood before his father. "It's going to be a shit job, isn't it?"

"It's a job, so wind your neck in. I need you to buy Natalia some clothes. Windproof jacket, thermal vest, jumper, lined waterproof trousers, pair of hiking boots, thick socks, gloves, and a woollen hat. The outdoor shop in Yaroslavl will sell what we need."

"What's her shoe size?"

Gregor looked at Sign.

Sign said, "I've no idea. Do you have a measuring instrument?"

Gregor rummaged in one of the kitchen drawers and handed Sign a tape measure.

Sign gave it to Yuri. "The ground outside is wet. Look at our footprints from our route to the lake. Discount the big prints. Measure the length of Natalia's prints."

Ten minutes' later Yuri was back in the house. "Twenty two centimetres."

Gregor asked, "What's that in shoe size?"

No one knew.

Gregor threw up his arms. "You'll just have to tell the shop assistant that her current shoes are twenty two centimetres long, that they are heeled work shoes, and you require boots that are a centimetre longer to accommodate thick socks. What's her clothing size?"

Yuri frowned. "Size?"

"You know – three, four, five, twelve, sixteen, all that stuff."

"No man knows what any of that means."

Gregor leaned against the workbench. "True."

"Shouldn't we just go upstairs and ask her what her measurements are?"

"She's probably sleeping. And even if she's not, the point of us solving this riddle is to supply her with a highly considerate and surprising gesture." Gregor grabbed his phone and searched women's clothes sizes on the Internet. When the results came up he exclaimed, "For the love of God, this is more complicated than trying to navigate a submarine through a minefield." He put the phone down. "It appears women come in all shapes and sizes, and none of the sizes are an exact science. Right – how tall is she?"

Yuri put his hand to his throat. "About up to here."

"That'll do. Tell that to the shop assistant. What about," Gregor waved his hands around his waist and chest, "women's body things? Do we need to factor that in?"

Sign was trying not to laugh. "No we don't. Buy her elasticated trousers, stretch thermals, and a baggy jumper. She won't look like she's on the front cover of Hiking Weekly, or whatever, but at least she'll be warm. Yuri – also, get herself something nice in Yaroslavl. If you're unsure, speak to a woman in one of the shops. Ignore them if they suggest perfume or any bathroom toiletries. Listen to them if they suggest anything more neutral but personal. If pushed, tell them that you're going out on a first date and just want to give your girlfriend something nice. Got it?"

Yuri nodded. "Got it." He took cash out of the safe and left.

Gregor said to Knutsen, "You and Lenin need to stay here and keep guard over her."

Knutsen angled his head, "Aye aye captain."

Gregor smiled. "The very best of my men were insolent." He patted Knutsen on the shoulder. "It was like herding cats. But you wouldn't want anyone else by your side if the shit hit the fan. Natalia's in the good hands."

The comment took the wind out of Knutsen's sails. Without a drop of sarcasm, he replied, "I'll protect her."

Gregor held his gaze for a moment, his eyes twinkling. He said, "Excellent. To your post." He turned to Sign. "Pick a rifle from the rack. We must now kill our dinner."

Sign and Gregor moved through the wood, their rifle butts firm in their armpits.

Sign whispered, "What are we hunting for? Anything that moves?"

Gregor replied, "I'll show you." He moved on.

Sign followed him.

Close to the lake's shore, Gregor crouched while still hidden amid the trees. He raised his fist, thereby silently indicating to Sign to also stop. He was motionless, on one knee, watching. He was barely audible when he said, "They carry a disease that humans are immune to but pigs can die from. We're hunting boar. We only need one. I have to cull them once a year, to keep numbers manageable and sustainable. They forage at this time of the day and at night. If we see one, I'll make a clean head shot. If there are other boars in the vicinity, fire shots over their head to scare them off. They're nasty fellows when they're angry."

"Why are we so close to the lake? Shouldn't we be deeper in the forest?"

Gregor smiled. "The boars like paddling in the shallow water. It's their playtime." His smile vanished. "This isn't sport. For every boar I cull I spend days constructing shelters and putting down food so they can reproduce and survive the winter. Like everything here, we coexist and help each other."

Three hours' later, Natalia came downstairs. She'd had a shallow sleep and a bath. Yuri was back. His face lit up when he saw her. He said, "I've bought you some things." He patted shopping bags that were on the table. "Things that will keep you warm. Apparently your route out of Russia might be a cold one. I've also bought you this." He handed her a book of poetry by Alexander Pushkin. "I struggle to read. Maybe you could read me a poem after dinner. Try on the clothes. I hope they fit."

Natalia looked at the bags. "You bought me these?"

"Yes. It was a difficult job." Yuri was now standing in the kitchen, chopping vegetables.

Natalia went to her room and changed into her new outdoors clothes and boots. Everything fitted perfectly. She returned to the kitchen, wearing her new attire. "Thank you, Yuri."

Yuri grinned. "You look perfect. Hey – have you got a boyfriend?"

Natalia wagged her finger. "Steady on tiger. Boyfriends are the last thing on my mind right now." She smiled. "But I appreciate you asking. Where is everyone else?"

"Just outside the house." Yuri wiped his brow as he dashed between pans of boiling water. "Here. Take this to my Dad." He handed her a basket containing a paint brush, large jar of homemade garlic marmalade, fresh herbs, bag of crushed ice, four tumblers, and a bottle of vodka.

Natalia wandered outside. The sun was going down, though the stunning surroundings were still visible. The torches on the lake-facing balcony had been lit. Others were dotted around the grounds. Sign and Gregor were standing next to a pit of coals. Above the pit was a boar that was skewered on a rotisserie. Gregor was slowing turning the swine. Knutsen was in the paddock, doing training with Lenin. He was throwing the boar's entrails high into the sky while screaming a variety of obscenities, including, "Why the fuck do I have to do this revolting job?!" Lenin was leaping, catching the guts and devouring them. The air was cold, but the heat from the torches and the fire negated any discomfort. Natalia thought she was in a dream. This place was magical. She handed the basket to Gregor.

"Did you sleep, my dear?" He asked.

"A bit."

"Then you are ready to fight another day." He opened the jar, poured the sauce over the rotating boar, used the brush to wipe the marinade around the skinned carcass, threw the herbs onto the coals to infuse the smoke, cracked open the vodka, placed handfuls of ice into the tumblers, and poured everyone a drink. He shouted, "Mr. Tank Engine! Drink time!"

Knutsen was now running around the paddock with the boar hide on his head and back. Lenin was chasing him. The wolf bowled him over, ripped off the hide, then looked confused. "It's okay, motherfucker," said Knutsen gently as he ruffled his head. "Apparently this is something to do with learning about how to spot a wolf in sheep's clothing. Except you're the wolf and all I had was a bloody enormous pig skin to teach you the lesson." He staggered to his feet. "One thing's for sure – if you can take me down you can take down a buffalo. Come on. Let's join the others." His body was throbbing as he limped to the roasting boar.

Sign asked, "Any broken bones?"

Knutsen grabbed his drink from Gregor. "Not fucking yet." He looked at Natalia. "Excuse my language."

"I don't mind." Natalia asked Sign, "Where are you taking me tomorrow?"

Sign assisted Gregor with the basting of their meal. "St. Petersburg. As you know, it's at least an eight hour drive. Yuri will take us there. He will be working through most of the night to ensure his vehicle can make the trip. The slightest vehicle impediment must be eradicated. We will be carrying spare canisters of fuel, food, bottles of water, and empty bottles to urinate in. We will not be stopping anywhere on route."

Gregor stepped away from his chef duties and addressed Natalia. "You're new clothes look good. Ben has brought me in to his confidence and told me how he's going to get you out of Russia. From St. Petersburg, you, Ben, and Thomas will sail on a ship that's bound for Liverpool. Ben knows the skipper. The journey will take seven days. Pack accordingly. Leave everything else here. We will burn what you don't need." He raised his glass and shouted, "Onwards, my friends!"

"Onwards," they all replied in unison before sipping their drinks.

Sign asked Knutsen to help Gregor with the boar. To Natalia he said, "Let's take our drinks onto the balcony." When the two of them sere sat there, looking at the lake, the roasting swine, and the torches, he said, "You are no longer a member of the SVR. You are no longer a spy for MI6. Soon your name will no longer be Natalia Asina. And once you're safely in Britain you will no longer be Russian. You'll be Ukrainian, though will have a British passport. In consultation with you, I will arrange all matters in relation to your living arrangements and your job."

The enormity of the changes hit Natalia. "Maybe I could be a teacher?"

"No. You would be listed on the school's staff list. Even though your name will be different, you must be invisible. You have seven days on our boat trip to think about suitable jobs. Don't reach for the stars. Take something that pays the bills and leaves enough left over to treat yourself now and again. Don't go on holiday outside of Britain. Under no circumstances use social media. Don't do Internet shopping, use courier services, and browse Internet websites containing political news. Ideally, don't use the Internet at all. Be constantly suspicious of people until you really get to know them. You will be financially secure. I will help you get a job. And you will receive a pension when you're sixty. It will come out of a government slush fund that has no links to the government. You are free to date and marry, but once again be very cautious as to whether to trust a lover. You will be able to contact me and Tom while we're still alive. It might be prudent to run a potential lover's name by us before you engage in a relationship. We'll do background checks and let you know if he's safe. Never, ever, speak to anyone about Russia. You've never been here and know nothing about the country beyond what you've seen on the news. You came to Britain after your parents died. You have no other family." He gave her more details about her new identity before concluding, "For the rest of your life, you will be off the radar."

Her voice was distant when she stated, "I must be held captive in Britain."

With kindness in his voice, Sign replied, "Don't look at it that way. It takes at least four lifetimes to experience ten percent of what Britain has within its shores. You will not be bored. On the contrary, it will be an adventure."

She nodded. "Will I see you and Tom again?"

"Only if there's an emergency."

"What will you do if Jayne Archer betrays me? And what about her fake English parents?"

"Her father's dead. Her mother and Jayne are close. I will deal with both of them."

"How?"

"By delivering them the truth." Sign didn't elaborate. He pointed at the others. "I'm retired from MI6 but still hold powerful sway within the highest circles in government. Tom is a former cop. Gregor is a former naval officer and assassin. You are now a former SVR officer. But, look at what you see. All of us are happy and carving a new life. Do not be frightened of the unknown. It can very often bring sublime joy."

"If you're retired from MI6, who's paying you to help me?"

"The person who's about to betray you."

"Then, how will you get your money?"

"I won't." Sign sipped his drink. "Money is considerably less important than a human life. Let's go and join the others. The meat smells delicious. It won't be fully cooked for an hour or so. But we can have another drink while we wait. I might even persuade Gregor to play his balalaika and give us a sing-song."

Natalia grabbed his arm. Her grip was tight. "If you'd already considered the possibility that Susan was going to be used as leverage against Jayne in order to flush me out, why did you send me to Moscow?"

Sign stared at the lake. "It was only a possibility. I needed to know the truth." He looked at her. "If I hadn't gotten to the truth, this time tomorrow you'd be dead. And we can't have that happening, can we?"

She released her grip. With a slight smile on her face and a lighter tone of voice, she said, "I'm actually a pretty good singer. Maybe Gregor and I could do a duet."

Archer served her mother shepherd's pie in her home in Putney. Elizabeth was now with her fulltime. The nurse had visited, supplied medicine and medical kit, made checks of the house, and departed after saying that everything in the property was perfect. Archer had made a real effort to make the house welcoming. Candles were lit; classical music was softly playing in the lounge; a bouquet of roses was in a vase adjacent to her mother's bed; the curtains were parted, revealing on one side of the house a view of the adjacent Thames and the old fashioned embankment lamps straddling the mighty river; a bottle of Elizabeth's favourite Rioja was in the centre of the dining table. It was evening. The sun had gone down. Daytime tourists had been replaced by evening revellers. The double glazing in the house meant they could barely hear them as they walked along the promenade. But, it was still good to see life in action.

Elizabeth ate her food. "I loved the peace and quiet in Godalming. But, I missed the vibrancy of London."

Archer poured them wine. "I've taken tomorrow off to help you settle in. Is there anything you'd like to do?"

Elizabeth shook her head. "Nothing special. I just want to get orientated. Depending on the weather I might take myself out on the scooter. How's your new job?"

"It's going okay. It's high pressure though."

"Any news on Susan?"

"Not yet. My team are still digging."

Elizabeth drank her wine. "Maybe I shouldn't have told you about her."

"Maybe you shouldn't. But you did and I understand why. If she's alive, I'll find her and bring her here." She added a few drops of Worcester Sauce to her meal. "What do I need to do to help you in the house?"

"Nothing. I can use the bathroom on my own; the bed is perfect; you've got a tumble dryer, so I don't need to worry about hanging up wet clothes; I'll get the measure of the local shops and if they're not up to scratch I'll order online; and I'm not stupid – I know my capabilities and limitations. I won't do anything that puts me at risk." She smiled. "Actually, there is one thing you can do to help – you can teach me how to use your TV. From what I've seen you've got three remote controllers and beneath the TV are electrical boxes of this that and the other. I don't know where to start."

"I'll write you a list of instructions." Archer was proud of the meal she'd cooked. "You know, mum, there are times I'm required to work odd hours. I don't travel so much these days, but there will still be times when I'll need to go away for a bit."

"I have two sets of spare keys. I won't be housebound when you're away."

"I know. But what I wanted to say is that most of the time I work during the day and come home in the evening. When I get home I have a bit of a routine. I cook or order a takeaway, have a bath or shower, pour myself a glass of wine or make a cup of tea, and watch something on Netflix or Sky. I don't tend to read because I spend a chunk of my day reading intelligence reports. I like to decompress by doing relaxing things."

"And you like to do so alone." Elizabeth fully understood. "Don't worry, dear. I won't get in your way. I get tired between seven and eight in the evening. Either the medication does that or it's just an age thing. Or it's a combination. Regardless, when I'm tired I go to bed. I won't be in your way and you won't be in my way."

"Sorry, I didn't mean it like…"

"I know. It'll be fine." She placed her knife and fork down. "You know I don't have long in this world. This is just a temporary arrangement."

"Don't speak like that."

"Face facts, Jayne. Soon – maybe months or maybe a year or so – I'll die in this house or while driving my scooter alongside the river. I'm just happy to be here for my closing chapter. By the way – tomorrow I'm going to cook us a lovely lasagne with some French beans on the side."

Archer smiled. "That will be lovely. Do you want me to buy the ingredients?"

"Don't you dare." Elizabeth finished her wine and smiled. "It will be liberating to A-Z prepare and cook a meal. I don't need fussing over." She yawned. "I'll load the dishwasher and head to bed. It's been a long day."

Archer squeezed her mother's hand. "It's good to have you home."

CHAPTER 10

At six AM the following morning, Sign, Knutsen, Gregor, and Natalia were outside of the house. Yuri backed his car towards them, stopped, and loaded the travellers' luggage into the boot of the vehicle. The air was crisp; there was frost on the ground; the lake was calm.

Knutsen crouched, gently wrapped his arms around Lenin's head, and held him against his chest. "I've got to go now, fella. Remember the training. You'll do fine when it's time for you to leave." He stepped back.

Lenin looked at him.

Knutsen nodded.

Lenin arched his back and howled at the sky.

Gregor walked up to Knutsen. "He knows you're going. It makes him sad, but also stronger. Now, more than ever, he wants his mate. He's just called to her and he will continue doing so for days, weeks, and months until she comes. If she doesn't come, he will leave to find her. I will let him." He held out his hand. "Goodbye Mr. Tank Engine. The journey isn't over just because you have sight of a port. You understand?"

Knutsen understood. "I'll look after her until the job's done." He shook his hand. "Thank you for being such a good host."

Gregor walked to Natalia and placed his hands on her arms. "You are British now." He smiled. "Learn to say please and thank you. Avoid black pudding and haggis." He kissed her on both cheeks.

Natalia and Knutsen got into the car.

Gregor walked to Sign.

Both men stared at the lake.

Gregor said, "When it happens, show no mercy."

"There'll be no mercy."

Gregor breathed in deeply and slowly exhaled. "You'll come back one day?"

"Of course." Sign turned to him. "My brother." He hugged him.

The two men didn't need to say anything else.

Sign got into the car.

Yuri drove them out of the farmstead.

Gregor watched them until the car was no longer visible. Then he whistled to Lenin. "Come on boy. It's just you and me for the day, until Yuri gets back tonight. I'm thinking we should go for a long walk. Maybe we could bag ourselves a couple of rabbits." When Lenin was by his side, Gregor looked at the empty lane and quietly said, "Keep moving; steady as she goes."

Five hours later the letter arrived.

It was addressed to Archer.

Her name and address were handwritten on the white envelope. Archer didn't like that. This wasn't a utility bill and she never received personal letters. She held it for a moment at her front door before going into the kitchen, sitting at the table, swigging her coffee, and opening the letter. She stared at in disbelief. Aside from the letter, there was a photo. The letter said:

Dear Miss Jayne Archer

I am writing on behalf of interested parties who live east of you.

You may or may not know that you have a twin sister, Susan Archer. I am happy to report that she is alive and well. She has just been made aware of your existence. She is unmarried, has no children, and works as a clerical assistant. I'm sure you'd like to meet her and return with her to your family home – either for a visit or for a permanent reunion. This can happen on one condition. You will be required to help me and my colleagues with a major problem. Your task will not be arduous. All I require is for you to give me a name. If you do that, your sister will be placed in your care. If you don't, the consequences for Susan will be dire.

You and I will meet tomorrow at midnight in the centre of Quaibrücke Bridge, Zurich, Switzerland. Susan will be close by. If you bring police or covert operatives, Susan will be instantly shot in the back of the head.

We know who you work for and we know your position within your organisation.

If you give me the name we desire, you and Susan will never hear from us again. If you give me a false name, you and Susan will have the Sword of Damocles hanging over you. One day that sword will fall with unforgiving accuracy.

Take a look at the photo. She looks just like you.

Travel under your own passport. Susan will be carrying her passport. It has a valid visa to travel to the UK. She will also be carrying one thousand dollars for flight and associated costs to get to your home. I look forward to seeing you tomorrow.

Archer looked at the photo and ran in to the lounge. Her mother was in there, reading a newspaper. "Is this her, mum? Do you think this could be Susan?" Her hand trembled as she handed the photo to Elizabeth.

"Where did you get this?"

Archer lied. "My team."

Elizabeth was unblinking as she examined the shot. "It's Susan."

"I know she looks like me but how can you be sure?!"

Elizabeth placed a finger on the photo. "It's not just the resemblance. She has a half-moon birthmark on her chin. Susan was born with the exact same birthmark." She looked up at Archer. Her eyes were watering. "Jayne – this is your sister."

Archer's heart was pounding.

Elizabeth asked, "Where is she?"

"Overseas. I can't yet tell you where. I can't tell anyone about this. But, I'm going to try to bring her here."

"Will there be a price to pay for getting her here?"

Archer slumped into a chair and held her head in her hands. "Yes."

"Is the price reasonable?"

Archer didn't respond.

In a sterner voice, Elizabeth repeated, "Is the price reasonable?"

Archer looked at her. "I don't know what the price is. But, whatever it is, I'll pay it."

It was late evening when Sign, Knutsen, and Natalia were told by the ship's captain that it was safe to leave the on-board container that was one of eighty five on the boat. The vessel had left Russian waters and the three of them were now free to move around the ship. They'd been given a three-bed cabin, close to the engine room; had access to a tiny bathroom that was shared by eight other sailors; and would eat breakfast, lunch, and dinner in the galley canteen. Sign had told the skipper that they must work their passage. Sign would help out in the galley, Knutsen would work in the engine room, and Natalia would help with any required repairs and maintenance. They'd start their chores tomorrow. The other sailors were a mixed bunch of Russian, Chinese, Indians, and Albanians. They didn't care about the presence of three strangers on their boat. They were used to smuggling people, drugs, exotic animals, cash, and precious metals. It's why they were loyal to their skipper. He paid them four times more than the normal salary for a sailor.

Knutsen, and Natalia were on the starboard side of the deck. It was dark, the only lights coming from the ship's electric bulbs. Russia wasn't visible. They were in open waters.

But, Natalia looked in the direction of Russia and said, "The divorce has come through. Sad really, isn't it?"

Knutsen replied, "Not when one of the parties in the marriage is a cunt."

"That's sort of true. But there are always two people to blame. I'm not some idiot woman who repeatedly mentally abuses her husband and goads him in to slapping her, then raises her voice three octaves when the cops arrive and pretends to be the victim so that they can arrest him and take him away. I betrayed my country. I'm anything but a victim. But, then there's the cooling down period. Husband and wife might have a moment to work out what went wrong." She raised her eyebrows. "It's too late now. No cooling down period. No reconciliation."

Knutsen nodded as he looked out to sea and felt the salty air on his face. "Where do you think you'll live in Britain?"

"I don't know. I like the countryside but I may be too exposed there. Maybe a big town or city. You can be more anonymous there. Do you have any recommendations?"

"Maybe Bristol, Bath, or Exeter. I grew up around there. It's a nice part of the country."

"Maybe." Natalia looked at him. "What will you do when you get back to England?"

Knutsen leaned against the ship's rail. "I'll help Ben close this job. After that, we'll shift to the next thing." He looked over his shoulder at Natalia. "It's funny when I hear myself using the word *job*. It sounds so impersonal, doesn't it?"

Natalia walked to his side and placed her hands on the rail. "Do you have a wife?"

Knutsen smiled but not because he was happy. "In my head, yes. In reality no. The woman I loved died."

"Ben told me the same about his partner. My brother killed himself. My parents are dead." She breathed in deeply. "The hardest part about grief is when grief no longer features."

"Yeah. We move on. It sucks." Knutsen turned and rested against the rail. "How do you fall out of love with a dead woman? Self-preservation, I guess. The memories become too painful."

Natalia touched his hand.

Knutsen looked at her. He wrapped his fingers around hers.

"I'm cold." She placed her body against his. "You smell of Lenin."

Knutsen laughed, placed his arms around her, and held her firm. "At some point in the next year or so, I'll go back and see the wolf. If he's in the wild, I'll find him. He'll recognise me. I hope he has a mate and cubs. And I hope he'll introduce me to his family."

"He will. He loves and respects you. You're his father. Or his big brother. Or his mentor. Certainly you're his pack leader." Natalia rested her head against his chest. "Very few men can achieve that with a highly intelligent savage beast. Lenin's frame of reference is not dissimilar to that of humans. When we left, he howled because he missed you and wanted love from a female wolf."

Knutsen was stock still, just holding her. "He's persistent. He'll find love."

"And you, pack leader?"

"I was an undercover cop. I lived for months, and sometimes years at a time, in the most godawful environments. The movies portray men like me as living on their nerves. It's not like that in reality. We become other personalities. We'll do anything to prove ourselves to the scumbags we have to mix with. We become a scumbag. That's how we survive the darkness and the fucking blood. There were no nerves, nor any room for love."

She touched his face. "But you are not that now, da? You are Thomas."

He looked at her. "No one calls me Thomas. My name's Tom Knutsen."

"Tom. Yes, that's a good name. Knutsen? You are Scandinavian?"

"In DNA only. I don't know. In fact I don't know much shit about any of my family background. Fucking orphanages will do that to a kid."

She stared at him.

He held her gaze.

They both smiled.

Then they walked inside.

Archer called the deputy head of the Russia Department and told him that she was urgently needed in Europe tomorrow to meet one of her agents. She instructed him to hold the fort while she was away and that she'd most likely be back in the office mid-afternoon the day after. After she ended the call she poured herself a glass of wine. There was nothing more that could be done today. Earlier she'd booked a hotel in Zurich and a flight, and packed an overnight bag. She'd be arriving in Switzerland at 1500hrs tomorrow.

She took her wine into the lounge and sat on the sofa. Her mother was sleeping in her room. Archer was glad. She wanted solitude so that she could collect her thoughts. What secret did the sender of the letter want from her? It had to be significant, given they were willing to exchange Susan for the information. And the letter used the word *name*. That could refer to a building or facility. More likely it was the name of a person. She was in no doubt that the letter was sent from the Russians; more specifically, SVR, FSB, or GRU. Her value in the Zurich meeting was because she had access to MI6 secrets about Russia. But, what secret did they want? Something that was hurting them the most. The name of a Russian traitor who was working for the British, Europeans, or Americans and selling out Russian assets.

Archer sipped her wine. She'd not heard from Sign during his trip to Moscow; ditto Natalia. But that wasn't unusual. They were only supposed to contact her if there was an emergency. Even then, Sign would deal with the emergency, rather than involve MI6. She was certain Sign had made no progress in tracking her sister. Now, that was a good thing. Another chess move was in play and it was to her advantage. She had to make her move with her unknown opponent. All that mattered was getting her sister to London. She'd lie about how she found her. It would be easy. If asked by the chief of MI6, she'd say some of her Russian agents – who couldn't be named – found Susan and got her out of Russia. It would be hushed up. She'd get a pat on the back from the chief. Susan would be given the right to abode in the United Kingdom. The matter would be closed.

Sign and Knutsen had failed, she decided. They were no longer of use to her.

Natalia's value to MI6 was now irrelevant. .

After all, she was the traitor who the Russians wanted to identify.

Forget trying to help her regain her courage.

Archer now had a wholly different use for Natalia Asina.

Archer had only become her case officer when she'd been recently promoted to run the department. And that's when Natalia had stalled. MI6 peers had acted sympathetic to Archer. These things happen, they'd told her. Try your best to get her back on track. But if you can't, no one will think of you as a failure. It was that word – *failure*. Everyone who'd spoken to Archer, and was cleared to know about Natalia, had dropped that word into their conversations with her. It was not only embarrassing. Her colleagues were very deliberately giving her a subliminal message.

We're judging you on the Natalia case.

Archer had spent a lifetime getting to where she was in MI6. And she didn't want her career to peak now. She wanted much more.

Natalia could be disposed of in a way that made Archer happy and everyone else happy. Archer would get her sister back. And, because Natalia was caught out by the Russians, the headache Natalia had created would vanish and no one would bandy around the word failure anymore. On the contrary, Archer would be branded a hero within MI6 and Whitehall because she'd inherited a lost cause but had still tried her best to give Natalia courage.

She finished her wine and decided she'd have an early night. Tomorrow was going to be a big day.

Knutsen and Natalia entered their cabin. Sign was lying on his bed, reading Moby Dick, by Herman Melville. He had a mischievous look on his face when he saw them. He held up the book so they could see the cover. "Do you think we'll spot a whale during our passage to England?"

"No," replied Knutsen. "Why have you got the single bed and left Natalia and I to have the bunk beds?"

"Oh, you know, dear chap. Man of my age gets achy joints. It's easier for me to get in and out of this bed."

"You're only bloody forty nine and you have the stamina and strength of a twenty year old athlete!"

"Ah, but it's night time when the creaks and groans set in." He chuckled and looked at the book. "It must have been cold on deck."

"It was."

Sign kept his eyes on the book. "Sometimes it's best to get warmth from wherever you can when the chill hits you."

Knutsen and Natalia said nothing.

Sign tossed his book to one side and looked at them. "When we boarded the boat, Thomas had three of Lenin's hairs on his jacket. They were loosely embedded in the fibres. Now he has two. The other one is on your jacket, my dear."

Natalia's face flushed red.

Knutsen replied, "Whatever. Just read your book and turn your fucking brain off. Seven days of listening to you will do my head in."

Sign gestured to the bunk beds. "Who's going to be on top and who's got to be underneath the other person?"

"Shut up, Ben." Knutsen looked at Natalia. "You choose."

"I'll take the bottom bed." She patted the mattress. "Sometimes I get seasick. I don't want to vomit over you."

Knutsen smiled. "Right oh. Top bed it is for me." He clambered onto the bed. "Ben – be a darling and turn the light out. We've all got early starts tomorrow."

Sign asked, "What about getting changed into our pyjamas?"

"We haven't got any frickin' pyjamas, and you know it."

Sign turned the light off and got into bed. "For seven days we must be like astronauts. They coexist, regardless of gender, in tight spaces. There is no privacy. They get changed in front of each other; go for a wee and poo in front of each other; clean themselves in front of each other. They become hermaphrodites. For the duration of this voyage we too have to become…"

"Shut up, Ben!" said Knutsen and Natalia in unison.

Knutsen added, "Just get some sleep, please!"

The room was pitch dark.

Five minutes later, Sign was snoring.

Knutsen rubbed his eyes and in an exasperated tone yelled out, "Ben – you're snoring!"

Sign giggled. "I never snore. But it did make you laugh."

"You bastard!"

CHAPTER 11

At four thirty PM, Archer arrived at the five star Zurich Marriott hotel. She was tired, but not because the journey was arduous – it was only a short hop, skip, and a jump from Heathrow – but rather because she had a mentally exhausting case of the jitters. Was this all some elaborate bluff? Was Susan really alive? Was Archer doing the right thing?

After checking in, she went straight to her room. Though luxurious, it was like so many other hotel rooms that Archer had stayed in around the world during her career. Luxury meant nothing to her. Only the most junior front-line MI6 officers got a thrill from travelling first or business class and arriving at a swanky hotel. Once you'd trawled the Earth, many times at unholy hours, the novelty of luxury was completely worn out. A bed was a bed; a bathroom a bathroom. No amount of chocolates on a pillow or complimentary this and that made a jot of difference. Hotels were places to get one's head down or to meet secret agents. That was their only purpose. Archer had booked the Marriott because she was pretending to meet one of her assets. It wouldn't make sense for a woman of her seniority to be assessed as slumming it when she handed in her expenses claims.

She showered, blow dried her hair, and changed into fresh clothes. She knew she had to eat to keep up her strength, though she wasn't hungry. At six PM she wandered down to one of the hotel restaurants and ordered *De Wildi* – saddle fillet of venison with a cranberry jus, hazelnut knöpfli, and red cabbage. When the food arrived she had to force it down her throat. After she finished, she returned to her room, drank a glass of wine, regretted doing so, drank two bottles of mineral water, and turned on the TV. She sat in the armchair, flicking through channels, unable to concentrate. But, there was nothing else she could do. As with so many of her MI6 missions, her hotel was her base camp. It was a safe place before she had to venture out. She was poised. The waiting was a killer.

Sign was serving dinner to the sailors in the galley. As he heaped food onto their plates, he told them to enjoy their food. To some, he communicated in Russian and Chinese; to the rest he communicated in English. Instead of the usual unrecognisable slop the crew were served at dinner time, he'd transformed the cuisine. Tonight the sailors were eating pan-fried chicken legs, cabbage and bacon, herb encrusted sautéed potatoes, and gravy that he'd made from chicken carcasses, fried onions, salt and pepper, and a dash of rum. It wasn't up to his usual culinary standard, but he had to work with the produce at his fingertips and the tiny kitchen at his disposal. The sailors had smiles on their faces as they asked for extra helpings. When dinner was complete, he cleaned the galley, made himself a coffee and went on deck to get some air.

Knutsen was sweating in the engine room. He was paired with a Chinaman who didn't speak English. The Chinaman had a rag around his head, was wiry, stressed, and had quickly realised that barking orders at Knutsen in Mandarin was of no use. For the majority of today's shift, the communication between the two men was conducted in crude sign language. The Chinaman tapped dials that registered the heat of the vessel's engines. He pointed at the red zone of the thermometers and wiped his flat hand against his throat. Knutsen interpreted this to mean that he had to monitor the dials and alert his colleague if the needle went too high. They also cleaned pistons while they were operating - Knutsen thought he might lose his hand in the process – and did a variety of other jobs all of which had the singular purpose of keeping the ship moving. When the two men working the nightshift arrived, Knutsen went on deck and joined Sign.

Natalia spent the day doing two jobs. The first was checking that all of the containers were secure on deck. The second was hanging from a rope over the side of the boat and applying rust treatment to the metal hull. The latter job was terrifying. Waves and foam were only a few feet beneath her. An Albanian called Edi lowered her down and pulled her up, and this went on for hours around the circumference of the ship. He had a permanent grin on his face. Natalia knew he was testing her. In fairness, what she did today was what he did day in day out. Still, it was arduous and Natalia was exhausted when she'd completed her tasks. When back on deck, Edi handed her a hip flask containing vodka. She took a swig and handed the flask back to him. He told her that she was an excellent worker. Tomorrow and the next few days would be considerably easier. Unless something went wrong on deck or on the hull, it would simply be monitoring the cargo and sides of the ship. He bade her goodnight.

. When Sign, Knutsen, and Natalia were back in their cabin, Knutsen sat on his bed and said, "Natalia is either already blown today, or she'll be blown in the next hour or so."

Sign looked at him. "Yes." He handed them disposable foil cartons containing warm leftovers from the galley dinner. "You'll have to eat with your fingers. I wasn't permitted to borrow galley cutlery." He tucked into his food.

Natalia sat next to Knutsen and ate. "I'd kill for a nice bath right now. Every muscle in my body aches. Instead, I'll have to use the bathroom sink to wash."

Sign smiled. "It's an adventure. Be thankful you have access to a sink." He sucked sauce off his fingers. "How do you feel, Natalia?"

"Like I'm living in a surreal dream."

Sign nodded. "Do not let reality become a distant concept. If you do, madness awaits." His tone of voice was stern as he added, "You are on a boat that is bound for England. You are in a cabin with Thomas and Ben. You were a traitor. You are no longer a traitor. You don't have a job. Your brother killed himself near St, Petersburg. Thomas has taken a shine to you. The Russians will shortly want you dead. These are facts. This is not a dream."

Natalia put her food to one side. "I know. Except the bit about Thomas."

"Eat. I will do my best with tomorrow's breakfast but don't expect miracles. You need fuel where and when you can get it." Sign finished his food. "We must also have some respite." He smiled. "I may not have been allowed to take some knives and forks out of the galley, but I did manage to nick this without the head chef knowing." He held up a bottle of rum. "The three of us will have a few drinks this evening and talk about pleasant things – the future; our favourite novels and films; the best restaurants in London; and whether Ben will ask you out on a date."

Knutsen sighed. "Give it a rest, Ben."

Natalia placed her hand over Knutsen's hand. "It's okay. I like pleasant thoughts." She looked at Sign. "Pour me a drink and describe to me the most beautiful part of Britain. I want it to be magical. Maybe that's where I'll live."

It was midnight in Switzerland.

Archer stood in the centre of the Quaibrücke Bridge, on the pedestrian walkway. Traffic was non-existent. And though the German quarter of Switzerland had bars, clubs, and restaurants that stayed open longer than their counterparts in the French cantons, there were few lights on in the regal buildings on the other side of the river. The air was still and cool. Her breath was steaming as she exhaled. Noise from the city was barely audible. There were no other pedestrians on the bridge.

She waited.

A car drove onto the bridge and stopped. A man got out and walked towards her. He was wearing a woollen overcoat and suit. He stopped by Archer and lit a cigarette. In a polished Russian accent he said, "You are Jayne Archer. I would like to see your passport."

Archer handed him her ID.

He gave it back to her. "Susan is in the car. She has a gun against her head. Do you want to see her without me and my men present?"

Archer nodded.

He went right up to her and put his face an inch from her face. "I want the name of the Russian who has been betraying my colleagues. You know that person. I don't want a code word. I want a real name."

Archer's heart was pounding fast. Was this the right thing to do? If she gave the name she'd be committing treason. Then again, who would find out that she'd committed treachery by giving the Russians the name of a traitor? And was it unethical to do so? By giving them a name, she'd be saving Susan. A traitor's life for an innocent's life. That was the equation.

She said, "Natalia Asina. She works in the SVR's London station."

"Give me the names of the men and women she's sold out."

Archer told him who was on the list of blown Russian agents.

The man made a call on his mobile phone. He supplied the name of Natalia Asina, then waited while listening. He nodded and ended the call. To Archer he said, "You are telling the truth. Wait here." He walked to his car.

Archer watched him.

The man didn't get in the vehicle. He opened the rear passenger door.

A woman got out.

She walked to Archer.

Archer held her breath.

The woman stood in front of Archer.

There was no doubt it was Susan.

Susan spoke in Russian. "You are my sister. Until two days ago, I didn't know you existed."

Archer hugged her. "Susan, Susan."

The woman frowned. "My name's Dina Vichneva."

"It's not your real name." Archer smiled and stepped back. "Do you want to see my home in London? My mother's there."

Susan had tears running down her face. "They threatened to kill me. I don't know what's going on. This is… so confusing. Yes. Let's go home."

Archer took her hand. "It's not confusing anymore. Come with me. I need to check out of my hotel and then we can get a night flight to England. You're safe now."

CHAPTER 12

Five days later, Sign, Knutsen, and Natalia arrived in the Liverpool docks. They travelled by train to London. Under normal circumstances, Sign would have suggested to Natalia that she stay at his house until she secured her own home. But, these were anything but normal circumstances. Natalia was blown. Archer knew where Sign lived. And though there was no reason why Archer would have told the Russians about Sign and his engagement by her, there was the possibility the Russians would re-contact her when they realised Natalia had vanished. Then, she'd give them Sign's name and address. His house wasn't safe. So, instead he paid upfront in cash for Natalia to stay in a B&B in Pimlico. It was walking distance from West Square. Sign and Knutsen would liaise with her on a daily basis and make sure she was safe. She wasn't registered with her real name in the temporary accommodation. Sign had taken the proprietor to one side and quietly said that she'd been battered by her husband and needed a safe place. He'd added that if any men came here asking about a woman with an Eastern European accent, the proprietor was to call the police and demand that an armed response unit was deployed to his B&B.

Day two after they'd arrived back in England, Sign and Knutsen were in the lounge of their apartment. Earlier today they'd gone to Sign's barbers in St James's where they'd been given a cutthroat shave and haircut. Now, Sign was in immaculate slacks, a shirt, and brogues. Knutsen was in jeans, a creased T-shirt, and flip-flops. They were sitting in their armchairs, adjacent to a lit fire.

Sign said, "We must establish where Natalia can live."

"It's her choice."

"She and I don't want it to be her choice, and rightly so. She knows parts of London, but everywhere else is a jungle to her." Sign placed the tips of his fingers together. "We must square the circle. She must live somewhere where she can be anonymous. But she must also have vibrancy and happiness."

"A rural town or city? I suggested to her the west country."

"That didn't help those Russians in Salisbury. It's too obvious to relocate her to a place like that."

"Why keep her in Britain?"

"Three reasons. First, I've pulled strings to get her a new British identity. I have no strings to attempt gaining a foreign nationality. Second, you and I must keep a weather eye on her welfare. Third, there is a ninety two percent chance that you and Natalia may become an item."

Knutsen smiled. "Ninety two percent chance? How did you come to that calculation?"

"I made it up, though I'm a millimetre either way from being correct." Sign was weary and not in the mood for banter. "She can't live in London in case…"

"Of a chance encounter with one of her former SVR colleagues."

Sign nodded. "But she can live close to London. Hertford springs to mind."

Knutsen agreed. "That's a great idea. Lovely town. Lots going on. Quick and easy access to London at the weekends when most of the SVR station is closed shop. Good rail links. It's a bit pricey though."

"She only needs a one bedroom flat."

Knutsen used his phone to browse the Internet. "I'm looking at Rightmove." After a few minutes he said, "Discounting the silly prices, we're looking at between seven hundred and a thousand quid per month."

"Perfect."

"How will she afford that? She's got no savings."

"I will pay until she has a salary coming in."

Knutsen stared at him. "That's very generous."

"I prefer to think of it as pragmatic."

Knutsen didn't need to tell his friend that he was lying through his teeth. "I'll get on to the real estate agents today. What about a job?"

"I'll arrange that. She'll work from home. I have one or two contacts that'll help her get on her feet and earn a living."

Knutsen knew that Sign had hundreds of valuable contacts in Britain alone. "We must take her out this evening."

"We will. I've bought us tickets to the Royal Albert Hall. We're seeing Verdi's Requiem at eight o'clock.. After, we will dine at Goya tapas restaurant in Pimlico. Then we'll walk Natalia to her B&B. You will need to change before this evening. You currently look like a beach bum on Mykonos." He smiled. "We only have a few hours so let's divide and conquer. I've already secured her a British passport. But, there are other matters to attend to. I need to open a bank account in her new name, make a few phone calls and get her a job, obtain a UK mobile phone in her new identity, and plant some misinformation that Natalia was spotted yesterday in Tokyo. Meanwhile, your task is to find her somewhere nice to live. It must be walking distance to the town centre. Preferably go for unfurnished. I'll deposit five thousand pounds in her new bank account to pay for new furniture and other set-up costs. Are you up to the task?"

Knutsen nodded. "Let's get it done. Deadline is six PM. Then I'll get showered and dressed into my best bib and tucker. We'll have time for a sharpener before we leave for the concert."

"Good man."

Knutsen stood. In a more hesitant voice he asked, "What are you going to do about Archer and her mother?"

"I'm going to deal with them tomorrow," was Sign's only reply.

Archer made a pot of tea and placed muffins onto a plate. She took the food and drink into the lounge. Susan and Elizabeth were in the room, playing cards. Archer sat with them and after two minutes poured the tea. In Russian she said to Susan, "Your British passport should be through tomorrow. You will have a permanent right to abode in Britain."

Elizabeth placed her cards down. "She can live here, can't she?"

"Of course." Archer looked at Susan. "Would you like that?"

Susan nodded. "I can't go back to Russia. And I don't know England. Plus, I want to get to know my real mother and sister."

"That's settled then." She handed Susan and Elizabeth mugs of tea. "I was thinking we should get some takeaway pizzas tonight. What do you think?"

Both nodded.

Archer smiled. Everything was perfect, though she wished her father was still alive to be part of this reunion. Fleetingly, she thought about Natalia. No doubt she was stopped at the airport when trying to depart Russia. The FSB and SVR would be merciless. She'd be tortured to within an inch of her life and executed. Still, that was the price to pay if one got exposed as a double agent.

She drank her tea. "I think we should all go for a nice stroll on the promenade before dinner." She looked at Susan. "I've booked an appointment for you tomorrow. It's with a neighbour who teaches English to foreign students. She's happy to see you for an hour a day at her home, until you've got a working knowledge of the language. She's not going to charge me. I'll show you where she lives when we go for our walk this evening."

Susan replied, "Yes, that would be good." She looked away, a tear rolling down her face. "Who were the people who raised me? The people I thought were my parents? Do you know?"

Archer shook her head. "I don't."

"It doesn't matter. They died a few years ago." Susan wiped away her tear. "How did you get to me? How did you get me released from the thugs who kept me in a cell for two days and held guns against my head?"

"It was Elizabeth who answered. "Jayne is in a powerful position in government. She exerted her influence with the Russians. She pulled out the stops to find you and to bring you to England."

Susan replied, "But there must have been a trade. Jayne must have given them something in return."

Archer said, "The British and the Russians do trades all the time. It's complicated. On this occasion, and with my prime minister's permission, I conducted what's called back-channel diplomacy. I told the Russians how Britain would be voting at the next UN summit. Simple as that. Me doing that served Britain's interest and Russian interests."

Susan breathed in deeply. "I don't know anything about politics." Her mood lightened. "Yes. Let's go for a walk." She looked at Elizabeth. "If I get tired on the way back, can I sit on your scooter?"

Elizabeth laughed. "Absolutely not, my dear! My scooter; my rules."

CHAPTER 13

The following morning, Knutsen fried bacon and eggs in the flat's kitchen. He felt invigorated, in large part because his trip to Russia and voyage home had been such a mind-blowing adventure. He'd never experienced anything like it before – the dramatic scenery, new friendships, constant fear over Natalia's safety, Gregor's amazing house and grounds, hunting for dinner, working like an oil-smeared naval lackey in the engine room during his passage home, and the look Natalia had given him as she'd briefly touched his hand when they were alone on deck together. Now, he felt more alive than he'd ever been. But it was good to be back in West Square. It was the same feeling he imagined most people had when they returned from an amazing holiday – great time, but comforting to be home and surrounded by familiar and personal accoutrements.

Sign emerged from his room. He was wearing a suit and looked pitch perfect – hair immaculate, clean shaven, shoes polished to the standards of a guardsman, trouser creases like blades, not a single piece of fluff on his Gieves & Hawkes royal navy blue suit, silk tie bound in a Windsor knot over a heavy cotton white shirt with a cutaway collar, and the aroma of expensive shower gel he'd purchased from Harrods and a bespoke cologne he'd bought from a perfumery in Chelsea. He sat at the dining table. "I have an appointment with Jayne Archer at ten AM. That gives me one hour."

Knutsen served up the food. "What have you told her?"

"My message to her was cryptic. I simply said I had news and no news and that we should meet at her house, alone." He ate his food. "Archer's mother will be out. If Susan is living with Jayne, she too will be out. I will be clearing the decks."

Knutsen sat opposite him with his plate of food. "Meaning?"

"Meaning the innocents maintain a rite of passage towards a wondrous world and the guilty starve to death on a cold rock." He looked at Knutsen. "As Gregor advised me, I will show no mercy."

"That was already your stance. Gregor didn't need to advise you."

"Correct. But sometimes it pays to have affirmation from a man one wholly trusts."

"Do you want me to help you today?"

Sign sliced his egg into two, allowing the yolk to flow over his pork. "I would like you to attend to Natalia. Before I leave, I will give you a plastic A4 folder. Inside is her British passport, the contact details of a woman who wishes to employ her as a freelance political analyst, a bank card and bank details, and a mobile phone. You will also furnish her with the details of the lovely flat you have secured her in Hertford. Take her there for a viewing today. She will want to make decisions about furnishings. I regret to say that you may have to go with her to Ikea or somewhere similar. I believe she moves in on Monday?"

"Yep. How did you get her bank card so quickly?"

Sign shrugged. "A bank card is only a bit of plastic and an account can be opened with a few taps on a keyboard. I know someone who can do these things in a matter of hours."

Knutsen eyed him. Sign seemed cold, distant, and utterly focused. "You have that look. You're about to mess with minds."

"I often do that for good reasons. But, sometimes... yes, sometimes..."

"It's okay. It has to be what it is." Knutsen finished his food and cleared up the plates. "Fucking Ikea?! Why do I get the shit job?!"

Sign smiled. He knew Knutsen was making light of the day's tasks. He also knew that Knutsen was trying in his own way to transfer strength to Sign, fully cognisant that Sign had the worst job of all. "Be happy today. Act excited in front of Natalia. Hold her hand when you go shopping." He stood. "I will get you the folder. Then I must leave."

At ten AM, Sign rang Archer's doorbell.

She let him in to her house.

They sat in the lounge.

Archer said, "My mother's gone shopping."

Sign was motionless. "And Susan? Where is your sister?"

Archer feigned ignorance. "I thought you were going to give me the answer to that."

Sign's voice was cold when he replied, "Tom and I didn't find Susan. We didn't need to. You found her with the help of the Russians."

"I... I don't know what you're talking about."

"You got Susan in exchange for giving the FSB or SVR the name of the person who'd been giving British Intelligence the identities of Russian agents."

"This is nonsense!"

Sign showed no emotion. "I withheld from you the real reason why I wanted Natalia to go to Russia. I tasked her to investigate what had happened to Susan. She found out everything, including why the Russians snatched her at birth. They wanted to use her as leverage against you. That event happened just over a week ago. You have betrayed an MI6 agent. Natalia is safe and far away from Russia. I made that happen. You and the Russians can't touch her."

Archer stood. "Get out of my house!"

But Sign didn't move. "Decades ago, your treachery would have put you in front of a firing squad. These days, you will face life imprisonment."

Archer paced back and forth. "I've done nothing wrong!"

"Your sister is living with you in this house." He tossed a photo onto the coffee table. "Mr. Knutsen took that yesterday. There are you, Elizabeth, and Susan, having a walk alongside the Thames. You all look very happy. There wasn't really a need to take the camera shot. I'd already spoken to the chief of MI6. He informed that you'd told him you brought your sister to England and had asked for the service to facilitate her legal status here. He was happy for you. He also told me that he was aware that Natalia was off the radar. He had no idea why. He assumed she'd gone back to work in Moscow. He doesn't suspect foul play on your part. That remains the case, because I didn't enlighten him. Sit down. There are things you need to know."

Fury remained on Archer's face. She sat.

"Elizabeth and Michael are not your real parents. They were KGB and SVR moles whose sole job was to raise you to hate Russia. Your twin sister was raised by KGB caretakers in Russia. They pretended to be Susan's parents. Your real parents were murdered immediately after your births. Your name is Anna Vichneva. Susan is Dina Vichneva. You are Russian. Elizabeth gave birth close to the time when you were born. She willingly let the KGB murder her child. It was all part of the plan. And Elizabeth knew there'd come a day when you'd be of use to her and her Moscow controllers. Susan/Dina was innocent throughout. Like you, she had no reason to suspect her parents were fake. Susan was just a pawn to be used someday to prompt you to betray the United Kingdom. You, however, are not innocent. You took the Russian bait. Were it not for my help, Natalia would be dead by now."

Archer sat in stunned silence. "My mother is a lie?"

"Yes."

"She knew the Russians wanted to give me the name of my double agent?"

"She knew everything."

Archer was trying to process the information. "I didn't... didn't give them Natalia's name."

"Yes you did! It was the only way you could get Susan. Don't make matters worse for yourself by lying to me!"

Archer bowed her head. In a barely audible voice, she said, "Natalia had dried up." She looked at him. "What would you have done? What would anyone in my position have done? This is my flesh and blood we're talking about. The Russians were threatening to kill Susan if I didn't help them."

"There is no doubting that you were placed in an impossible situation. You have my sympathies. You were forced to attempt the murder of Natalia Asina. This is what's going to happen. In two hours, Special Branch will arrest you. In a closed court hearing, I will testify to your otherwise good character. It won't result in a lenient sentence, but it may help your life imprisonment be a little more comfortable. Don't attempt to flee the country on your real or alias passports. You would be arrested at any port.. He stood. "The reason I'm giving you two hours is to allow you a brief window of time to sort out your affairs." He stood. "Do you understand what I mean? Good day to you Miss Archer." He left the house.

Archer was shaking when he was gone. She called Elizabeth. "Mum – are you on your way home?" She listened to her reply. "Good. I need to travel at short notice, but we've got a problem with the heating. I need to give you the number of the repair man I use."

Ten minutes later Elizabeth was back home. Archer helped her sit in an armchair.

Elizabeth asked, "Is Susan at her English lesson?"

"Yes. She won't be back for another thirty or so minutes. I need to pack and then I'll tell you about the heating." She went upstairs, picked up a pillow from Elizabeth's bed, returned downstairs, and stopped at the entrance to the lounge. "You're not my mother. You lied to me for all of my life. You're a Russian agent. You made me betray my country and a woman who had barely started her adult life."

Elizabeth's mouth opened; her eyes were wide. "How did you know..?"

"Shut up!." Archer walked quickly to her and shoved the pillow against Elizabeth's mouth and nose. She pressed hard and held the pillow in place.

Elizabeth was twitching, but unable to do anything because her limbs were so weak.

Archer held the pillow there for three minutes. Her face was red from the exertion and from stress. She removed the pillow. Her mother was dead.

She returned upstairs and placed the pillow back on to Elizabeth's bed. No doubt the pillow had Elizabeth's saliva on it, but almost certainly a police forensics examination of the cushion would conclude that any secretions were simply as a result of night time sleep. And Archer's fingerprints on the pillow would be totally explainable. After all, Archer had to regularly change Elizabeth's bedding.

But, it was highly unlikely the police would be involved. Elizabeth was dying; she'd returned home, sat in her chair, had a nap, and stopped breathing.

Archer regretted that Susan would have to find Elizabeth dead. There was no alternative to that. She grabbed her handbag, left the house, and walked to East Putney tube station. She was in a daze. After buying a ticket, she stood on the platform. There were only a handful of other travellers on the platform. She walked to one end, away from the other commuters, and waited. The electronic information unit announced that the next train was due to arrive in one minute.

One minute.

That's all she had.

A rush of wind coursed through the tunnel. The train was going to arrive at speed in seconds.

She waited.

She saw the train's headlights.

Timing was everything.

When the train was two yards away, she leapt in front of it.

Her body and head were mangled into pieces.

CHAPTER 14

Three days' later, Sign lit the fire in his lounge and poured two glasses of calvados. He handed one of them to Knutsen and sat in his armchair. Both men were facing each other. They were quiet for a while. Knutsen had been busy during the last forty eight hours, helping Natalia move furniture in to her new home. The men had barely had a chance to spend time together, Knutsen having arrived home at close to midnight during the preceding two days, and departing at six AM the following mornings. Knutsen had done his job. Natalia was happily ensconced in her new place. He'd see her in a week's time, after she'd settled in. She'd invited him over for dinner. He was looking forward to that.

Sign sipped his drink and looked at his colleague. "All that could be done is now done. Natalia is safe. Susan has legal ownership of the Putney house, thanks to a few tweaks in the property deeds. It's always good to have a dodgy lawyer on my books. MI6 Welfare Department will check on her regularly. Susan won't know they're MI6. Probably they'll pose as Social Services or Home Office. She'll be fine."

"Will you see Susan?"

"No. There's no need. It would serve no purpose."

"Plus, just sight of her would remind you of Jayne."

"I could handle that. Jayne was a professional acquaintance. Nothing more, nothing less. Susan must lead her own life now. The less she comes into contact with our murky world, the better. Ergo I must stay away."

Knutsen eyed him. "Did you know Archer would kill her mother and take her own life?"

Sign hesitated. "I gave her a two hour window for a reason. What she did with that window was up to her."

"In other words, you knew." Knutsen frowned. "I can't quite work out if I'm glad Archer's dead."

"Jayne wouldn't have lasted in prison. She knew that. Every second of every day she'd have been tortured by the demons of circumstance – knowledge that her mother was not her mother, not seeing her sister, the arm lock that forced her into betraying Natalia."

"Susan could have visited Jayne."

Sign shook his head. "Jayne knew the drill. She'd have been placed in a top secret military facility. She wouldn't be allowed to see other prisoners, let alone visitors. All she'd have to keep her company would be the silent memories in her head." Sign sighed. "What a tragedy." He placed his glass down, clapped his hands, and said in an upbeat tone of voice, "Let's take a stroll to Borough Market. I'd like to check out what my favourite veg and meat stalls have to offer. Grouse is in season, so maybe we could pick up a brace. Plus, they'll be quick to cook for this evening's supper. After dinner we could grab a pint or two at our local."

Knutsen smiled. "You're on, mate." He finished his drink. "Are we having a few days off work?"

Sign's eyes twinkled as he replied, "Oh no, my dear chap. Tomorrow we are being visited by a new client." He was brimming with energy as he added, "We must catch a serial killer whose victims don't want to be found by anyone."

THE END

Printed in Great Britain
by Amazon

14515695R00130